SMOKE
SNORT
SWALLOW
SHOOT

LESSER
GODS

FIRST PUBLISHED IN THE UNITED STATES OF AMERICA IN 2017 BY:

LESSER⩗GODS

15 W. 36ᵗʰ St., 8ᵗʰ Fl., New York, NY 10018

An imprint of Overamstel Publishers, Inc.

PHONE (646) 850-4201

WWW.LESSERGODSBOOKS.COM

DISTRIBUTED BY:

Consortium Book Sales & Distribution

34 13ᵗʰ Ave. NE #101, Minneapolis, MN 55413

PHONE (800) 283-3572

www.cbsd.com

FIRST EDITION MARCH 2017 / 10 9 8 7 6 5 4 3 2 1

PRINTED AND BOUND IN THE U.S.A.

ISBN: 978-1944713034

LIBRARY OF CONGRESS CONTROL NUMBER: 2016939177

**Legendary Binges, Lost Weekends,
& Other Feats of Rock 'n' Roll Incoherence.**

Featuring:

Aerosmith
Marilyn Manson
Mötley Crüe
Slash
Dee Dee Ramone
Johnny Cash
Phil Spector
Lemmy
Gregg Allman
The Rolling Stones
Marianne Faithfull
Mike Doughty
Rex Brown
Steven Adler
Al Jourgensen
NOFX
Anthony Kiedis

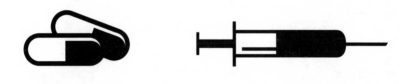

CONTENTS

JACOB HOYE
INTRODUCTION

There's simply nothing quite like a vividly recollected drug story. I've always relished in their telling, just as David Letterman rejoiced when Richard Harris (the original Dumbledore) or Peter O'Toole shared with him their drunken misadventures. There's something about the extremity, the depravity, the guts, to push something as near to the edge as humanly possible.

For a number of years, I knocked around the idea of doing a collection of remarkable drug stories by regular people, the kinds of wilder tales I've cajoled friends into sharing around a late-night fire, or while playing music, or at a spirited lunch. When you get someone talking about that first experience, for example, there's so often a joy in the telling that is palpable and transferable. Maybe it's my dad and all his stories from the Sixties. Maybe it's all the music I've ingested over the years and the friends I've made. Maybe it's the books I read, from Jim Carroll and Hubert Selby to William S. Burroughs and Denis Johnson. Whatever the sources, I always find myself circling back to stories like these. People with long histories of experimentation tend to remember at least a handful, often much more, of those times in vivid detail. I've bonded with more than a few over these recollections. Sadly, an original collection was difficult to assemble. But as

I was catching up on a number of musician memoirs that I had been meaning to read over the previous couple of years, I saw a new way to achieve this idea.

Marilyn Manson's deranged trip on LSD was the piece that made me think an anthology of rock star drug stories could be achievable. It wasn't just a sustained piece with a complete narrative, it was wonderfully composed, a modern gothic full of humor and horror. After that, it was simply a research project to see who else had similarly sustained stories that might shock and entertain. The hope was always that these would be the kinds of pieces to make readers laugh. I was never keen on stories loaded with misfortune and regret. There are plenty of books full of those, and some quite good. Nevertheless, I prefer reading about the wonder, the ride up as opposed to the ride down, which is so often laden with other baggage. Give me Keith Richards, Aerosmith and Mötley Crüe. I'm definitely going to lean in closer if your story begins with a line like this from Lemmy: "We were all sitting around waiting for the speed to arrive."

Moderation is key in life but these are not stories about regular life. Sex, drugs & rock 'n' roll is not about moderation. Go ahead check it out. And remember. They did it so you don't have to.

PROLOGUE / MARILYN MANSON
DRUGS

There is a stereotype among people who have never gotten high that anyone who has ever done drugs, no matter what that drug is, is an addict. The truth is that addiction has little to do with what drugs you use or how often you use them. There are other factors, like the extent to which you let them run your life and your ability to function normally without them. I make no secret of my drug use. But at the same time I have nothing but utter contempt for anyone who is addicted to drugs. It is the people who abuse drugs that make the people who use them look bad. Here are a few simple rules to help you determine whether you are a user or an abuser of cocaine, pot and other substances. Consider yourself an addict if…

1   YOU ACTUALLY PAY FOR DRUGS.
2   YOU USE A STRAW AS OPPOSED TO A ROLLED-UP DOLLAR BILL.
3   YOU USE THE WORD BLOW.
4   YOU'RE A GUY AND YOU'RE BACKSTAGE AT A MARILYN MANSON CONCERT
    (UNLESS YOU'RE A DEALER OR A POLICE OFFICER).
5   YOU OWN MORE THAN ONE PINK FLOYD RECORD.
6   YOU DO COCAINE DURING A SHOW. (IF YOU DO IT AFTER A SHOW, YOU'RE OKAY.
    IF IT'S BEFORE, YOU'RE TEETERING ON THE BRINK.)
7   THE MERE MENTION OF COCAINE MAKES YOU PASS GAS OR THE SIGHT
    OF IT MAKES YOU WANT TO TAKE A SHIT.
8   YOU'VE WRITTEN MORE THAN TWO SONGS THAT REFER TO DRUGS.
9   YOU GET KICKED OUT OF A BAND FOR BEING A DRUG ADDICT.
10 YOU'RE FRIENDS WITH A MODEL.
11 YOU LIVE IN NEW ORLEANS.
12 YOU PAY FOR YOUR GROCERIES WITH ROLLED-UP DOLLAR BILLS.

13   YOU'VE EVER BEEN IN DR. HOOK OR KNOWN THE LYRICS TO A DR. HOOK SONG.

14   THE EMBOSSED NUMBERS, PARTICULARLY THE 0'S, 6'S AND 9'S, ON YOUR CORPORATE CREDIT CARD ARE FILLED IN WITH A MYSTERIOUS WHITE POWDER.

15   YOU'RE ALONE IN YOUR HOTEL ROOM ON TOUR AND YOU DO DRUGS.

16   YOU DO DRUGS BEFORE 6 P.M. OR AFTER 6 A.M.

17   YOU HATE EVERYBODY. (IF YOU LIKE EVERYBODY, YOU'RE ON ECSTASY AND I'M AGAINST YOU.)

18   YOU KNOW THE NAME FOR THE FLESHY CREVICE BETWEEN YOUR THUMB AND INDEX FINGER.

19   YOU'VE EVER SAID, "THIS IS MY LAST LINE" OR, CONVERSELY, "WHICH LINE IS THE BIGGEST?"

20   YOU INVITE PEOPLE TO STAY AT YOUR HOME WHILE YOU'RE ON DRUGS.

21   YOU TELL ANYBODY ABOUT YOUR CHILDHOOD WHILE YOU'RE ON DRUGS.

22   YOU'RE NOT THINKING ABOUT TITS RIGHT NOW.

23   YOU SAY, "I ONLY DO THIS WHEN I'M WITH YOU."

24   YOU HAVE YOUR BODYGUARD WATCH THE DOOR WHEN YOU GO TO THE BATHROOM.

25   YOU'RE A GUY AND YOU TALK TO A GIRL WHO HAS A BOYFRIEND FOR MORE THAN FIVE MINUTES BECAUSE SHE HAS DRUGS.

26   YOU'RE A CHILD ACTOR.

27   IF YOU MAKE THIS BOOK INTO A GAME AND DO A LINE EVERY TIME DRUGS ARE MENTIONED, THEN NOT ONLY ARE YOU AN ADDICT BUT YOU MAY BE DEAD.

RULES I'VE BROKEN: 1, 4 (but that doesn't count), 5, 6 (and I came back onstage with the dollar bill hanging from my nose), 7, 8 (I've written dozens), 12, 13, 14 (unless I've cleaned it out because I'm crossing a border), 15, 16, 17, 19, 20, 21 (but only for this book), 24, 25.

The urge towards love, pushed to its limit, is an urge towards death.   —Marquis de Sade

CHAPTER ONE / MARILYN MANSON
DIRTY ROCK STAR

EXCERPT FROM
The Long Hard Road Out of Hell

AUTHORS
Marilyn Manson and Neil Strauss

COPYRIGHT © 1998 by Brian Warner and Neil Strauss
REPRINTED BY PERMISSION OF ~ HarperCollins Publishers

Marilyn Manson is the lead singer and songwriter for Marilyn Manson, one of the most controversial bands of all time.

✕ ✕ ✕ ✕

"This is not the kind of mistake you can get away with.
Fucking a psycho is as good as killing one."

THE PLACE IS Fort Lauderdale, Florida. The date is July 4, 1990. The thing in the palm of a hand stretched out in front of me is a tab of acid, and in a moment it will obliterate all these facts.

Teresa, my girlfriend, has done acid before. Nancy, the psycho, has done it. I haven't. I let it sit in my mouth until it annoys me, then swallow it and return to packing up the remains of Marilyn Manson and the Spooky Kids' first backyard performance, confident that my will power is stronger than whatever this tiny square of paper has in store for me. Andrew and Suzie, the couple who gave me the tab, smile conspiratorially. I wink back, unsure of what they're trying to communicate.

Minutes pass, and nothing happens. I lie in the grass and focus on figuring out whether the acid is working, if my body seems different, if my perception has changed, if my thoughts are warping. "Do you feel it yet?" comes a voice, breathing sticky and sickly on my ear. I open my eyes to see Nancy grinning masochistically through her black hair.

"No, I don't," I say briskly, trying to get rid of her, especially since my girlfriend is around.

"I need to talk to you," she insists.

"Fine."

"I'm just starting to realize some things. About us. I mean, Teresa's my friend and Carl, I don't care about Carl anymore. But we need to tell them how we feel about each other. Because I love you. And I know you love me, even if you don't know it. It doesn't have to be forever. I know how you are about things like that.

I don't want this to get in the way of our band—"our band"—and the chemistry we have onstage. But we can try it. I mean, love . . . "

As soon as she says love that last time, her face appears lit up against the grassy background, like a billboard advertising self-deception. The word love seems to hang suspended in the air for that moment, masking the rest of her sentence. It's all very subtle. But I realize then that I'm going on a trip, and there's no way back.

"Did you feel that—the difference?" I ask, confused.

"Yes, of course," she says eagerly, as if we're on the same wavelength. I do need somebody on my wavelength because I think I'm about to freak out. But I don't want it to be her. Oh, God, I don't want it to be her.

I stand up and start to look for Teresa, walking through the house slightly disoriented. Everyone is huddled in corners talking in small groups, each cluster of people smiling at me and beckoning me to join them. I keep walking. The house seems endless. I explore about a hundred rooms, not sure whether they're all the same one or not, before giving up, confident that my girlfriend is having a good time somewhere that I'm not. I reemerge in the backyard. But it's not the same backyard. It's dark, it's empty and something feels wrong. I'm not sure how long I've been inside.

I step outside and wander around. Intricate designs, like sketchy pencil drawings, appear in the air, only to be erased moments later. I trip out on them for a while before I realize it's raining. It doesn't really matter. I feel so light and uncorporeal that the rain seems to be dropping through me, penetrating the layers of light my body is emanating. Nancy comes up to me and tries to touch me and understand. Now I'm definitely freaking out.

With Nancy in tow, filling the air with the store-bought scent of dead flowers, I walk downhill to a small, man-made creek. Everywhere there are gray-skinned toads, jumping on the rocks and in the grass. Each step I take, I squish several of them, squeezing out gray-blue blood. Their entrails stick to my shoe, discolored, dead and yellow like blades of grass trapped under the metal rails of lawn furniture. I'm driving myself crazy trying not to kill these things, who have kids and parents and lives to get back to. Nancy is trying to relate to me and I'm trying to pretend like I'm paying attention. But all I can think about are the dead toads. I feel pretty confident that this is what a bad trip feels like—because if this is a good trip, then Timothy Leary has a lot of explaining to do.

I sit down on a rock and try to collect myself, to tell myself that this is all just a drug thinking for me, that the real Marilyn Manson will be back in a moment. Or is this right now the real Marilyn Manson, and the other one just a shallow representation?

My mind is spinning like the wheel of a slot machine around my consciousness. Some images I recognize—the creepy stairs to my old basement room, Nancy playing dead in a cage, Ms. Price's flash cards. Others I don't—a leering police officer wearing a Baptist church cap, photographs of a blood-drenched pussy, a scab-covered woman tortuously tied up, a mob of kids tearing up an American flag. Suddenly, the wheel stops on one image. It bobbles up and down blurrily in my mind several times before I can make it out. It's a face, large and expressionless. Its skin is pasty and yellowish, as if jaundiced from hepatitis. Its lips are completely black, and around each eye a thick black figure, like a rune, has been drawn. Slowly, it dawns on me that the face is mine.

My face is lying on a table near a bed. I reach to touch it, and notice that my arms are stippled with the tattoos I've been thinking about getting. My face is paper, it is on the cover of a big, important magazine, and that is why the phone is ringing. I pick it up, and notice that I am not anywhere I recognize. Someone who identifies herself as Traci is trying to tell me that she saw the magazine with my face and it makes her excited. I am supposed to know this person, because she apologizes for not having been in touch for so long. She wants to see me perform tonight at a big auditorium I've never heard of. I tell her I'll take care of it because I am glad that she wants to come but disappointed it is only because she saw my paper face. Then I roll over in a bed that is not mine and go to sleep.

"The cops are here!"

Someone is yelling at me, and I open my eyes. I hope that maybe it's morning and this is over, but I'm still sitting on a rock surrounded by dead toads, Nancy and a guy shouting that the police are busting the party. I can't figure out which of these things is worse.

I've always been paranoid about the police, because even when I'm not doing anything illegal I'm thinking about doing something illegal. So whenever I'm around a cop, I get uncomfortable and nervous, worried that I'm going to say the wrong thing or look so guilty that they'll arrest me anyway. Being completely out of my mind on drugs doesn't help the situation any.

We start running away. The rain has stopped and everything is wet and soft under my feet, so I feel like I'm sinking into the ground instead of running. Utterly acid-addled, the situation grows to enormous proportions in my mind, and I feel like I'm fleeing for my life. My entire future depends on not getting caught. We arrive and stop dead in front of a Chevrolet covered from hood to trunk with fresh, dripping blood. I'm in too deep.

"What the fuck is going on?" I ask everyone around me. "What is this? What's happening? Somebody!"

Nancy reaches out to me, and I push her away and find Teresa. She takes me into her car—dark, factory-scented and claustrophobic—and tries to soothe me, telling me that the other car is just painted red, and the red looks like blood because of the wet rain on it. But I'm completely paranoid: dead toads, cops, a bloody cat. I see the connection. Everyone's against me. I can hear myself scream-ing, but I don't know what I'm saying. I try to get out of the car. I do it by punch-ing the windshield, putting my fist through the supposedly shatter-proof glass. The cracks in the glass spiderweb around my hand, and my bleeding knuckles look like a row of open sewer pipes gushing waste.

Then we sit, and Teresa whispers things in my ear and tells me she knows what I'm feeling. I believe her, and I think she believes herself too. We enter that acid mind-meld where we don't have to talk anymore to know what each other is thinking, and I begin to calm down.

We return to the party. People are still there, though there are less of them, and there's no evidence that the cops have ever been there. Just as I'm beginning to cross the border from bad drug experience to tolerable one, someone—not real-izing I'm tripping my balls off—tries to push me in the pool as a joke. It doesn't take a math major to figure out that acid plus swimming pool equals certain death. So I panic and start flailing. Soon, we're locked in a fistfight, and I'm tear-ing at him like he's a doll I'm trying to mutilate. I punch him in the face with my raw, skinless knuckles and don't even feel the pain.

After he stumbles out of range, I notice everyone staring at me slack-jawed. "Listen, let's just go over to my house," I say to the people around me. We pile into the car—it's me, my girlfriend, Nancy and her boyfriend—the exact four ingredients necessary in a recipe for personal misery. Back at my parents' town house, we make our way to my room, where we find Stephen, my keyboardless keyboardist, lying on the bed like gasoline waiting for a match. He tries to interest us in the video he is watching, Slaughterhouse Five, the kind of strange, discon-nected head-trip film you don't want to think about when you're on acid.

Carl instantly gets engrossed in the movie, the television glow playing on his open, drooling jaw. Without saying a word, Nancy stands up hastily—annoyingly—and marches to the bathroom. I'm sitting on the bed with my girlfriend, my mind flashing in the same way the movie is flickering on Carl. Stephen is babbling about how the special effects in the movie were done. From the bathroom, I hear a spastic scratching sound, like the claws of dozens of rats skittering around the bathtub. In a rare moment of lucidity, I realize that the sound is of a pencil writing furiously on paper. The sound grows louder and louder, drowning out the TV, Stephen and everything else in the room, and I know that Nancy is writing something that is going to completely make me miserable and ruin my life. The louder the sound surges, the more crazy and twisted I imagine the words getting.

Nancy emerges from the bathroom in a blaze of vindictive glory and hands me the note. No one else seems to notice. This is between us. I look into the television to gather my strength. I'm staring at it so hard that I can't even focus on the picture anymore. In fact, it doesn't even look like a TV. It looks like a strobe light. I turn away, and look at Nancy. But I don't see Nancy. I see a beautiful, pouty woman with long, blow-dried blond hair and an Alien Sex Fiend T-shirt hiding her curves. It must be the woman from the telephone . . . Traci.

Instead of pencil scratching, I hear David Bowie: "I, I will be king. And you. You will be queen."

I have Traci's fingers in one hand and a bottle of Jack Daniel's in the other. We're standing on a balcony at a party, which seems to be in my honor. "I never knew you were all this," she purrs, apologizing for something in the past I'm unaware of. "I thought you were something different."

There are lights and flashbulbs, Bowie is singing "We could be heroes just for one day," and everybody is smiling ingratiatingly at us. She seems to be as famous as I seem to be.

"I spent my adolescence masturbating to that bitch," a roadie—mine?—cackles in my face.

"Who?" I ask.

"That."

"What's that?"

"Traci Lords, you lucky fucker."

On the floor beneath us there is a tall, slouched man with long black hair and a face painted white. He is wearing platform boots, torn fishnet stockings, black leather shorts and a shredded black T-shirt. He looks just like me, or a parody of me. I wonder if he is me.

A fat girl with metal rods and hoops stuck through half of her face and lipstick smeared over the rest notices me staring at the tall man. She comes upstairs, pushes past a stocky bodyguard—mine?—and, as her face strobes grotesquely in the light, explains, "You wanna know who that guy is? Nobody really knows his name. He's totally homeless. He makes his money hooking, and then spends it trying to look like you. He always comes in here and dances to your records."

I listen to the music again. The DJ has put on "Sweet Dreams" by the Eurythmics. But it's slower, darker, meaner. And the voice singing is mine. I need to get away from this surreal scene, away from all these people who are treating me like I'm some sort of star they can suck a little brightness out of. Traci takes my hand and leads me away, moving like mercury through the admiring rubble. We step behind a shite, gauzy curtain to an empty VIP room full of untouched deli sandwiches and sit down. There is something in my hands . . . a piece of paper. I try to focus on the thick, smudged lines. "Dear, Lovely Brian," it begins. "I want to kick my boyfriend out, and I want you to move in with me. You said last week that you weren't happy with the way things were going with Teresa"—fuck, it's from Nancy—"I will make you so happy. I know I can. No one will take care of you like I will. No one will fuck you like I will. I have so much to give you."

I put it down. I can't deal with it right now, not while I'm on this trip. Will I ever get off this trip? Nancy is standing in the bathroom doorway looking at me, her bare midriff slightly distended below her tight, navy T-shirt. Her thumb is thrust into the waistband of her jeans and she is biting her lower lip. She doesn't look sexy. She looks freakish and misshapen, like a Joel-Peter Witkin photograph. I stand up and walk over to her. Teresa and Carl sit on my bed watching the movie, completely oblivious to us and Stephen's freakish chatter.

The breeze blows in cool and logical from the open window of my bathroom, which is pitch black, though the lights in my head strobe on. I grope for the porcelain edge of the bathtub and sit down, trying to still my spinning head and remember what I was going to say to Nancy. I can hear music now, far too big and loud for my bathroom. I feel myself blacking out and try to fight it.

The music grows louder in my head. "This is not my beautiful house! This is not my beautiful wife!"

The music is not just in my head anymore. It's the Talking Heads, "Once in a Lifetime," and it's all over me, vibrating against my back. I'm lying on the floor, blinking open my eyes and trying to regain consciousness.

"And you may ask yourself, 'Well, how did I get here?'"

She—Traci—is leaning over me, pulling my shirt over butterflied lacerations I never knew I had. Her other hand is working on the buttons of my pants. Her mouth is hot and syrupy, and I can taste cigarettes and Jack Daniel's. She begins to do things with that mouth and those tiny hands and pomegranate red nails that millions of men have watched on second-generation videotapes for years—films I was never interested in, despite my fascination with her life. She lowers my pants and, with arms perfectly crossed, pulls off her top. She hikes up her skirt, not to remove it but to show me she's not wearing any underwear. I'm transfixed. She doesn't seem dirty, as if she's playing a role in a porno movie, even when she's giving me head. She is delicate, protective and angelic, a feather suspended in midair above an inferno of debasement and carnography. I'm drunk and, for that split second, I'm also in love. Through the thin lace curtain separating our tangle of tongue, fingernail and flesh from the rest of the club, I can see the bodyguard silhouetted against the strobing light, guarding the gate like St. Peter.

"Once in a lifetime . . . '"

I am thrusting into her now, and she screams. I grab her hair, but instead of long tresses of yellow, I get something short, clumped and stiff that tears out in my hands. My arms are shorn of tattoos, and the moans, muffled by my hand, reverberate against the silence. Shit, I'm fucking Nancy. What am I doing? This is not the kind of mistake you can get away with. Fucking a psycho is as good as killing one. There are consequences, repercussions, prices to pay. In strobing flashes, I see Nancy's face gazing up at me as she sits on the bathtub, her legs opening and squeezing shut, foaming wet like the jaws of a ravenous dog. With every flash, her face grows more and more distorted, more twisted and inhuman, more . . . demonic. That's the right word. My body keeps moving, fucking her hard, but my mind is screaming for it to stop.

This is it. I'm fucked. I'm screwing the devil. I've sold my soul.

"And you may ask yourself, 'Where does that highway go?'"

Someone bites the cartilage of my ear. I think it is Traci, because I like it. She grabs my choker and pulls my head toward hers. Her breath, hot and moist on my ear, whispers: "I want you to come inside me."

The music stops, the flashing stops and I come inside Nancy like a bouquet of milk white lilies exploding in a funeral hole. Her face is dead and emotionless. Her eyes are like burned out flash bulbs. Is that where the flashing was coming from?

"And you may ask yourself, 'Am I right? Am I wrong?' And you may tell yourself, 'My God! What have I done?'"

✕ ✕ ✕ ✕

CHAPTER TWO / LEMMY
BELLADONNA

EXCERPT FROM
White Line Fever

AUTHORS
Lemmy with Janiss Garza

COPYRIGHT © 2002 by Ian Fraser Kilmister and Janiss Garza
REPRINTED BY PERMISSION OF ~ Simon & Schuster UK LTD

Lemmy (1945-2015) was a bassist and songwriter who founded and fronted the band Motörhead.

". . . it calmed us down too much,
so we took some acid, and then we took some
mescaline to make it more colorful."

THIS PERIOD OF TIME, THE LATE SIXTIES, was brilliant for rock 'n' roll in Britain. There hasn't been such a wealth of talent in one era since. The Beatles, the Stones, the Hollies, the Who, Small Faces, Downliners Sect, Yardbirds had all come out of the same three-year period. The "British Invasion" had changed the face of rock music for all time, so in London we were sitting on top of the world. There was a lot of blues going on: Savoy Brown (which was much bigger in the States than in England) and Foghat started off as blues bands, and the jazz-blues thing came in for a little while. There were people like Graham Bond, who had Jack Bruce in his band, and Ginger Baker, both of whom went on to be in Cream. The Beatles had just come out with Sergeant Pepper, so they were certainly flavor of the fucking month! Two of them had just gotten busted, too, so they could do no wrong—John Lennon as icon-martyr, and Yoko looking violated at his side.

Everywhere you looked, there were good bands coming up. It's depressing nowadays because you have to dig to find a really great band, and there seem to be thousands of awful ones. There were thousands of bands then, too, but really, at least half of them were great. Just to give you an example, I was along for Hendrix's second UK tour, which ran from November 14,1967 until December 5. Co-headlining were the Move, who'd also just had two No. 1s in a row; then Pink Floyd with Syd Barrett—his last tour; Amen Corner, who were then at No. 2; the Nice, featuring a young organ player called Keith Emerson; and the Eire Apparent, later to become the Grease Band backing Joe Cocker. All for an entrance fee of 7 shillings and sixpence (70 cents American). And that was normal for the era.

You didn't think I'd get to talking about sixties London without mentioning drugs, did you? Oh no, not I. Our whole crew was just on acid during the entire tour. And we all got the job done just fine. Orgasms on acid, by the way, are fucking excellent, really unbelievable, so I was doing plenty of that, too. As a matter of fact, acid was still legal back then. There weren't any laws against it until the end of '67. And as for marijuana—well, you could have passed by the average copper on the beat, smoking a joint, and he wouldn't have known what it was. In fact, a friend of mine once told a cop it was a herbal cigarette, and the guy went for it. It just seemed like all of London was out of their heads back then. We used to get high and go down to the park and talk to the trees—sometimes the trees would win the argument. We were told that acid didn't work on two consecutive days, but we found that if you double the dose, it does!

There were some great clubs in London, like the Electric Garden and Middle Earth. You'd go there and everybody would be tripping. There was a chick who used to stand in the doorway of Middle Earth, by the cash register, handing out acid. She'd give one to each person as he or she walked in, free. One thing we used to do was get a crystal of acid, which had a hundred trips in it, and dissolve it into a hundred drops of distilled water in a bottle. Then we'd take a dropper and lay the mixture out in rows on a sheet of newspaper. Then when it was dry, we'd put the page back in the paper, go out, rip off the corners and sell them to people for a quid. Sometimes, if you were lucky, you'd get a piece of the treated newspaper that had two trips in it; other times, a soggy bit of paper!

Real acid tripping, in those days, wasn't all groovy-like, peaceful shit. The first trip I look lasted for eighteen hours, and I couldn't really see. All I saw were visions, not what was actually around me. Everything, every sound—you could snap your fingers and it would be like a kaleidoscope—doomph! Your eyes would just turn into noise-activated, colored strobes. And all the time your mind felt like you were on a rollercoaster, sometimes slow at the approach to the top of each drop and then—wheee! Your teeth would kind of sizzle, and if you started laughing, it was incredibly hard to stop. You could say I liked acid. But acid is a dangerous drug—that is, if you're complacent because it will wake your ass up! If you were a little uneasy about yourself, you would either be catalyzed by it or you wouldn't show up again—you know, they'd take your tie and shoelaces away, and your belt, and put you in a room with no windows in it and a lot of soft walls. A lot of people I knew went to the basket-weavers' hotel on acid.

Everybody was taking pills, too. Uppers, like Blues, Black Beauties and Dexedrine. It was all pills—I never took powder for years and years. Really, if you're in a band, or especially if you're a roadie, you need to take them things because otherwise you can't keep up with the pace. You can't go on a three-month tour without being on something. I don't give a fuck what they say—keep fit, eat your greens, drink juice—fuck off! It's not true! I don't care if you eat two hundred artichokes, you still won't last through a three-month tour, doing a gig a day.

Everybody did downers as well. We were doing Mandrax (the same as Quaaludes in the States). Once we bought a canister of a thousand Mandrax, but when we opened it, they had all melted—they must have got wet somehow. There was just this mushy mess of Mandrax at the bottom of this thing. So we laid it all out on the breadboard, rolled it down with a rolling pin and put it under the grill and we wound up with this white sheet of Mandrax, and we'd snap a corner off and eat it. Sometimes you just got a mouthful of chalk (the binding) and sometimes you'd get three Mandrax—sort of opiate Russian Roulette! I had a prescription for Dexedrine and Mandrax. In those days, there were a lot of doctors who'd prescribe you anything if you gave them the money. Harley Street doctors at that. And the doctor I went to took me off Mandrax, because a law had just been passed against it, and put me on Tuinol as a substitute. They were horrifying, really. Fuckin' Tuinol was seven or eight times worse than Mandrax. Mandrax is a little baby boy compared to Tuinol! That was dumb as shit. As usual.

✕

So I knew from personal experience that heroin was the most awful drug to get involved with, but that doesn't mean I didn't go through a few harrowing experiences involving the search for my own substance of choice. One time, about '69 or '70, I really came unstuck. A bunch of us were sitting around, waiting for the speed to arrive. This guy was going out with a nurse, see, who worked at a dispensary, so he bribed her into getting us some amphetamine sulphate. Finally, she came in with a mason jar with what looked like amphetamine sulphate written on it. And we, greedy bastards that we were, dug in immediately. But it wasn't amphetamine, it was atropine sulphate—belladonna. Poison. We'd all done about a teaspoonful of it, which is like 200 times the overdose, and we went berserk, the whole lot of us.

I was walking around with a TV under my arm, talking to it. Somebody else was trying to feed the trees outside his window. It was really interesting for a while, actually. Then we all passed out and somebody called Release, the firm with the free drug rescue van, and they loaded us all in the back like bundles of wood and took us to the hospital. I woke up in this bed and I could see through my hand. I could see the wrinkles in the sheet under it. Then I saw the institution walls. "Fuck me!" I thought. I was convinced I'd landed in the loony bin. Then I realized it was a normal hospital because the sleeves on the jacket weren't long enough. And I saw, across from me, my friend Jeff, just waking up.

"Psst! Jeff!"

"What?"

"We're in hospital."

"Wow."

"We've got to get out of here. Are you okay?"

"Yeah."

"Be quiet!"

So we got out of bed and I was just pulling up the jockeys when:

"AAAAARGHII! THEY'RE ALL OVER THE FLOOR!"

And he was leaping and screaming, eyes like organ stops, "Worms and grubs and ants—WAAARGH!"

I got back in bed.

Eventually the doctor showed up. "If we'd got to you in another hour, you would have been dead."

I was thinking, "I bet you're sorry, you miserable bugger."

He said we'd had the antidote, and that it would take a while to wear off. Well, it took two weeks and it was a really strange time. I mean, I would be sitting, reading a book, and I'd turn to page 42—but there was no book. Or I'd walk down the street, thinking I was carrying a case and suddenly—oops! I'd have nothing in my hand. Weird . . . but interesting. Not interesting enough to do it again, though!

Finally, after dossing around for some months, I wound up in another band, Opal Butterfly. I met their drummer, Simon King, at a place called the Drug Store in Chelsea. The Drug Store was a big flash gaff, about three floors high. There was a restaurant at the top and a boozer on the ground floor and a record store in the basement. All these boutiques and other stores, too. It was one of the first mall-type places. It was rather expensive, but it was an all-right place. The guys in Opal Butterfly used to hang out there to drink, and I hooked up with Simon and just sort of drifted into the band. I don't really know why I was hanging out with him—I never got along with him all that well. But you will be hearing more about Simon later.

Anyhow, Opal Butterfly was a good band, but they never went anywhere. They'd been around for years when I got in and it was only a few months after that that they gave it up. One of the guys, Ray Major, went on to be in Mott the Hoople. The breakup turned out to be rather timely, because it was only a couple of months later that I wound up in Hawkwind.

✕

Anyhow, we made for one hell of a show. Hawkwind wasn't one of those hip-pie-drippy, peace-and-love outfits—we were a black nightmare! Although we had all these intense, colored lights, the band was mostly in darkness. Above us we had a huge light show—eighteen screens showing things like melting oil, war and political scenes, odd mottoes, animation. The music would just come blaring out, with dancers writhing around on stage and Dikmik shaking up the audience with the audio generator. It was quite an experience, especially since most of our fans were tripped out on acid to begin with . . . not to mention everyone in the band. That included me and Dikmik, of course—just because we were Hawk-wind's only speedfreaks, it certainly didn't keep us from indulging in anything else we could get our hands on! There's one legend about how I was so loaded that supposedly I had to be propped up against my amp onstage so I wouldn't fall over. Well, as loaded as I may have been, I remember that show and it's not true about my having to be propped up.

That gig was at the Roundhouse in 1972, when we recorded the songs "Silver Machine" and "You Shouldn't Do That." That was a big venue. It was once an old engine shed, where they used to turn the trains around on a huge turntable. These rock 'n' roll people leased it and turned it into a venue by taking the turntable out and putting a stage at one end. There were still bits of locomotive lying around inside and shit. It was a great place, but now it's used for theater troupes—you know, Japanese acrobats and shit. Very interesting culturally, I guess, but . . . back to my story.

Dikmik and I had been up for about three days prior, whacking down Dexedrine. Then we got a bit paranoid and took some downers—Mandrax—but we thought it wasn't very interesting because it calmed us down too much, so we took some acid, and then we took some mescaline to make it more colorful. It started getting a bit freaky, so we took a couple more Mandrax . . . and then we took some more speed because we got too slowed down again. Then we went to the Roundhouse. Dikmik was driving and he was really interested in the side of the road, so he kept steering over to look at it. Finally, we got up there and we walked in the dressing room and it was full of smoke—everyone was smoking dope. So we sat there for a while and somebody came in with some cocaine and we had some of that, and then some Black Bombers (or Black Beauties, as they're known in the States—uppers) arrived, so we each had eight of them. Oh yeah, and we took some more acid as well. By the time we had to go onstage, me and Dikmik were like boards!

"Fuckin' hell 'Mik," I said, "I can't move. Can you?"

"No," he replied. "It's great, isn't it?"

"Yeah, but we've got to get onstage soon."

"Oh, they'll help us," he assured me.

So the roadies hooked our bootheels on to the back of the stage and pushed us up, and they strapped my bass on me.

"Right, okay," I said. "Which way is the audience, man?"

"That way."

"How far?"

"Ten yards."

So I stepped up—"One, two, three, four, five, right. Hit it."

And that was one of the best live gigs we ever taped. The jamming between me and Brock was great. But I never saw the audience! We got "Silver Machine," our only hit—and a No. 2 that!—from that gig! My vocals wound up on the recording, even though Bob sang it at the show. Bob wasn't on that night and he sounded horrible, so everybody tried overdubbing it later and I was the only one who sang it right. That was really my only time singing lead, except for "The Watcher" on Doremi Fasol Latido, "Lost Johnny" on Hall of the Mountain Grill, and "Motorhead," which was a B-side for the single "Kings of Speed" and later appeared on the rerelease of Warrior on the Edge of Time.

But I did sing a lot of backups.

It was magical, the time I spent with Hawkwind. We used to go to this huge, deserted estate and trip out. It had immense, overgrown gardens surrounding little pathways, ornamental lakes and tunnels all around this burned-out house. It was like madness in there. The whole band with about ten chicks and a couple more guys would all climb over the wall and we'd get high and wander around—you'd find the occasional person, tied in a knot under a tree, gibbering. That was a great time, the summer of '71—I can't remember it, but I'll never forget it!

Maybe you're wondering, with the massive amounts of drugs I consumed in those days, why I never became a casualty. I did die once—well, the band thought I had, at least. But I hadn't. The whole thing started when we were going home from a gig in the van. This guy, John the Bog, was our driver—actually, he died, about two years after this incident, come to think of it. He was going down the road, dropping everyone off, and I was the last one. We were in the midst of dividing up about a hundred Blues (pills that had speed with downer mixed in them) between us. I had the bag on my lap and I'd just handed him fifty and I had fifty. Right then, a carload of cops pulled in front of us. Brilliant timing, that.

"Look, Lemmy," John said, "we're getting busted!"

Well, no shit! But I wasn't about to let that happen. So I said, "Fuck this," and ate all my blues—John did the same. So here we were, chewing fifty blues apiece. Let me tell you, that was fucking foul! And we couldn't exactly take a drink to wash them down, either, because the cops were standing right outside.

"Step out of the van."

"All right, officer," we mumbled through the mush in our mouths.

"What were you doing in the front of the van there?" one cop interrogated me. "You were doing something with your hands when we pulled you over."

"No I wasn't," I insisted, drooling blue shit all the while.

But they missed that somehow and let us go. So John dropped me off in Finchley, where I was living in a house with the rest of the band. Apparently, I fell asleep and my metabolism hit an all-time low. It looked like I had stopped breathing, although I hadn't. But I was lying there with both eyes open, and it scared the shit out of Stacia. She freaked out.

"HE'S DEAD! HE'S DEAD!" she began screaming. Then she got Dave, and he was standing over me too, screaming, "HE'S DEAD!"

Meanwhile, I was lying there thinking, "What the fuck is the matter with these people?—Can't they see I'm trying to get some sleep?" I wanted to tell them to shut up, but I was having kind of a hard time speaking. Eventually they figured out I wasn't dead and after a while, I was all right again.

× × × ×

"We call them the 'wonder years' because we wonder what happened to them." —Steven Tyler

CHAPTER THREE / AEROSMITH
THE WONDER YEARS

EXCERPT FROM
Walk This Way: The Autobiography of Aerosmith

AUTHORS
Stephen Davis

COPYRIGHT © 1997 by Dogeared Publishing, Inc. and Stephen Davis
REPRINTED BY PERMISSION OF ~ HarperCollins Publishers

Aerosmith is Steven Tyler (vocals), Joe Perry (guitar), Brad Whitford (guitar), Tom Hamilton (bass), and Joey Kramer (drums), one of the most popular, influential and successful rock groups of all time.

"I kept a straw in a vial of coke so Joe could snort during the blackouts between songs, while Steven would leave lines on the amps. If a roadie put his flashlight down on the lines by mistake, he was fired."

IN EARLY 1976, Aerosmith woke up to find itself one of the most successful bands in America. Tireless road warriors, Aerosmith was beloved by millions of kids as the band you could actually see. Led Zeppelin, its empire in collapse, was injury-plagued and off the road, while the Rolling Stones were in a creative eclipse. John Lennon had retired to Central Park West. New bands like Boston took over album-oriented FM radio with "More Than a Feeling," while Lynyrd Skynyrd's "Free Bird" challenged "Dream On" as an American radio anthem. Two sisters from Washington State formed a band called Heart that outranked everybody except maybe Aerosmith. Little Feat and the Meters from New Orleans were the most respected bands, at least by their peers and the critics.

But the biggest successes in 1976 would be Peter Frampton's live album and Aerosmith's old idols Fleetwood Mac, former Brit blues scholars transplanted to Southern California in a later incarnation. The new thing was called soft rock and it began to sell, big time. Radio stations changed their formats to play Frampton, Fleetwood Mac, the Eagles, Elton John.

The rebellious spirit of rock 'n' roll lived on in unreconstructed hard rockers Aerosmith and Ted Nugent, who sold out almost every show they would play for the next three years. "In 1976 only Kiss and ZZ Top can rival Aerosmith's claim as the hottest new band in America," opined Circus magazine. "What sets the five Yankees from Boston apart from the other sensations of '76 is the purity of their roots. They are virtually the only natural heirs to the hard rock tradition founded by the Yardbirds and passed down into the seventies through Led Zeppelin."

Meanwhile in London, underneath the complacent, drug-soaked pop music structure, there was a new current of young bands that hated Elton, Zeppelin, the Stones, and other big rock icons, reviling them as rich, totally irrelevant junkies and Boring Old Farts, completely out of touch with youth. Soon the punk bands—the Sex Pistols, Clash, Generation X—would stage a revolution of their own.

In January, with the three-year-old, rereleased "Dream On" a Top 40 single all over America, Aerosmith and Jack Douglas began preproduction on the band's fourth album at the Wherehouse. In February, Brad Whitford married his girlfriend Lori at her family's home in Florida. Then the band moved to the Warwick Hotel in New York to begin recording the tracks that would ship platinum three months later under the title *Rocks*.

BACK IN THE SADDLE

BRAD WHITFORD: We started working on *Rocks* by backing the Record Plant's mobile recording truck into our Wherehouse and just letting it fly. The Wherehouse was just a good place to hang out and rehearse; a long white corrugated steel building that you could drive right into. Local kids spray-painted messages to us on the outside walls. Inside there were pictures of Chuck Berry, Rod Stewart, and Mick Jagger. One whole wall was a photomontage composed of Mick and Keith's faces. There were five trays for fan mail in the office—four usually contained five or six letters. Steven's tray was always overflowing.

When the other guys were late for rehearsal, Joey and I could wash our cars. The place was our clubhouse and lab. We could get a real organic sound from the Strats and the Les Pauls and Nick Speigel, our crew guy, was building the switching systems for our guitars and effects that we later used all year on the road. Our fan club was upstairs, with Raymond selling T-shirts through the mail, people designing things and spending our money, stealing us fucking blind, people padding bills, stuffing their pockets. Poison was running right through the system, from Leber-Krebs down to the lowest guy on the totem pole.

We were living the high life and not paying attention to anything except making this record. I had the beginnings of "Last Child" and "Nobody's Fault." Tom had "Uncle Tom's Cabin" that became "Sick as a Dog." We had "Tit for Tat," based on "Searching for Madge," which turned into "Rats in the Cellar." We cut all the basic tracks except two there.

JOEY KRAMER: That's when it all happened for us. There was a lot going on. We were beginning to get into drugs, the meat of getting high as a way of life. We weren't overwhelmed yet and I was living my fucking dream. I felt so content. How could I ever ask for anything more? But that's what I did, and that's what I got—more. Even "Dream On" was a hot record! Now I listen to *Toys* and *Rocks*, and they reek of the time and the fun we put into them.

Preproduction was me, Tom, Brad, and Jack Douglas at the Wherehouse. We worked hard and we laughed all the time. Jack would say or do something and I'd fall off my drum stool from laughing so hard. Example: Jack convinced me that if I ate nothing but greens for two weeks, I'd smell like a freshly mowed lawn. This went great until I got really constipated, so Jack had me drink a quart of prune juice to push it all through. He hid a new prototype sound-activated tape recorder in the bathroom. When he rewound the tape, there was a full day of horrible gas and flushing toilets. We laughed ourselves sick.

There were constant practical jokes around the studio all the time. One of the classics happened in the Record Plant, where the engineer had to cross the darkened studio to switch on the light to start the sessions. So Jack hung dozens of live crabs from the studio ceiling so Jay Messina would get clawed as he fumbled toward the light switch.

The main thing for me was I was really beginning to establish my style of play. "Nobody's Fault," "Combination," "Get the Lead Out" they were just so much fun to play on.

JOE PERRY: There's no doubt that we were doing a lot of drugs by then, but you can hear that whatever we were doing, it was still working for us.

We were experimenting and getting into heroin. We got good dope because now we could afford it. All the big dealers started hanging around us, so we only got the best stuff. We found good, steady connections, at least until our guy in New York got murdered. I snorted the stuff, and it felt great. I'd be lying if I told you anything different.

Then my father died. Elyssa and I were living in a condo her mother set up for us at 135 Pleasant Street in Brookline. I was depressed, in great emotional pain over losing my dad at too young an age—both for him and for me. Anyone who's gone through this might be able to understand. I knew these two coke dealers who had just come back from Thailand with twenty-eight ounces of Golden

Triangle pure heroin for their own use. It was the kind of shit you could step on four times and it would still be good. They turned me on to their stash and I was gone. When you first fall in love with heroin, it's like discovering God. I started studying the folklore of opium as a sacrament and really got into it. It helped me to concentrate on my work and became a good writing tool for me at the time . . . before it turned into this fucking monster.

For me, the agony you put up with when you don't have it was worth the ecstasy you felt when you did have it. Paying the piper when you're dope-sick was something I learned how to handle. I preferred to withdraw painfully rather than trying to cop on the street. I bought grams and half ounces. I'd take a couple of hits on the road with me and just get sick and stay in the hotel when I ran out. That's how I managed it for a few years. I never even saw a dime bag until 1980.

I wrote the main riff to "Back in the Saddle" on a six-string bass guitar I'd just bought, lying on the floor, stoned on heroin. Quite a few of the songs that Steven and I wrote for the Rocks album started out that way. When it came time to record the song later that year, Elyssa and I had moved to a big house on Waban Hill Road in Newton, and I drove over to the Wherehouse in Waltham and played this six-string bass like it was a "lead bass." We had so much fun rehearsing at the Wherehouse we figured: Why not try to record there too?

STEVEN TYLER: When we're doing our albums, I listen to Joe. *Rocks* comes from a time when we used to jam and I'd hear something and go, "STOP! WAIT! WHAT WAS THAT? PLAY THAT AGAIN!!" I'd hear something really good and I'd write the lyrics down right there. It doesn't happen that way anymore and it hasn't since we put the drugs down. We were more free then, more creative as a band. We still haven't solved some of the problems that the drugs cloaked.

Then we'd do thirty takes—forty!—because we were *gacked.* Jack Douglas would then take half of this take and half of that take and the bridge from Take 23 and put it all together and nobody knew what was what when we finally heard the record. Today I listen to those albums, some of our best, and all I can hear are the drugs.

DICK "RABBIT" HANSEN: I started working with bands when I got out of high school in Chicago. I started out with [the British group] Yes and worked for a whole lot of other bands. In fact, Aerosmith were the first nonheadliners I ever worked for. I started out baby-sitting Joe and Steven at the Wherehouse in the fall of '75. They were nice guys, wild guys, fun to be around. When they went on the road that fall with Nugent and REO Speedwagon, I did the monitors and NightBob did the outside sound.

My first show with them was in Detroit. They invited me to fly to the next gig in Indiana with them on their chartered plane: Steven, Joe, Elyssa, Kelly, Night-Bob, and me. They were chopping coke and passing a mirror around the cabin. Kelly snorted the whole thing and when Steven yelled at him Kelly blamed it on an air pocket, which got to be a big joke. "Sorry—air pocket." We all had luggage tags that said WTB in big letters. This meant "Where's The Blow?" (To outsiders, it stood for "World Touring Body.")

Kelly was a great road manager, the best in the business, with a great sense of humor. He took care of the band and crew and knew how to get what was needed out of promoters. He'd book the tour into hotels as the Shakespearean Players or the Globe Theatre Company. We'd get to a town out in the boondocks and the motel sign would read: WELCOME SHAKESPEAREAN PLAYERS.

It was Steven Tyler who started calling me Rabbit, because I was a vegetarian and liked what he called "rabbit food." Soon no one called me anything else. They were a pleasure to work for because they had the most advanced equipment in the business, everything custom-built and way ahead of its time. Joe and Brad had these rack-mounted effects with foot switches for their phasers, phlangers, digital delay, color sound, distortion, graphics, the air bag, whatever. There was another set of switches at my station, so an effect could be deployed by me if Joe forgot to turn his on.

They always played music through the PA before they went on. When I started it was [Bernard Hermann's] music from the shower scene in the movie *Psycho*, but we also used *The William Tell Overture* and *The Ride of the Valkyries*. The stage was always set up a certain way. Naked pictures of groupies in hotels were pasted to the amps; an old doll was on Joey's drums; a model of the Starship Enterprise had its own place. I kept a straw in a vial of coke so Joe could snort during the blackouts between songs, while Steven would leave lines on the amps. If a roadie put his flashlight down on the lines by mistake, he was fired.

You had to be careful around Aerosmith.

There was always a bottle of Jack Daniel's on the drum riser, as well as a bottle of

150-proof white rum, a total mind-fucker. Steven's little joke was to take one hit off this bottle and pass it down to the teenage kids in the first row. Five minutes later they'd all be vomiting because they weren't used to the overproof firewater. Nothing more hilarious than a row of puking fans.

The great thing was how close the band and the crew were. We called ourselves the Country Club Crew—Kelly, Nick Speigel, Henry Smith, NightBob, and myself—because we always wore these neat little Lacoste polo shirts and Gucci belts that Elyssa bought us. When we got sick of the road and had a few days off, we'd spend our per diems on drugs and take the crew bus to a campground by some lake and just spend our time water-sling and live on the bus while the band went home. We called them "camping trips."

The crew got a lot more girls than the band, who were more interested in dope than the girls who showed up backstage to blow them on the bus. So we got them instead. A day where I didn't have two girls was rare. The rule was, of course: "No head, no backstage pass."

Another rule was nothing but blowjobs ten days before coming home so you wouldn't pass on the clap to your girlfriend. This was the Ten Day Rule, alluded to in "Last Child" on *Rocks*.

THE COUNTRY CLUB CREW'S 21 ROCK 'N' ROLL LIES FOR ALL OCCASIONS

1:   Of course I remember you.
2:   It sounds great out front.
3:   I'll fix it in the mix.
4:   They're prepaid at the airport.
5:   I'll call you on Monday.
6:   I only use a third of a bottle.
7:   One more line, and we'll go to bed early.
8:   There'll be bonuses at the end of the tour.
9:   Ask me.
10: I won't get drunk onstage tonight.
11: I usually don't do this with girls.
12: Your name is on the list.
13: I'm all packed.
14: I'll turn down tonight.

15: We'll have a sound check tomorrow.
16: There's enough T-shirts for everyone.
17: I'll be down in five minutes.
18: I've got some in my room.
19: Yes, I turned you up.
20: I'll do it in the morning.
21: The check? It's in the mail.

LOS ANGELES: *At the last minute, Joe and Elyssa and Steven and Diana decide to attend the Don Kirshner Rock Awards TV broadcast, because Aerosmith has been nominated for Best New Group, which they think is pretty funny. Bored out of their minds (except when watching Jeff Beck's band writhe in mock agony during Rod Stewart's big number) they leave after Hall and Oates wins Best New Group. "Sounds like a cereal," Elyssa complains.*

The Perrys head for New York, where Joe will play on David Johansen's debut solo album. Steven repairs to a beach house in Malibu owned by the guy who leases jet aircraft to rock stars. The house is equipped with one-way mirrors so guests can watch the sex shows the owner likes to put on. Another guest, Mick Jagger, tells Steven Tyler, tongue in cheek, about the Stones' plans to hang parachutes around the halls of their next tour to get a better sound. Steven bothers NightBob about this for the next year.

Steven then flies to Boston, where he's met at Logan Airport by Harold Buker, Sr., Zunk's father, former campaign pilot for Jack Kennedy and now commander-in-chief of the Aeroforce, the band's flight wing. Light rain as Buker murmurs into the radio and the twin-engine, six-seat Cessna Citation clears the runway and heads north over the flaming golden carpet of New England in September to Sunapee, where Steven is living in a rented house on the lake while waiting for his new house, a former steamboat landing and yacht club, to be renovated. Exhausted after four months on the road, he dozes until Mount Kearsarge looms into view and the plane begins to fall into a steep bank as it approached Eagle's Nest, the Bukers' private airstrip in New London. Diana is there to meet him in his own red Porsche.

STEVEN TYLER: It was one of those houses I'd see when I was a kid driving around the lake in a little putt-putt boat that kids could rent down in the harbor. It was on Lovers' Point; it had a boathouse, a boardwalk, wooden stairs leading up the house. I'd admired this place for years, and I heard it was for sale and I had some money for the first time. "Seventy-five thousand? Yeah, I'll do it." I had this friend, a Vietnam vet who would bring up needles and coke to the house and we'd shoot coke all night. I'd get so high that the downstairs of the house always looked distorted to me, like it was elongated. When I finally got sober, I had to have the whole house gutted and rebuilt to get it out of my past.

THE CENACLE

BRAD WHITFORD: We had a new album to make, the follow-up to *Rocks*, and so the pressure was definitely on. We wanted to do a remote recording, out of the normal studio grind, and so though the Record Plant people we found the Cenacle, an isolated estate on 100 acres in Armonk, New York [in Westchester County, north of New York City]. It was built by Broadway showman Billy Rose in the 1920s and was reached by a half-mile-long driveway up a small mountain. Its most recent incarnation was a nunnery; the mansion had these wings for nuns' dorms, libraries, chapels, refectories—the whole convent scene.

By the time we got there, Jack Douglas, Tom, Joey, and I had been working for a month in Boston without Steven and Joe, who were both three sheets to the wind. We just kept working when we got to Armonk, figuring that (hopefully) Steven and Joe would start writing in the studio.

TOM HAMILTON: The Cenacle [the name was the French word for the Last Supper] was now owned by a psychiatrist who wanted the place to become a treatment center for disturbed adolescents. Instead he got us. We had to build a studio but weren't allowed to drive any nails into the walls, so they built a room within a room. They laid down a lot of cable and we recorded in the chapel and various other rooms of the big house.

BRAD WHITFORD: We explored the house and picked out our rooms on the second floor, each a little suite with its own bathroom. We looked at all the old cubicles for the nuns and listened to the caretaker's innuendos about their nocturnal habits. We brought in cooks to do the catering—the place was so big the food was about a quarter mile from the bedrooms-and settled into a routine of eating, driving our Ferraris and motorcycles on the Merrit Parkway, playing with our various toys, and getting high. One night early on, we turned out the lights and had a huge squirt gun fight. Jack went crazy and took it to extremes, stalking us on hands and knees in the house's giant attic, pitch-black, lit only by the lights of a digital watch. It was nuts. We were all soaked.

A couple days later, Joe Perry arrived in his black Porsche Turbo Carrera, toting one of his new toys, a semiautomatic Thompson submachine gun. Joe and Elyssa had driven down from Boston at a very high rate of speed with this thing in the trunk. Loaded. They went up to their room and disappeared for the next three days. Steven came in his 911 Porsche and he disappeared too. The three of us just kept working with Jack.

JACK DOUGLAS: They came to the Cenacle almost right off the road—no rest, no songs, no ideas, talking about maybe doing some cover versions. Never a good sign. The band had a chance to solve its problems by staying off the road and out of the studio, but they wanted to work. I thought they were crazy. The idea of the Cenacle was for them to rest, play with their new toys, eat well, and supposedly stay away from drugs right off the street. Jay Messina and I designed and built a control room with video monitors so we could see the guys while they were recording. Joey's drums were in the chapel, Steven was up on the second floor, Brad was in the living room, and Joe was in this big walk-in fireplace. That's how we did the record.

RABBIT: They'd brought at least twenty guns with them, cars, motorcycles, two bodyguards. There was constant target practice. Joe Perry set up a rifle range in the immense attic and basically opened fire. They liked to blow cymbals apart with shotguns. Everyone was fucked up on coke all the time. The caterers were former cooks for the Grateful Dead, so they were dosing the food. If they ran out of dope, crew guys would be sent into Manhattan. David Johansen was bringing in heroin, so not a lot of work got done. Sometimes the shrink who owned the place would materialize out of the fog wearing a long cape. The whole trip was pretty weird, and we were there for six weeks.

JOEY KRAMER: The Cenacle had been built by Billy Rose in the Gatsby days, and we had our own version of the Gatsby lifestyle going. We had girls catering the meals, a big table in the hall where we ate. After dinner, they left coffee and dessert for us and we'd work and record at night, because during the day we were too busy getting high and driving our cars and having a good time.

TOM HAMILTON: It was a rough period, because the band was split in two. Brad, Joey, and I would work all evening, rehearsing, tightening up. Steven and Joe wouldn't come down until midnight. So the band was fragmented. Heavy drug use was in the picture now, a really sick, very evil corrupt thing was happening. The vibe started to happen when Joe would be working on "his" songs, as opposed to "ours." We had some fun there, but no one was too happy.

BRAD WHITFORD: One night Joe came down to play with us. He said he wanted to practice the slide guitar part for the track that became "Draw the Line." But he was way out of it, slurring, nose running.

But he wanted us to lay down some rhythms so he could play over it. After ten minutes, he staggered to the nearest bathroom and puked his guts out. Then he came back, played for an hour, went back up to his room, and we didn't see him for five days.

JACK DOUGLAS: Joe and Elyssa were just totally wrecked. Joe would show up, glassy-eyed, and I'd throw him out because he couldn't play. I told Joe he should be ashamed of himself, coming to the session in that condition. He didn't give a shit. He'd just shrug and go back upstairs—for days at a time. Steven was a less-obvious junkie than Joe, but he had his own problems. He'd done some pre-production at my house in New Jersey but hadn't really written anything because he was on tour when he should have been writing. Most of the lyrics and vocals were done later at the Record Plant. It took us six months and half a million dollars to make that record.

JOE PERRY: There was an amazing line of Ferraris and hot Porsches in the Cenacle's driveway, but I never even drove mine after I got there because I was burnt-out and didn't need to go anywhere. Joey would wash my car for me because he hated to see it look bad.

We got there—me, Elyssa, Rocky (our Lhasa)—and checked out the studio they'd built on the first floor, the drums set up on the altar of the chapel. We went into our room, did a lot of dope, and basically went to sleep because we were exhausted from being on the road for two years. Rocky pooped in the closet. He was pretty good about it.

I'd shipped down my motorcycle, a Thompson submachine gun, a bunch of

.22 rifles, pellet guns loaded in holsters. When I woke up, I'd go up to the attic, pull out the Ruger and shoot off a bunch of rounds to let off steam, clear the cobwebs out. Downstairs, I'd have a big White Russian for breakfast. That's how I'd start off the day.

RABBIT: At one point we got an ounce of bad coke from some mob guys and we decided to try to return it. Steven gave it to Henry Smith to hold. Henry put it into a manila envelope, but later switched envelopes because we knew that Steven would decide he wanted the coke at 4AM. Next day Steven was pissed off and asked why we switched envelopes on him. I said to him, "Steven, we did it because you just don't know when to stop. You don't know where to draw the line."

JOEY KRAMER: Every night before dinner, Steven would go up to his room and lay out two big lines of blow to do afterward. Raymond was around and he started to poach these lines while Steven was eating.

Steven would go up and we'd hear him yelling, "WHAT THE FUCK!!!" One day someone saw Ray snorting these lines, but without Ray knowing it. Steven says, "OK, I am gonna really fix his ass good." So Henry Smith scraped some loose plaster off the wall, chopped it up into little lines, and baited the trap. We all went down to dinner. Raymond slipped away. We looked at each other and waited. Soon we heard terrible coughing sounds. Raymond tumbled downstairs, screaming, with all this shit up his nose. He had to deal with it all night.

TERRY HAMILTON: Steven was there with his girlfriend Dory. Joe and Elyssa were off in their separate attic and rarely came down. Joey was with his girlfriend Nancy Carlson, and Brad was with his wife Lori. One night Tom and I were eating and Joe came down with Elyssa. He was out of it, and he says to me, "I'd like to introduce my wife Elyssa." It was so silly I just started laughing, because I'd known her for years. We hated each other. She ran away in tears. Then she came back and everything was "normal."

JOEY KRAMER: Steven and I stayed up for days at a time. Day and night was the same thing, a blur. One morning at 5AM. Steven wanted to shoot some .22 rifles, so he and I went all the way to the end of the yard and set up some cans. He started to line up so he was shooting back towards the house. I said, "Steven, you've been up for three days, you can't even talk, why do you want to shoot?" But he wanted to shoot. He loads the rifle, lies in the grass, and he's aiming, aiming, aiming.

"Steven! Shoot the fucking gun already! Let's go!"

He keeps aiming. "Steven! C'mon!"

That's when I heard him snoring. He'd passed out. I picked him up, threw him over my shoulder, carried him up to the house and put him to bed.

RABBIT: Steven Tyler was a great guy who turned into Mondo when he did drugs. He liked to come in, piss off the crew, and walk out, having left a cassette recorder secretly running so he could hear what we said about him after he left. He was always walking around with one hand over his eye because he was seeing double. One day at Armonk he told me, "I've reached a new high—I'm seeing triple!"

STEVEN TYLER: We were out there at the Cenacle. Those were my Tuinal days where I'd buy a bottle of Tuinals, a hundred to the bottle, and I could only eat four or five a day because they were so strong, so I'd be good for a couple of months. I'd stash 'em in my scarf with a little hole in the bottom. I'd stuff twenty Tuinals in there and could go anywhere for a week. I was stoned on pharmaceutical drugs—much stronger than street drugs, which is why that period is blackout stuff.

JOE PERRY: The Beatles recorded their White Album, right? Well, *Draw the Line* is our "Blackout Album."

SCOTT SOBOL: I visited Joey a couple of times at the Cenacle and came away with an outsider's perspective. People who knew the band liked to trade Cenacle stories because it was basically one long party: lots of food and blow, driving the respective Ferraris and Porsches around quiet little Armonk, down into White Plains, and up into Mount Kisco. Lots of weird relationships going on: Steven with a girlfriend, Elyssa making everyone she came into contact with miserable, Joey breaking up with longtime girlfriend Nancy in the middle of everything.

On my first visit, I wanted to drop off some posters I'd gotten for Steven. Joey directed me upstairs to Steven's room at the end of a long hallway. The door was closed, guarded by a piece of notepaper (printed FROM THE BED

OF STEVEN TYLER) with the scrawl DON'T FUCKING KNOCK IF IT'S CLOSED. I knocked, because he'd asked me for these posters.

The door swung open quickly and there's Steven with this amazed look on his face that anyone had ignored his note. He saw me and lightened up instantly as I handed him the posters. "Hey, man. Thanks! Cool!" He was like a kid getting fresh posters of his favorite band, which I guess was what was happening. Over his shoulder I could see a pair of beautiful bare female legs stretched out on the bed, a mirror with some residue on it, and a rolled-up bill of large denomination, which made me feel awkward and I said good-bye.

When I got down to the front door, I heard footsteps bounding down the hall and Steven appeared at the top of the huge main staircase, bounded down two steps at a time, and stuffed a wad of cash in my hand. "Hey," I said, "the posters were a gift." He said, "Fuck you. I didn't used to have money and now I do, so take it and when you have the money you can give it to me." Typical, unpredictable, wonderful Steven.

You hear a lot of horror stories about Steven in those days, but nobody tells the ones that show him as he usually was. If you spent time alone with him, he was just the best. I remember him showing me the endless hallways in the huge basement one afternoon before we grabbed a couple of Heinekens out of the walk-in coolers in the kitchen. (One was for food, the other was full of beer and champagne.) We went upstairs and sat in one of the small rooms off the hallways.

Steven peered out one of the castle windows and looked across the great lawn behind the monastery, lost in thought, sipping his beer. "Here we are," he said a couple of times to himself, softly, with not a little sadness to it. "Here we are." It blew my mind because it seemed like something was hitting him at that moment, that they—and he—had really made it, and now they didn't quite know what to do with it.

SELF-DESTRUCTIVE WITH A SENSE OF HUMOR

JOE PERRY: If a band is like a river, an album is a bucket of water you take out of it, a moment in a band's life. *Draw the Line* was untogether because we weren't a cohesive unit anymore. You could tell we weren't in the same room when the tracks were done. The only thing linking us together were headphones. We were drug addicts dabbling in music, rather than musicians dabbling in drugs.

A lot of people had input into that record because Steven and I had stopped giving a fuck. "Draw the Line," "I Wanna Know Why," and "Get It Up" were the only things Steven and I wrote together. Tom, Joey, and Steven came up with "Kings and Queens," and Brad played rhythm and lead. Brad and Steven wrote "The Hand That Feeds," which I didn't even play on because I'd stayed in bed the day they recorded it and Brad played great on it anyway. Tom Hamilton and Steven wrote "Critical Mass." David Johansen worked on "Sight for Sore Eyes." In the end, we didn't have enough for a whole record, so we covered Otis Rush's "All Your Love" and reached back into the Jam Band for Kokomo Arnold's "Milk Cow Blues," which had been done by Elvis and the Kinks, whose version we modeled ours on. Brad played the solo and it made it onto *Draw the Line.* "All Your Love" didn't.

Before we went to Armonk, I worked for about a month in the eight-track studio I'd built in the basement of my house, which was filled with Stratocasters, Gibson Les Pauls, a B. C. Rich Mockingbird, a double-neck, and custom guitars by Dan Armstrong. I was into an "A" tuning for slide guitar and was writing and arranging things on a six-string bass tuned that way. I was way into the energy of the Sex Pistols, which I thought was another important thing from England that we should absorb. "Holiday in the Sun" and "God Save the Queen" and "Pretty Vacant."

That's where "Bright Light Fright" came from. We'd work all night, crash at dawn, when the only thing on TV was the good morning news. (This was before cable, right?) You write about what you know, so I put this on tape, along with some demos and various raw things. I put a bunch of these cassettes in a cookie tin, brought them to the Cenacle and forgot about them. A month later, we ran out of material and Elyssa reminded me of the cookie tin. There were all these slide riffs that caught Steven's ear and became "Draw the Line" and "Get It Up." I'm scratching my head, going, "Gee, I knew I had more songs." I brought "Bright Light Fright" to the band, complete with words and everything, ready to go. They didn't like it. I said, "Do you want to do it or not?" They said no.

In the end, Jack talked them into it.

JOEY KRAMER: "Kings and Queens" was a typical session at the Cenacle. It was recorded in the chapel with the pews out, the drums on the altar. Jack was in the confessional, hitting a snare drum by himself.

We were playing a lot of practical jokes on each other, so I snuck up behind him and yelled boo and scared him so much he chased me around the house for ten minutes before I lost him in the warren of nuns' cubicles.

JACK DOUGLAS: By the time we left the Cenacle at the end of May, I felt pretty bad. *Toys* and *Rocks* had helped me to another level of success. I had discovered and launched Cheap Trick, produced Patti Smith's *Radio Ethiopia*, and was turning down a lot of offers. I could have done Kiss and made a lot of money, but that would've been unfair to Aerosrnith because by 1977 Kiss was their only competition, at least among American rock bands.

So I started Draw the Line, and for a while gave it my all. But because they were halfhearted about the record, I was too. Steven wasn't writing at all. The lyrics to "Critical Mass" came from a dream I had at the Cenacle. I never expected Steven to record it, but he didn't have anything else, so he used my lyrics as written. Same with "Kings and Queens." Steven and I wrote the lyrics together, which was like pulling teeth. After the Cenacle, we spent from June to October either in the Record Plant, trying to finish the album, or on the road, where we recorded some of the live stuff that came out on *Live! Bootleg* and occasionally snuck into local studios trying to finish *Draw the Line*.

STEVEN TYLER: Why did it take so long? Because I wasn't Patti Smith writing poetry. I write exactly to the music, and when the music ain't coming, neither were the lyrics.

TOM HAMILTON: One afternoon we posed for Al Hirschfeld, the famous theatrical caricaturist, who came up to Armonk to do a line drawing of us for the album cover. *Draw the Line.* Get it? Hirschfeld was this quiet, bearded, bohemian artist, about seventy. He said he used to draw theater sketches inside his pocket during performances. I asked him if this used to get him thrown out of the theaters, but he didn't laugh. A week later, he produced this caricature that I thought captured us with wicked cruel accuracy. I liked it so much I bought the original.

LAURA KAUFMAN: Ray Tabano and I went up to the Cenacle to work on the tour book because they were going back on the road that summer without finishing the album. By that time, the drugs had taken over all our lives. I mainly remember that I did a lot of blow and never heard a note while I was there. One night we had a slide show for the band to approve photos, and Steven yelled at me yet again about some of the photos of him that were getting into the press. I finally solved this problem once and for all by going to CBS and stealing the whole Aerosmith photo file.

JOE PERRY: I couldn't wait to get away from the Cenacle. The day before we left, we had five U-Hauls lined up in the driveway for our motorcycles, amps, and guitars. I was pretty wasted, but I tried to drive my bike up the little ramp into the back of the truck. I got on the thing, gunned the engine, drove onto the fuckin' ramp and right off again, careening into some bushes. I got up, dusted myself off, looked at the crew, and said, "You guys take care of it."

RABBIT: Last day at the Cenacle, a TV crew shows up to make a promotional video for the album. This was Aerosmith's first video. Joe was so fucked up on heroin that we had to put a couple of grams of coke up his nose, just to get him to stand up. The video was never used.

TOM HAMILTON: Then there was the insane ride home from the Cenacle. We'd been up all night shooting this video and drinking Jack Daniel's. Joey got in his Ferrari and left immediately after we were through. "Be careful," I told him.

A couple of hours later, I'm driving up I-86 [now 1-84] without a radar detector because I couldn't plug mine into the Ferrari's weird cigarette lighter. So I limited myself to 80—nothing faster, or slower. I get on the Mass. Pike, and at Framingham I saw a black shape on the side of the road, an unmistakable Ferrari mashed against the guardrail. My heart sank when I realized it was probably Joey's.

JOEY KRAMER: I was almost home and doing about 135 because the car was finally broken in. We'd been filming a commercial under hot lights, and I was tired. Brad had offered some keep-me-awake powder, but I refused. At 4AM., I fell asleep and smashed into a guardrail. My head rammed into the glass, nicked an artery, and I started to bleed. Tom, an hour behind me in his Dino, saw the wreck and at first was afraid to call the hospital because he thought I was dead.

TOM HAMILTON: I pulled into a rest stop, called the state police, and went over to the hospital as Joey was released, soaked in blood, his head bandaged, and cut up from the glass. We went to the police barracks and Joey pulls out this deck of registrations, because he owned nine cars and carried all the paperwork with him. I watched this cop watch this bruised and bandaged, pissed-off, burnt-out, half-stoned, Ferrari-driving punk shuffling through the registrations, and I just knew he was thinking, *Who the fuck is this guy?*

JOEY KRAMER: The damage report? Seven stitches and $19,000 for the car. Plus, we had to cancel some shows. Then Joe Perry completely totaled his Corvette.

JOE PERRY: I was doing 90 on Route 9 in Newton, passed a slower car, swerved, hit the guardrail, spun around, and sideswiped an unmarked cop car. I walked away from the wreck without a scratch, started picking up pieces of fiberglass all over the road. The cop told me to get the hell out of there. He must have felt sorry for me. He even dropped me off at Dunkin' Donuts.

STEVEN TYLER: All this time we were out on the road. With the album unfinished, we played a show at Cleveland Stadium that was later voted worst show of the year by the local stations. Then Omaha. Fort Worth, Texas, on Joey's birthday (June 21, 1977), in front of a rabid, hardcore audience. In August, we started a three-week mini-tour to honor some concert dates, with the record still unfinished. Everywhere we went people told us they'd heard rumors Aerosmith was breaking up.

AERO KNOWS, VOL. 1, #3 [Official fan club newsletter]
We're getting organized for the big one, AEROSMITH EVERYWHERE on tour '77. It should start right around Labor Day and most major cities across the land are planned stops. Listen up, you loyal fans out there. No matter what you hear, there is only one AEROSMITH, we're going to be playing everywhere constantly. "Accept no substitutes" and let me add this! (Ahem, *Aero Knows* is about to get heavy.) If you hear any kind of weird rumors, stories, concerning AEROSMITH as a group or the lads individually, unless you hear it here, baby, somebody's only exercising their jaw! (Ray Tabano, July 1977)

CIRCUS
Performing their last mini-tour date at Baltimore's Civic Center, Aerosmith had

technical problems as Joe Perry's guitar amp kept cutting out. After the fourth breakdown, Perry took off his guitar and walked over to Steven Tyler, and the two square-danced while waiting for the repair job. During the group's encore, "Train Kept A-Rollin'," the amp [quit again.] Perry walked over to the mike and held the guitar over his head.

"This is a 1957 Stratocaster," he said. "It's been in my family for generations, and this is how we used to solo back then." The precious stringed relic of the pioneer days of rock 'n' roll flew fifteen feet in to the air and crashed to the floor unattended. The group finished the show without Perry. (September 15, 1977)

JOE PERRY: I was throwing monitors into the audience. When a string on my Strat broke, I must have snapped. But I had the presence to grab a fake Strat, which is the one that got smashed. I mean, we're not talking about schizophrenia here, just self-destructive with a sense of humor.

CHAPTER FOUR / GREGG ALLMAN
COME AND GO BLUES

EXCERPT FROM
My Cross To Bear

AUTHOR
Gregg Allman

COPYRIGHT © 2012 by Gregg Allman
REPRINTED BY PERMISSION OF ~ HarperCollins Publishers

Gregg Allman is one of the original members of the Allman Brothers Band, a member of the Rock and Roll Hall of Fame, and a recipient of a Grammy Lifetime Achievement Award.

"Goddamn it, they're coming after us. Everybody eat what you got, or throw it out, but do something."

WHEN I THINK BACK across my life, I usually come up with positive stuff—like the fun times with my brother, the great times I had with Allen Woody, and all that. My memories aren't about being in jail or my ex-wives. I imagine that most people have enough negative shit in their life that if they dwelled on it long enough, they'd probably blow their brains out, and I'm no different. I just naturally don't dwell on the negatives, just like I naturally don't eat the white part of the turnip—because I can't stand it. Thinking about drugs at this point is another negative, but there's no denying that drugs were a big part of my life.

If you check the records, the most consistent thing about my drug use was that I kept on trying to get straight. I kept coming back, and coming back, and coming back, trying to quit. I must have gone into treatment eighteen times, and the time between each visit got to be a little longer, which I saw as a good thing. That little voice telling me to clean up was always in my head, even though there were times when I could barely hear it.

I started using pills in Daytona, because I had to go to school after playing gigs at night. They were red-and-blacks—they had a little phenobarbital, so they'd take the edge off a little bit. In New York, there was a bit of speed, and I believed in my speed. As long as I had my speed, I was okay, but I never took too much. You know when you're young like that, before you're thirty, you're fucking bulletproof.

When we weren't playing music, we'd do speed and drink or do downers and fuck. We had Nembutals, and we'd grind them bad boys up, sit and wait a bit, and then just fuck for hours. One time, I was visiting Daytona, and we had to go all the way down to Deland to pick up a prescription that somebody had for Nembutals. It was me and these two real pretty girls. We got those pills and chopped them up, put just a bit of water in them, set them up on the dash, and I'm thinking, "Boy, I'm fixing to have me a hell of a time!"

"We pulled off on an old country road, did them Nembutals, and then we fucked until the sun went down. I did both of them, one at a time—my dick was like a damn oak tree all day. There weren't no mosquitoes, neither! We didn't have any AIDS back then; there was none of that. Fucking didn't kill you, but it might just make you a little sick or itchy.

I was turned on to cocaine by King Curtis, during the Brothers' first trip out in Los Angeles. I had done a fair amount of speed before I tried cocaine, and to tell you the truth, coke didn't really work on me. It seems that people who had taken speed, when they tried coke, it wouldn't work, and the people who took cocaine, when they tried speed, it wouldn't work. When I first tried coke, it just gave me cottonmouth, and not much else.

I didn't get into coke real serious until I moved up to Macon. This guy who had robbed a drugstore gave me a full sealed ounce of pharmaceutical cocaine, and between me and the band, we about blew our brains out on that shit. You'd do a little bit of coke, you'd pour a real stiff drink so you could level out, and you'd go play some music. Then, when you came back down, you wanted another hit of that damn cocaine, even though you realized that you felt like shit it from it and needed that drink to cool out. Doing the same thing twice and expecting a different outcome is the definition of insanity.

Whoever came up with that slogan, "Cocaine is a lie"—well, it is a lie. I don't know how many times I got high on coke, and then sometime between eleven and one o'clock, I felt so fucking bad. I'd be paranoid and jittery, and thinking, "Man, I paid $125 to get like this?" The thing is, then I'd do it again the next night.

After we had gotten into cocaine, we were playing one gig, and we went to count off "Statesboro Blues," and my brother went, "One, two—the band needs some coke!" At intermission, there must have been nine cats come back there with shit to sell. I thought for sure we were all gonna get popped, but we got lucky.

I never did like cocaine by itself, because it made me too nervous. But a little coke and two Percodan and I was ready to fight three lions at once. Then it would stop working, and that was the problem.

Bad as all those were, they were no heroin, man—and it was smack in the middle of that crazy year of 1970 that heroin made its first appearance. We'd been playing so many fucking gigs we couldn't count them all, and by summer we'd found ourselves back in Macon. Back then in Macon, it was really hard to find a nickel bag of reefer, let alone an ounce, but you could buy heroin in a snap—seven dollars a bag.

The first time we scored heroin, we were having a little party over at Duane's house on Bond Street. We had just come in off the road, and we had done pretty good—we each had a couple hundred dollars to show for it. A black dude who was a friend of Chank's came over to me and said, "Hey, bro, try a whack of this." He had a pocketknife that he dipped down into a little plastic bag of off-white powder, and the tip of the knife just barely touched it. He put the point of the blade right under my nose, and I snorted the powder off of it.

It hit me with a big rush, because back then they would cut heroin with quinine, so that it would surge through your blood real fast. I started drifting, and I didn't give a shit about nothing. I felt relaxed, so I sat down in this big leather chair, which was so cool. I remember seeing big purple hippos kinda floating through my head, and that's about all that was going on up there. I thought, "Man, this is neat," because it shut up all the noise in my head.

This cat let me keep enough for about two more little tastes, and then we hit the road for about a month, so I didn't see him. When we got back to town, I ran into him, and the same thing happened again—same amount, same result. It was just as much of a groove, because it hit and I went, "There's that feeling again!"

After that, this cat would kinda be around all the time. After about a month or so, all the band and all the roadies were participating. It wasn't long until everybody associated with the Allman Brothers Band, with the exceptions of Twiggs Lyndon and later Joe Dan Petty, from our road crew, was addicted to opiates. The thing is, no one ever used the word "heroin." The only word that was ever said was "doojee." If I'd had any idea of what it really was, I don't think I would have done it. I honestly didn't know that this doojee stuff was heroin. Maybe I should have, but I didn't.

Heroin is a musician's drug, because you work till you drop, and this stuff would just ease you down off the mountain. You don't think people sneak around and put needles in their arms for nothing, do you? You've never been high till you've been high on heroin. A lot of people who try heroin for the first time will barf up a lot of air and have the dry heaves for about four hours, and it's so terrible that it stops them from taking it again. That didn't happen to us, because we must have taken just enough not to get sick.

At first, there were no needles. We were just snorting it, and we didn't have any accidents. Oakley just loved that stuff. He was an Aries, a fire sign, and the doojee brought him down just enough, but he had enough smarts to never do it two days in a row. Duane liked doojee all right, but blow was much more his thing, and, he did a lot of it. Me, I had to learn the hard way about doojee; that shit brought me nothing but pain and agony, and it almost took me from this world about six times.

In the beginning though, I never thought we were real junkies—we were just trying to keep a buzz going. We never got too high to play, at least while my brother was alive. Even though those drugs are real habit-forming, it does take a while for the shit to really get into the marrow of your bones, to the point where you wake up and that's the first thing you think of. Thank God that didn't happen but to two of us, but the money we laid down for that shit was unbelievable.

We went to Nashville to play Vanderbilt University in October 1970, and we were staying right across the street from the hospital where Duane and I were born. We had a day off, and my brother was out looking to score some doojee. He didn't find any, but he did find a guy who had some Tuinals and he took one. Then here comes a dude, and he's got a ball of opium with him that's about the size of a baseball. Tuinals and a narcotic do not mix; that's what killed Allen Woody and many, many others. It almost got me a couple of times, until I got wise to it.

As soon as the opium got there, my brother bought a piece about the size of a golf ball and took a big chunk of it off and ate it. A while later, the rest of us were down in the Winnebago getting ready to go, and no one had seen Duane. Red Dog went up to the room to check on things, and he came back down and said, "Man, he won't wake up, and half of his body is turning blue," because his blood was settling—he was almost dead

"Oh my God, he's going to die, right here where he was born." I was freaking. I'm getting ready to spring like a damn black panther, and Dickey goes right over the top of me. When that guy needed to run, he could really move. He was over me, through me, and past me, up to the third floor. He loved Duane—I've got to say that about Dickey Betts. I also have to say that he probably saved Duane's life that night. You've got to give the devil his due, but the thing is, Dickey ain't no devil. He's just a mixed-up guy.

Dickey got to Duane first, with Payne and Callahan right behind him. I was just standing there, frozen in prayer. I got down on my knees in prayer, probably for the first time in my life. They got him downstairs, and he was not moving. The lights were on, but no one was home—hell, the lights weren't even on. Thank God we were parked right across the street from the hospital, because they got him over to the emergency room, and he was in there for the longest fucking time, but they were able to revive him.

God was looking down on us, man, and so were his Angels of Mercy. They say you got two guardian angels; well, I think Duane borrowed both of mine, and a few more from everybody else. My brother must've stayed high for three days, but he actually played the gig the next night in Atlanta. It's too bad we don't have those tapes, because that was a rather slow night.

The whole thing really scared my brother, man. He had the fear of God in his eyes after that, and he didn't do drugs again for a long time. He might have drunk a beer now and then, beer or cheap wine, but that was it.

The first time I got dosed with acid was in January 1971 at the Fillmore West, where we were playing four nights with Hot Tuna. I set my drink down, and some Prankster dosed it. I didn't know where I was—it was like Alice in Wonderland. There were these big fuzzy things floating around, and everything looked like something out of an R. Crumb comic, I guess because I had gotten turned on to Zap Comix right around that time. These R. Crumb images were coming out of my brother's amp, right along with the notes, and I was like, "What the fuck is going on here?" But it didn't take me long to realize what had happened.

Acid is a brain douche, if you ask me; I've got no use for it, because it just scrambles your brain. It would take me three days before I could even think straight, so I haven't tripped in over thirty years.

We were aware of what was going on in society at that time, and we cared about what was happening with the war in Vietnam and what happened at Kent State. The original title of *Eat a Peach* was *Eat a Peach for Peace*, but it got shortened. In truth, though, we were sheltered by the music and the traveling, and, especially, for myself, by the songwriting. Writing throws your whole and complete attention into the process, and you get into it so deep, nothing distracts you. Someone would have to inform you that your house was ablaze.

Still, sometimes things would happen that you couldn't ignore. We didn't have any run-ins with the law in Macon, but it seemed like every time we went to Alabama, we got in trouble. One time, when Twiggs was still with us, we were in the Winnebago heading through the hills of northern Alabama, and I had just got done smoking a joint. We heard the sirens and saw the blue and red lights, and this guy pulled us over.

He opened the door and said, "All right, who do we have here?"

"Sir," Red Dog said, "we've got the Allman Brothers Band, a rock and roll band on Atlantic Records, thank you."

The cop said, "Then let me see Mr. Allman, in the back of my car—now."

So my ass got up, and I got my wallet, and I go and get in the back of the car. He asked me a bunch of questions—where we had been and where we had played, where we were going, where we were planning on staying—and this was back when I was up on everything, so I spit it right out to him. He looked over at me, moved his clipboard, and pulled out a big old syringe and started flipping it up and down, catching it.

Then he said, "You know what, Mr. Allman? The judge would absolutely go crazy out of his mind if he knew what you fuckers was out here doing."

"How much, man?" was all I asked.

"Don't rush me—I'm not through with my story." So he finished his lecture. Then he said, "As for the price, I think $300 would be fine. Just drop it over the seat, and I'll give you back your license. And please, be discreet."

"I went back to the Winbag, and Twiggs was waiting. He just asked, "How much?" I told him it was $300, and he said, "Man, that's almost going to clean us out." That's when I should have written that song: "That's just the way it is, some things will never change."

Then there was the time we were on our way from Macon to the Warehouse in New Orleans, and we were in a real hurry. We were driving in two rental cars, and Jaimoe was sitting in the back of one of them—keep in mind, this was 1971. We passed through Grove Hill, Alabama, and we were all hungry, so we pulled off the road and went to a restaurant. All of us—that is, except for Dickey, who'd had too much to drink, so he stayed in one of the cars. We sat down, and we were looking pretty rough. Right away, you could tell that people were checking us out.

While we were inside, I looked out the window, and there's Dickey—he's gotten out of the car, and he's barfing like crazy, and the whole place can see him. I thought, "Oh shit," but said, "Okay, guys, I'll have pancakes, and cook the bacon well."

I went to the bathroom and flushed the four or five reds I had on me. I had one bag of doojee, and I wasn't going to throw that away, so I put it in my wallet and walked back out and sat down. When I got back out, I noticed that one of the waitresses was talking on the damn phone and glancing over in our direction. By this point, Dickey was back in the car, horizontal in the backseat, but the door was still open. I told everyone, "Guys, let's eat up, pay the check, and get out of here." So that's we did.

We were riding along, and I was in the back with Jaimoe, while Willie Perkins was driving and my brother was up front with him. Suddenly Duane said, "Goddamn it, they're coming after us. Everybody eat what you got, or throw it out, but do something."

Jaimoe pulled out this bag of reefer that would have choked a mule, and he starts to eat it. It was this big bag of green that looked like a beer you get on St. Patrick's Day—there was no way he could finish it, and the more he ate, the bigger it got in his mouth. Then he couldn't spit it out, so it was like, "Hey, here I am!" Here he is with a bunch of long-haired white guys, and one of them is throwing up.

When I saw they were behind us, I took out that bag of doojee and, instead of snorting it and cooling my jets and making everything easy, I threw it out the back window, and them sons of bitches found it. They saw it in the sunlight when I threw it, and we could hear them going, "Well, it looks like hair-o-win to me, boy. Hey, look out now—don't spill it. You asshole, you're about to spill it." This one guy must have touched the bag, and half of it went out.

They arrested us all and threw us in jail, and I'm in the same cell as Red Dog, so he gets over in the corner and quietly takes off all his clothes. He's got a nut sack that hangs way far down, and legs that are no bigger than a pair of pool cues—I don't know how the hell they hold his body up. He's up on the bars and he looks like the damn Wild Man from Borneo with all that red hair, and that big old dick and them balls. A bunch of old ladies had gathered around the jail, and they just knew he was a heathen!

I knew there was safety in numbers, so I wasn't sweating shit while we were in there. I was hoping that it wouldn't hit the news, but sure enough, that town was so small that word spread right away. We got out of there after one night, charged with disturbing the peace, and we were only fined twenty-five dollars, because Mr. John Condon, the lawyer who'd helped us out when Twiggs stabbed that guy, came to the rescue again. At one point, we stopped playing in Alabama—except for Birmingham, and even that was pretty rare.

Another time we were playing New Orleans. We were staying at the Pontchartrain Hotel, and I had the bottom suite. I had an eight ball in my Levi's, and I had on a blue velvet coat, a white silk shirt with black roses on it, and a pair of blue velvet boots. I had taken my boots and socks off and was having a glass of wine. All of a sudden, here come six guys, banging on the door. "Let us the fuck in, this is the law."

I opened the door and jumped back as they came pushing in. All of them start going through the suite, and one of them got in my face and said, "We're going to sit here and bust you, and then we're going to let you watch us go upstairs and bust all your little Allman friends."

One of them came over and said, "All right, where's the shit?"

I started to say, "If you bust your head open, man, we can dip it out," but I just went, "Where's what? We're not smoking anything in here but cigarettes."

"You just stay here," he ordered, and they never even looked in my pocket—they never shook me down.

Then they went up to Jaimoe's room, and Jaimoe has on a dress! His friend Juicy Carter was there with him, but I don't know why he had on a dress. The cop opened the door, took one look at him in that dress, and turned around. He just walked away and didn't bother to fuck with him.

Butch had half an ounce of blow, and he put it under the mattress. Boy, how original can you get? This cop picked up the mattress, and if he had picked it up half an inch more, he would have seen it, so Butch got really lucky. Dickey was in bed with his wife, Sandy Bluesky, and as soon as they busted the door open, he jumped up and popped the first guy who came in the room. Another one pulled out his billy club and bapped Dickey across the head and knocked him out cold.

This whole thing happened because the promoters had changed. One promoter had fucked us, so we found a new one, and the first promoter made a call to the police. You should have seen what this fucking warrant said: "Possible possession of barbiturates, amphetamines, hallucinogens, hallucinogenic mushrooms, peyote, heroin, cocaine and marijuana." They also listed some shit I've never heard of, but all they ended up getting us for was Dickey taking that swing at them. It was a dirty, dirty trick, man—somebody really tried to set us up.

X X X X

Of the strange, improbable, and often excretory adventures that befall our heroes on a journey with the minstrel Ozzy Osbourne and his delightful consort, Sharon.

CHAPTER FIVE / MÖTLEY CRÜE
NO FUN

EXCERPT FROM
The Dirt: Confessions Of The World's Most Notorious Rock Band

----

AUTHORS
Tommy Lee, Vince Neil, Nikki Sixx, Mick Mars and Neil Strauss

----

COPYRIGHT © 2001 by Tommy Lee, Vince Neil, Nikki Sixx, and Mick Mars
REPRINTED BY PERMISSION OF ~ HarperCollins Publishers

Mötley Crüe is Nikki Sixx, Vince Neil, Mick Marrs and Tommy Lee. Multiplatinum recording artists, international rock stars, and legendary raconteurs, they defiled a generation.

"From that moment on, we always knew that wherever we were, whatever we were doing, there was someone who was sicker and more disgusting than we were."

NIKKI SIXX: WE THOUGHT WE WERE the baddest creatures on God's great earth. Nobody could do it as hard as us and as much as us, and get away with it like us. There was no competition. The more fucked up we got, the greater people thought we were and the more they supplied us with what we needed to get even more fucked up. Radio stations brought us groupies; management gave us drugs. Everyone we met made sure we were constantly fucked and fucked up. We thought nothing about whipping out our dicks and urinating on the floor of a radio station during an interview, or fucking the host on-air if she was halfway decent looking. We thought we had elevated animal behavior to an art form. But then we met Ozzy.

We weren't that excited when Elektra Records told us they'd gotten us the opening slot on Ozzy Osbourne's Bark at the Moon tour. We had played a few dates with Kiss after *Too Fast for Love*, and not only were they excruciatingly boring but Gene Simmons had kicked us off the tour for bad behavior. (Imagine my surprise seventeen years later when ace businessman Gene Simmons called as I wrote this very chapter, asking not only for the film rights to *The Dirt* but also for exclusive film rights to the story of Mötley Crüe for all eternity.)

We started warming up for the Ozzy tour at Long View Farm in Massachusetts, where the Rolling Stones rehearsed. We lived in lofts and I begged them for the one where Keith Richards slept, which was in the barn. Our limousine drivers would bring us so many drugs and hookers from the city that we could barely keep our eyes open during rehearsals. Tommy and I kept a bucket positioned midway between us, so that we'd have something to throw up into. One afternoon, our management and the record company came down to see our progress, or lack thereof, and I kept nodding out.

Mick, our merciless overseer of quality control, bent into the microphone and announced to the assembled mass of businesspeople and dispensers of checks, per diems, and advances: "Perhaps we could play these songs for you if Nikki hadn't been up all night doing heroin." I got so pissed off that I threw my bass to the ground, walked over to his microphone, and snapped the stand in half. Mick was already at the door by then, but I chased him down the country lane, both of us in high heels like two hookers in a catfight.

The tour began in Portland, Maine, and we walked into the arena to find Ozzy running through sound check. He wore a huge jacket made of fox fur and was adorned with pounds of gold jewelry. He was standing onstage with Jake E. Lee on guitar, Rudy Sarzo on bass, and Carmine Appice on drums. This wasn't going to be another Kiss tour. Ozzy was a trembling, twitching mass of nerves and crazy, incomprehensible energy, who told us that when he was in Black Sabbath he took acid every day for an entire year to see what would happen. There was nothing Ozzy hadn't done and, as a result, there was nothing Ozzy could remember having done.

We hit it off with him from day one. He took us under his wing and made us comfortable facing twenty thousand people every night, an ego boost like no other we've ever had. After the first show, a feeling came over me like the one I had when we sold out our first night at the Whisky. Only this was bigger, better, and much closer to the victory line, wherever and whatever that was. The little dream that we had together in the Mötley House was about to become a reality. Our days of killing cockroaches and humping for food were over. If the performance at the US Festival was a spark illuminating what we could become, then the Ozzy tour was the match that set the whole band ablaze. Without it, we probably would have been one of those L.A. bands like London, surefire stars who never quite fired.

Ozzy hardly spent a night on his tour bus: He was always on ours. He'd burst through the door with a baggie full of coke, singing, "I am the krelley man, doing all the krell that I can, I can," and we'd snort up the krell all night long, until the bus stopped and we were in the next city.

In one case, that city happened to be Lakeland, Florida. We rolled out of the bus under the heat of the noonday sun and went straight to the bar, which was separated from the swimming pool deck by a glass window. Ozzy pulled off his pants and stuck a dollar bill in his ass crack, then walked into the bar, offering the dollar to each couple inside. When an elderly lady began to cuss him out, Ozzy grabbed her bag and took off running. He came back to the pool wearing nothing but a little day dress he had found in the bag. We were cracking up, though we weren't sure whether his antics were evidence of a wicked sense of humor or a severe case of schizophrenia. More and more, I tend to believe the latter.

We were hanging out, us in T-shirts and leather, Ozzy in the dress, when all of a sudden Ozzy nudged me. "Hey, mate, I fancy a bump."

"Dude," I told him, "we're out of blow. Maybe I can send the bus driver out for some."

"Give me the straw," he said, unfazed.

"But, dude, there's no blow."

"Give me the straw. I'm having a bump."

I handed him the straw, and he walked over to a crack in the sidewalk and bent over it. I saw a long column of ants, marching to a little sand dugout built where the pavement met the dirt. And as I thought, "No, he wouldn't," he did. He put the straw to his nose and, with his bare white ass peeking out from under the dress like a sliced honeydew, sent the entire line of ants tickling up his nose with a single, monstrous snort.

He stood up, reared back his head, and concluded with a powerful right-nostriled sniff that probably sent a stray ant or two dripping down his throat. Then he hiked up the sundress, grabbed his dick, and pissed on the pavement. Without even looking at his growing audience—everyone on the tour was watching him while the old women and families on the pool deck were pretending not to—he knelt down and, getting the dress soggy in the puddle, lapped it up. He didn't just flick it with his tongue, he took a half-dozen long, lingering, and thorough strokes, like a cat. Then he stood up and, eyes blazing and mouth wet with urine, looked straight at me. "Do that, Sixx!"

I swallowed and sweated. But this was peer pressure that I could not refuse. After all, he had done so much for Mötley Crüe. And, if we wanted to maintain our reputation as rock's most cretinous band, I couldn't back down, not with everyone watching. I unzipped my pants and whipped out my dick in full view of everybody in the bar and around the pool. "I don't give a fuck," I thought to steady myself as I made my puddle. "I'll lick up my piss. Who cares? It comes from my body any way."

But, as I bent down to finish what I had begun, Ozzy swooped in and beat me to it. There he was, on all fours at my feet, licking up my pee. I threw up my hands: "You win," I said. And he did: From that moment on, we always knew that wherever we were, whatever we were doing, there was someone who was sicker and more disgusting than we were.

But, unlike us, Ozzy had a restraint, a limit, a conscience, a brake. And that restraint came in the form of a homely, rotund little British woman whose very name sets lips trembling and knees knocking: Sharon Osbourne, a shitkicker and disciplinarian like no other we had ever met, a woman whose presence could in an instant send us reeling back to our childhood fear of authority.

After Florida, Sharon joined the tour to restore order. Suddenly, Ozzy turned into a perfect husband. He ate his vegetables, held her hand, and went to bed promptly after each show, with neither drugs in his nose nor urine in his mouth. But it wasn't enough for Ozzy to behave. Sharon wanted us to behave. When she walked into our dressing room to find a girl on her hands and knees, and the four of us standing there with our pants around our ankles and guilty-little-boy grins on our faces, she laid down the law. She wouldn't let us do drugs, invite girls backstage, or have fun in any way that didn't involve a board game. To make sure her rules were followed, she eliminated alcohol from our tour rider and appointed herself as sole keeper and distributor of backstage passes. We grew so frustrated that we had the merchandising company traveling with us make a new T-shirt. The front consisted of a smiley face riddled with bloody bullet holes. The back was a circle with a vertical column containing the words "sex, fun, booze, parties, hot rods, pussy, heroin, motorcycles." A big red line was drawn through the circle, and below it were the words "No Fun Tour: '83–'84." We gave a shirt to everybody on the tour, including Ozzy.

Eventually, I was reduced to crawling up to Sharon on my hands and knees and pleading, "I really have to get laid. I'm going crazy."

"No, you can't, Nikki," she said firmly. "You're going to get a disease."

"I don't care about diseases," I cried. "I'll get a shot. I just want to get laid."

"Okay," she relented. "Just this once."

"Thanks, Mom."

She led me by the hand to the side of the stage and said, "So, which one do you want," as if I were a little kid picking out sweets.

"I'll take the one in red, please."

That same night, Carmine Appice left the tour. He had played with Vanilla Fudge, Cactus, and Rod Stewart, and was somewhat a star in his own right, so he thought he should be selling his own T-shirts. With uncharacteristic magnanimity, Sharon granted him permission. But when fans brought T-shirts back for Carmine to sign, all of them had a big hole over the breast: Sharon and Ozzy had cut Carmine's face out of all his T-shirts. They got in a big fight, which concluded with Carmine quitting and Tommy Aldridge returning to the band to replace him on drums.

Whenever Sharon left the tour, Ozzy returned to complete decadence. In Nashville, he shit in Tommy's bathroom and wiped it all over the walls. In Memphis, he and Vince stole a car with the keys still dangling from the ignition, terrorized pedestrians on Beale Street, and then destroyed it, smashing the windows and gutting the upholstery. Days later, we happened to arrive in New Orleans on the second night of Mardi Gras. The town was on fire. Tommy, Jake E., and I got into a knife fight at a bar on Bourbon Street while Vince and Ozzy toured the strip clubs. When we all returned to the hotel, drunk and covered with blood, Mom was waiting for us: Sharon had flown into town, and she forbade us to hang out with Ozzy again.

Sometimes, when Sharon was gone, Ozzy would break down like a child lost without his mother. In Italy, he bought a blow-up doll, drew a Hitler mustache on it, and kept it in the back room of our bus. On the way to Milan, he kept talking to it, like it was his only friend. He told the doll that there was some kind of conspiracy, and everyone had turned against him and was plotting to kill him. When he went onstage that night, he was wearing Gestapo boots, panties, a bra, and a blond wig. He seemed to be having a great time at first, but after a few songs, he snapped and started crying. "I'm not an animal," he sobbed into the microphone. "I'm not a freak." Then he apologized to the audience and walked offstage.

That night in the hotel room Mick and I shared, he asked if he could use the phone. He picked it up and said, "England, please."

I grabbed the receiver out of his hands and hung it up. "Dude, you can't call England. I don't have that kind of money."

So he called collect. Sharon accepted. "I'm just calling to tell you that I want a divorce," Ozzy said, as soberly and seriously as he could.

"Shut up and go to bed," she snapped back, then hung up on him.

For some reason, our tour manager had the bright idea of putting obnoxious me and quiet Mick Mars in a room together: We were like *The Odd Couple*. I'd get frustrated writing a song and take my guitar into the hallway, where I'd smash every single light. Then I'd come back into the room, trailing my broken ax behind me and asking Mick, "Say, can I borrow your guitar?" We regularly came to blows, usually because I was partying or bringing girls to the room. After I pulled a clump of his hair out when he wouldn't let me borrow his guitar, I was finally given my own room. It didn't help Mick find any peace and quiet, though, because not long afterward, a hotel guest called the police after she saw Tommy streaking down the hall, and the cops accidentally arrested Mick instead.

We toured with Ozzy on and off for over a year, taking time off to play solo shows or gig with Saxon. In the meantime, we received our first gold and platinum record awards, heard ourselves on the radio for the first time, and started getting recognized in the streets outside Los Angeles. It was all happening quickly and, as a result, all of our relationships began to break down. The day the tour ended, the bus dropped me off in front of the house where Lita and I lived. I stood outside for ten minutes with my suitcase in my hand, unsure whether to walk in or not. When I did, I hugged her and didn't say a word. I just stood there. I wasn't sure what I was supposed to do. Something had turned off inside of me during the tour, and I had no idea how to turn it back on.

When Lita left a few days later for her own tour, I was relieved. I was in no shape to carry on a relationship with her, especially with both of us constantly traveling, and I had no idea how to interact with a woman I respected anymore. By the time she returned, I had already arranged to move across the street and live with Robbin Crosby. The day I moved in with him, life returned to complete destitution and depravity. He had just one bed, and was kind enough to let me sleep in it while he crashed on the floor. Instead of a refrigerator, he had a Styrofoam chest filled with bags of ice. It had a hole in the bottom, and the water constantly leaked all over the kitchen floor. The manager of the building hated me and warned every day that if he caught me throwing loud parties or drinking alcohol by the pool or misbehaving in any way, he'd throw me out on my tattooed ass.

Though I couldn't afford a new Styrofoam ice chest or a real refrigerator for the house, I had no problem buying a brand-new Corvette. The day I drove it off the lot, I went to the Reseda Country Club and picked up a girl. We walked out to the parking lot, and I placed her on the hood, spread her legs in the air, and started fucking her. Slowly, a crowd gathered, and the only thing I remember them saying was: "Yeah, dude! Nice car!"

To forget about Lita, I buried myself between the legs of other women. A small college girl who was attractive in a nerdy, bespectacled way moved into the other side of the building complex a few weeks after I started living there with Robbin. So one night, instead of going out with Robbin, I stopped by her house with a bottle of champagne, a bindle of cocaine, and a bunch of quaaludes. We partied all night and, as planned, ended up fucking. When I walked back to my apartment at seven in the morning, the manager was outside watering the flowers. Trying to suck up, I waved and smiled at him, as innocent as could be. He turned, looked at me, and dropped the hose. He just froze. I couldn't figure out what his problem was. I walked into the apartment and accidentally stepped on Robbin. "Dude, what happened to you?" he exclaimed once his eyes adjusted to the light.

"I was fucking that nerd chick. What's the big deal?" I asked.

"No, dude, go look in the mirror," he said.

I went over to the mirror, which was a giant broken pane someone had probably smashed out of a building lobby one drunken night, and looked at myself. My whole face was covered in blood, from my chin to my nose. Evidently, she had been having her period when I went down on her, and I was too fucked up to even notice. By the look of it, it must have been her first day.

After a few weeks of fucking everything I could, I heard that a little punk rocker had introduced Lita to her new boyfriend, some guy named Don from a band called Heaven. Sure, I didn't want her anymore, but that didn't mean someone else was allowed to have her. Raging with illogical and hypocritical jealousy, I called Tommy. We met at my house, each grabbed a two-by-four plank, and walked over to Lita's house to assess the situation. We unlocked the door and stood in the middle of the room with our weapons. The only person home was the little punk rocker, who cowered in the corner as we rushed him, beating him mercilessly over the head and chest, until finally breaking the boards over his back. We left him in the corner, with blood streaked all over the walls.

A few hours later, the phone rang at my new place. "Fuck you!" It was Lita. "You are such a fucking asshole."

I explained my side of the story, and then she cut me down with a few well-chosen words that still ring in my head to this day: "That punk you just beat up didn't even introduce me to Don!"

I felt especially bad that I had involved Tommy, because the night before I had fucked his girlfriend, Honey. She had called to tell me she had drugs. I went over to partake, and one thing led to another, which led to me naked in the bathroom looking for some kind of ointment to put on the scratch marks on my back. It was yet another image to keep out of my mind at their engagement party. He was my best friend, and probably would have understood. But I've never been able to bring myself to tell him about it.

✕ ✕ ✕ ✕

CHAPTER SIX / JOHNNY CASH
NICKAJACK CAVE

EXCERPT FROM
Cash: The Autobiography

AUTHORS
Johnny Cash and Patrick Carr

COPYRIGHT © 1997 by John R. Cash
REPRINTED BY PERMISSION OF ~ HarperCollins Publishers

Johnny Cash (1932-2003) was an American icon and country music superstar.

✕ ✕ ✕ ✕

"They had a whole bunch of nice little names for them to dress them up, and they came in all colors. If you didn't like green, you could get orange."

I CLEARLY REMEMBER the first mood-altering drug to enter my body. When I was just a kid, probably eleven years old, I was wrestling at school with a friend of mine, Paul East. Paul was a big guy, with big feet in big clodhopper shoes, and in the process of rolling over, his heel caught me in the side and broke a rib. It hurt really bad at first, but after a little while it didn't hurt at all, and I had no idea my rib was broken—until, that is, I woke up in the middle of the night. I had turned over, and that rib had gone ahead and broken in two or splintered and was sticking me in the lung. The pain was terrible; every time I took a breath, I screamed.

Daddy hitched up the mules, wrapped me up in blankets and pillows, put me on the wagon, and drove me the two and a half miles to the Dyess Hospital and old Doc Hollingsworth. At that point I wasn't screaming with each breath, but only because I was working so hard not to; the pain was still excruciating, worse than anything I'd ever felt. Doc Hollingsworth took one quick look and went straight to work. "Well, we'll stop that, right quick," he declared, giving me an injection that killed the pain just as soon as the needle went in. Not only that, but I started feeling really good. That's what morphine did, said Doc Hollingsworth; it worked well.

I thought, *Boy, this is really something. This is the greatest thing in the world, to make you feel so good when it was hurting so bad. I'll have to have some more of that sometime.* Strangely enough, though, I didn't think about morphine again until many years later, when I was given it for postsurgical pain. Then I remembered how good it felt, and in time that got to be a problem.

And as I've said before, all mood-altering drugs carry a demon called Deception. You think, *If this is so bad, why does it feel so good?* I used to tell myself, *God created this; it's got to be the greatest thing in the world.* But it's like the old saying about the wino: he starts by drinking out of the bottle, and then the bottle starts drinking out of him. The person starts by taking the drugs, but then the drugs start taking the person. That's what happened to me.

I took my first amphetamine, a little white Benzedrine tablet scored with a cross, in 1957, when I was on tour with Faron Young and Ferlin Husky, and I loved it. It increased my energy, it sharpened my wit, it banished my shyness, it improved my timing, it turned me on like electricity flowing into a light bulb. I described the new world it opened to me in *Man in Black*:

> With all the traveling I had to do, and upon reaching a city tired and weary, those pills could pep me up and make me really feel like doing a show. . . . Those white pills were just one of a variety of a dozen or more shapes and sizes. . . . They called them amphetamines, Dexedrine, Benzedrine, and Dexamyl. They had a whole bunch of nice little names for them to dress them up, and they came in all colors. If you didn't like green, you could get orange. If you didn't like orange, you could get red. And if you really wanted to act like you were going to get weird, you could get black. Those black ones would take you all the way to California and back in a '53 Cadillac with no sleep.

And so it went. The journey into addiction has been described so often by so many people in recent years that I don't believe a blow-by-blow account of my particular path would serve any useful purpose. Perhaps in the late '50s or early '60s, it could have. Now it's just one tale among many, the details different but the pattern, the steps, the progression the same as any other addict's. So while I do have to tell you about it, I'll try to avoid being tedious. Hit just the lowlights, so to speak.

The first and perhaps the worst thing about it was that every pill I took was an attempt to regain the wonderful, natural feeling of euphoria I experienced the first time, and therefore not a single one of them, not even one among the many thousands that slowly tore me away from my family and my God and myself, ever worked. It was never as great as the first time, no matter how hard I tried to make it so.

That doesn't mean it didn't feel good, though, and for a while the pills did their job just fine without too many obvious consequences. Doctors were prescribing them freely in those days for just the reasons I said I wanted them—to drive long distances, to work late hours—and though in truth I was taking them for the feeling they gave me, I started by taking them only when I had to travel and/or do shows. People in the music business, the people I worked with, got the idea right from the start that I was high all the time, but that was only because I was high all the time when I was around *them*. In fact, in those early days I was the equivalent of what alcoholics call a "binge drinker." I don't know what addicts call it.

It felt great while I was high, but even in those first days the mornings after weren't so hot. I'd wake up and the guilt would slap me in the face. I'd remember something truly stupid I said to somebody, something insane and destructive I did. I'd realize that I'd forgotten to call home and say goodnight to my girls. Of course, sometimes that would feel so bad that I'd have to take another pill or two just to feel okay again. The amphetamine would kick in and I'd start feeling okay, and then it would kick in a little more and I'd start feeling good, and then I'd start feeling *good*, and so on into the next cycle. Gradually the binges grew longer, the crashes worse, the periods of sobriety shorter. Everything just got ratcheted relentlessly up its scale.

It wasn't long until the crashes got really bad. As soon as I woke up, I started feeling little things in my skin, briars or wood splinters, itching so badly that I had to keep trying to pluck them out; I'd turn on the light to see them better, and they weren't there. That kept happening and got worse—they started to be alive, actually twitching and squirming in my flesh—and that was unbearable. Then I *had* to take more pills. I talked about it to other people who used amphetamines, but nobody else had the problem for the simple reason that nobody else was taking as many pills as I was. I tried cutting back a little, and it quit happening. So I thought, *Okay, I'll push my doses right up to the line, but no further.* Sometimes I managed that. Other times I'd forget—well, I never forgot; I just didn't *care*—and I'd go ahead, get as high as I wanted, and end up trying to pull little creatures out of my body.

Some people were trying to steer me away from what they could see was self-destruction. On the road there were performers like Sonny James and Jimmie C. Newman, both of whom warned me repeatedly that I was killing myself. I'd humor them. My feeling was that I knew a whole lot more about drugs than they did and about whether or not I was killing myself, and so I really didn't have to pay much attention to what they said. I went along and agreed with them, then did what I wanted.

With Vivian it was harder, just as it's difficult for me to describe now. Many parts of my life are painful to recall—this book is hard on me in that respect— but as you'd expect, my first marriage is especially tough to speak about. I've made my apologies to Vivian and tried to redress the damage I did, and these days I don't carry any guilt about those days, so I *can* tell the stories (which wasn't always so). But still I find myself resisting. Old pain dies hard.

I met Vivian at a skating rink in San Antonio, Texas, before I shipped out overseas with the air force and began a romance that grew by mail. We wrote to each other almost every day, and as time went by more and more passion and intimacy went onto the paper—every word of mine written in green ink, a color reserved just for her. Vivian still has those letters in a trunk in her house, all but twenty-four of them; last Christmas she gave six to each of our four girls. That scared me at first, but I guess it's fitting.

By the time I came home from the air force on July 4, 1954, ex-Sergeant Cash and Miss Liberto knew two things: we were going to get married and have a family, and I was going to be a singer. She encouraged me all the way in both ambitions, even though the only singing she'd heard me do was on a disk I'd made in a booth at the railroad station in Munich for one deutsche mark—my first record, an unaccompanied rendition of Carl Smith's "Am I the One?" She wore it out. Unlike the Barbarian tapes, that one's not in the archive. "Am I the one who'll always hold you, 'til the end of time . . ." In retrospect it's strange that I chose a Carl Smith song; he was June Carter's husband at the time.

Vivian and I were married on August 7, 1954, by her uncle, Father Vincent Liberto.

Between then and mid-1955 we had a good time. Vivian would come along on the dates I'd arranged for Luther and Marshall and myself around the Memphis area in places like Lepanto and Osceola, then farther afield in Tennessee, Arkansas, and even Mississippi, and that was fun. Marshall's wife, Etta, and son, Randy, came along too, and so did Luther's wife, and we were at each other's houses all the time, a happy gang. Vivian learned to make cornbread, buttermilk, navy beans, pork chops—farmer food, the kind that'll make you fat if you're not out there plowing all day—and I began learning how to live with a wife. We were okay.

The first big problem between us began on August 5, 1955, the night I played the first big concert of my career, at the Overton Park Band Shell, with Elvis headlining. I still have the newspaper ad, framed. THE ELVIS PRESLEY SHOW was in big bold type with *Extra—Johnny Cash Sings "Cry, Cry, Cry"* down below. The show went well, and Elvis asked me to go on tour with him. I accepted and took Vivian along, as usual, and it scared her. Once she saw how women went nuts over Elvis and realized that I was heading into that world, she cooled considerably on the whole idea of my recording and touring career.

By the time our second daughter, Kathy (Kathleen), was born, I was well on my way to living the life of a rambler, and although life is a matter of choices, I didn't feel I had any control over that. Being a recording artist meant you had to tour, which meant you had to leave your family. My kids suffered—Daddy wasn't there for school plays, Fourth of July picnics, and most of the smaller but more significant events in the lives of children. Although Vivian handled it really well, being as much of a sister as a mother to the girls and taking very good care of them, my absence was a loss that can never be made up.

The pills were of course a big issue. She saw them as deadly right from the start, when she'd get up in the morning in the little house on Sandy Cove in Memphis and there I'd be, wide awake and red-eyed after staying up all night in the den, writing and singing and putting things down on tape. She urged me not to take them, and of course that just drove a wedge deeper between us. I shrugged her off. Then, as my habit escalated, she actually begged me—"Please, *please* get off those pills. They're going to destroy us both!"—but I hunched up into myself and let it roll off my back.

By the time we left Memphis for California in early 1959 we had three daughters and a marriage in bad trouble. At first I rented a house on Coldwater Canyon; then I bought Johnny Carson's house on Havenhurst Avenue in Encino when he left for New York to start *The Tonight Show*—$165,000 then, worth a few million today—and finally, because Rosanne was allergic to the smog, coming home from school every day with tears running off her chin, we moved to the Ojai Valley about fifteen miles inland from Ventura. I built a house for us and bought one for my parents, and I loved it there. It was beautiful land. "Ojai" means "to nest." Nesting wasn't what I did, though.

Touring and drugs were what I did, with the effort involved in drugs mounting steadily as time went by. As well as with increasing demand I also had to deal with diminishing supply. In the early 1960s the American Medical Association began waking up to the perils of prescribing unlimited amphetamines for anyone who wanted them, and getting drugs started getting to be work, especially for a traveling man. It got harder than simply calling the hotel doctor and having him send over sixty pills. If I was going on a ten-day tour, I had to plan accordingly, and that could be complicated. How many prescriptions did I have? Four? Four times sixty divided by ten, make that twelve just in case, hmmmm, maybe not enough. Maybe I need another local source. Maybe I should call another doctor before I left. Maybe I should drive to that druggist forty miles away and get a hundred or two under the counter. Maybe I should call a friend, or friends, and ask them to go get a new prescription. Ultimately, I might have to rely on whatever I could find on the road.

By 1960, Vivian's resentment against my commitment to the music business was very strong. Our experience together at the Disc Jockey Convention in Nashville that year was typical. I wanted to go room hopping, dropping into all the various record companies' and song publishers' hospitality suites, hanging out with my friends, singing songs and playing guitar, having fun and doing what you do, but that wasn't Vivian's idea at all. *She* wanted to be my priority. We had one of our worst fights that night. It didn't help at all that June Carter called our room to say that she and Don Gibson were singing and writing songs together, and why didn't I come over and join them? "Sure," I said, and hung up, planning to go, but Vivian threw a fit (which wasn't surprising, given how it all turned out between me and June and her). I ended up room hopping anyway and stayed up all night.

That was the night I heard about Johnny Horton getting killed. I took a lot of pills and drank a lot, too. I was a mess, and the light of the following day made it worse. Hungover, strung out, in shock, full of remorse, my best friend dead, my wife hurt and sad and bitter and angry…

✕

It was a sad situation between Vivian and me, and it didn't get better. I wasn't going to give up the life that went with my music, and Vivian wasn't going to accept that. So there we were, very unhappy. There was always a battle at home. It was hopeless for her because I just *wasn't* going to do what she wanted, and it was hopeless for me because she'd sworn that I'd never be free from our marriage. She was a devout Catholic; she said she'd die before she'd give me a divorce.

Everything just got more difficult as time went on, with Vivian and with drugs too. Amphetamines are hard to handle, and once you're into them to any extent you find out very quickly that you have a pressing need for other chemicals. I soon had to drink alcohol, usually wine or beer, to take the edge off my high if it got too sharp or knock myself out after being up for days, and after a while I got into barbiturates, too.

I wasn't high *all* the time. Sometimes nothing I did would keep me in pills, and I'd be stuck somewhere out on the road, having to go clean. I feared that more than I feared my own death, but when it happened, I'd begin to feel pretty good after two or three days without drugs. Then, though, I'd get home, usually on a Monday, and I'd find the stress of my marriage so hard that I'd drive to that druggist, get two or three hundred pills, head out into the desert in my camper, and stay out there, high, for as long as I could. Sometimes it was days.

Vivian, my preacher, and some of my friends fought for me, trying to make me save myself, but that just infuriated me, and I started staying away from home even more. I'd go out on tour and stay out when it was over. All the time my habit just got worse, never better.

I knew that, but it wasn't something I wanted to admit to myself. The crashes were coming closer together and I was burning myself out more often, going up to and past the point of total exhaustion, doubling and tripling and quadrupling my intake and getting a smaller and smaller margin of advantage. That would all reveal itself to me, as would the logical destination—death—when I got to the end of a binge and found myself shaking, sweating, cramping, hurting, and scared beyond the ability of any chemical on earth to take away my fear. Those states were temporary, though. The alcohol and barbiturates would knock me out eventually, and after a while, hours or days, I'd be able to get high again.

✕

One of the worst times came early: my concert at Carnegie Hall in May of 1962, which apart from being an event in itself was the final stop on one ride and the beginning of another.

When I got to New York I was already burned out. I'd been in Newfoundland with Merle Travis and Gordon Terry on a moose hunt sponsored by a company introducing walkie-talkies to the civilian market. One of the things a walkie-talkie would be good for, they figured, was communication between hunters in the woods, and we were there to publicize that proposition. As it turned out, the radios didn't get much use. I shot a moose about three hundred yards from the cabin and called Merle on the walkie-talkie to tell him so, and it went something like this:

"Merle, I got a moose."

"That's nice. I might get one too if you'd stay of this thing."

That was about it for the walkie-talkies. You don't need them when you're holed up together in a cabin taking drugs and drinking, which is what we were really doing those three days. We all had our own preferences in that regard— Merle was on sleeping pills while I was on amphetamines—but it worked out, more or less. If Merle could keep his dosage right, he'd stay in what he considered his mellow mood, not nervous, for long periods of time. In that state he could be hilarious, a wonderful conversationalist and raconteur. He took so many pills that eventually they'd start working like they were supposed to and put him to sleep, but sometimes that took three or four days. For me, the trick was to match my biochemical schedule, running on the fast track, to his. Sometimes it worked and great stories were told, great thoughts exchanged; sometimes it didn't and there was a lot of dead air.

Merle was truly one of the most interesting men I've ever met, certainly one of the most talented in many areas. He was a brilliant singer, songwriter, and guitar innovator—he developed "Travis picking," a step further on from the style Mother Maybelle introduced. On the side, so to speak, he drew wonderful cartoons, told fabulous stories, possessed authoritative knowledge in many different areas, and was a skilled taxidermist, master watchmaker, and expert knife thrower (he's the one who taught me how to sink a bowie from twenty paces). That's an odd-sounding combination, I know, but Merle was indeed a man for all seasons, in many ways the ideal companion. After three days in that cabin, however, I was about ready to kill him, he probably felt the same way about me, and Gordon Terry felt likewise about both of us. It was a relief to get ourselves and our moose meat out of there and go our separate ways.

I took myself and mine to New York City and met up with the regular gang, but by that time I was shot: voice gone, nerves gone, judgment gone. I did an interview with Mike Wallace during which I almost tore his head off (Question: "Country music at Carnegie Hall. Why?" Answer, snarled: "*Why not?*"). We made an arrangement with the chef at the Barbizon Plaza and served moose meat at our press party, which may have been a miscalculation (and may not; I don't recall). Then the concert itself came up on me. Merle Kilgore went on and did well, then Tompall and the Glaser Brothers, then June and the Carter Family. Finally it was time for the headliner, me.

I was deep in my Jimmie Rodgers obsession at the time, so I'd thought up something special. Mrs. Rodgers, before she died, had given me some of Jimmie's things. When I walked onto that stage that night, not only was I intending to sing only Jimmie Rodgers songs, I was also wearing his clothes and carrying his railroad lantern. I lit it backstage, had all the stage and house lights turned off, and made my entry in the dark with just the flame of the lantern on me. The plan was to set the lantern down on a chair at center stage, prop my knee up on the chair just the way Jimmie did, start into "Waiting For a Train," and wait for the roar of recognition.

It didn't work our that way. If there were any people in the audience who knew about Jimmie Rodgers (and I'm sure there were at least a few), they were slow to make the visual connection. Nobody else had a clue. I thought they were going to be in awe—*This must be something special. What's he going to do?*—but they weren't. They were yelling for "Folsom Prison Blues" before I even got to the microphone. So I turned around, handed the lantern to somebody, and went into my regular opening number, whatever that was at the time. Which would have been fine, I guess, if I'd been able to sing. But I couldn't. I was mouthing the words, but nothing was coming out. All the people were hearing from me was my guitar.

At first they laughed. They thought I was kidding, that this was a joke. Then they went quiet, and I had to do something. I stopped the song. "I have laryngitis tonight," I said. "I have no voice. I don't know if I can sing anything."

I couldn't, but I tried to. I kept asking for glasses of water to ease my dry throat, but it didn't help. I kept hoping the pills I'd taken would boost me up to where I didn't care anymore, but they didn't. It was just a nightmare, and I remember all of it with perfect clarity. June came out dressed in a beautiful white robe with a heart sewn into it for when I did "Ballad of the Heart Weaver." I did "Mr. Garfield," which isn't very funny if you're not on the right wavelength, and nobody was. I whispered my way through "Give My Love to Rose." I went back again and again to Jimmie Rodgers songs, hoping to pull it together somehow, but I failed. It was awful, start to finish. The memory of it still gives me a headache.

After the show June came up to me backstage, obviously depressed, and said, "I thought you were very good, but your voice just wasn't there, and I really feel sorry for you about that."

I was in a very bad mood, angry with everybody and everything. "Well, I don't feel sorry for me," I snapped. She backed off.

The next encounter I remember was similar. A man I didn't know who'd been watching me from the corner of the dressing room came over and said, "It's called Dexedrine, isn't it?"

"What is?"

"What you're taking."

"Yeah. Why?"

"I just kinda recognized it. I'm of a kindred spirit. I've been into all that stuff myself. I'm in a program right now and I don't take anything, but I recognize Dexedrine. That stuff will kill you, y'know."

I had a whole arsenal of flippant little dismissals for occasions like this. "Yeah?" I said. "Well, so will a car wreck."

He wouldn't give up. "You know, man, you can learn to sing around laryngitis a little bit. I'm a writer and a singer, I've been in this business all my life, and I've learned some stuff like that. If we spent a little time together, maybe I could show you how to take care of yourself a little better."

I rejected them out of hand, but something about the man made an impression on me. After learning who he was—Ed McCurdy, the singer of Irish and Scottish folk songs, especially the bawdier ballads—I told him to come by the hotel in the morning.

I was off for a while after Carnegie Hall, so I started hanging out with Ed, and for a few days I didn't do any amphetamines. One afternoon, though, Ed came by with a friend of his, Peter LaFarge, a Hopi Indian and a songwriter, and invited me to go down to the Village with them to hear some folk music at the

Bitter End.

"Okay," I said, "but I'm not going down there without taking some Dexedrine."

That was okay with Ed, it seemed. "Go ahead, take some," he said. It was more than okay with Peter, whose reaction was to take some, too.

I'll always remember a conversation we had at the Bitter End. "Cash, you're getting screwed up again," Ed told me. "You know that, don't you? You're losing it. You're going to blow it. You're just getting your voice back, and now you're going to lose it again."

I'd had two or three days of being relatively straight, so I was perfectly serious when I told him, "Hey, it's all right. I can handle this."

Ed and Peter just looked at each other and started laughing.

I bristled. "I don't know what's so funny, but I *don't* like to be laughed at!"

"Oh, Cash, you are a funny man," said Ed. "What you're saying is funny—so stupid, you have to laugh. You can't *handle* it. There's no way you can handle it. *It's* handling *you*, and eventually it'll kill you."

I discounted that—I'd heard it all before, time and time again—and the night went on. Peter got up and sang some of his Native American songs and Ed got up and sang an archaic Irish version of "Molly Malone." I took some more Dexedrine and gave Peter some more. I also handed him some Thorazine I'd gotten someplace, for use when he needed to come down and crash.

The next day I got a call from Ed. Peter had taken all the Thorazine I'd given him, he said, eight or ten pills, and now he couldn't be awakened. We were really worried, but while Peter slept for three or four days, he didn't die. He and I went on to work together; he inspired me to do my *Bitter Tears* album and wrote "The Ballad of Ira Hayes." The son of Oliver LaFarge, whose novel, *Laughing Boy,* won a Pulitzer Prize, Peter was a genuine intellectual, but he was also very earthy, very proud of his Hopi heritage, and very aware of the wrongs done to his people and other Native Americans. The history he knew so well wasn't known at all by most white Americans in the early 1960s—though that would certainly change in the coming years—so to some extent, his was a voice crying in the wilderness. I felt lucky to be hearing it. Peter was great. He wasn't careful with the Thorazine, though.

After he and I had become friends, he stayed in Nashville a while and he and Pop Carter formed a bond. Pop even went down to the reservation in New

Mexico with him. Then Peter went back to New York, and the next news was another phone call from Ed McCurdy. Peter hadn't woken up again, Ed told me, and this rime he never would.

I wrecked every car I had in those days. I wrecked other people's, too. I wrecked June's brand new Cadillac. In fact, I managed to get fired from the Grand Ole Opry and total my future wife's car all in the same night.

Technically, I wasn't fired from the Opry because I wasn't in fact a member when they asked me not to come back again. The Opry at the time required that performers who'd been invited to become members commit themselves to appearing on the show twenty-six times a year, the equivalent of every other Saturday night. I'd never been willing to take that deal, which would have placed drastic limitations on my touring and therefore my income, and so my status with the Opry management was that of a frequent guest star. Technicalities aside, however, there was no mistaking the message that was imparted to me as I walked off stage on the night I smashed all the footlights with my microphone stand. "You don't have to come back anymore," the manager said. "We can't use you."

I was pretty angry about that. This was just the same stuff I'd been doing for a long time, I thought, so why were they getting so upset about it now?

June, as usual, tried to insert the voice of reason into the equation. "Go back to the motel and go to bed," she said. "You'll feel better tomorrow."

Fat chance. Instead, I asked to borrow her car.

She didn't think that was a good idea, especially since I'd been drinking a lot of beer as well as taking amphetamines. But I wasn't too concerned about what she thought, so I kept at her until she relented, and off I went in her nice new Caddy. I didn't know exactly where I was going, or even *vaguely* where I was going, but it didn't matter. I was just angry and driving and speeding. A blinding electrical storm was in progress, with torrential rain, and that fit my mood. I couldn't see the road ahead, but I wouldn't have been able to see it anyway, even on a clear, crisp night with unlimited visibility.

I hit the utility pole head on. My face smashed into the steering wheel, breaking my nose and bashing my front teeth up into my upper lip. Stunned as I was, I looked up and watched as the pole snapped and began falling toward me. It smashed into the roof above my head, and the wires it was carrying spread out on the wet pavement around the car and lit up the scenery with high-voltage electricity. It looked like Christmas or hell, take your pick, a warm fiery glow all around the car.

Being intelligent and sensible, I decided against stepping out. As long as the rubber of the tires was between me and all the volts, I reasoned, I might be okay. And besides, I had a lot to do in the car. There were beer bottles and pills aplenty to hide, somehow or other, before the police arrived. Which they did very soon. I was in the heart of Nashville, just a couple of blocks from Vanderbilt Hospital.

My main concern was that June would be mad at me, so while I told the police whose car I'd destroyed, I didn't tell them where they could find the owner to give her the news. I also had my own way with the doctor who set my nose. It was going to hurt, he said, avoiding euphemisms like "this may cause you some discomfort," so he was going to give me morphine.

"No," I growled. "Don't give me any morphine. Just set my nose!"

"You won't be able to stand it if I don't," he argued.

I wasn't having any of that. I'd show *him* how much I could stand. "Yeah? Well, go ahead. I want to experience it."

He went ahead. I could hear the little bones cracking in there, and yes, it really was excruciating. I thought it was a fine test of manhood. I could *really* take it.

June learned about her car soon enough, of course, and found me even though I'd gotten my friend David Ferguson to hide me away at his house, lying in the dark with my face wrapped on bandages. She didn't try to come see me because she knew I didn't want to see her. She waited until I'd emerged back into the world, and even then she didn't harass me about it.

"You know you totaled my car out?" was all she asked. "I guess I get a new Cadillac now. " And she did. Insurance paid for it, not me.

I felt kind of bad about it all, especially since the police officer investigating the wreck had been Rip Nix, who at the time was June's husband. I didn't hear directly from him about it, but June mentioned that the incident didn't go over too well at home.

June said she knew me—knew the kernel of me, deep inside, beneath the drugs and deceit and despair and anger and selfishness, and knew my loneliness. She said she could help me. She said we were soul mates, she and I, and that she would fight for me with all her might, however she could. She did that by being my companion, friend, and lover and by praying for me (June is a prayer warrior like none I've known), but also by waging total war on my drug habit. If she found my pills, she flushed them down the toilet. And find them she did: she searched for them, relentlessly. If I didn't like that and said so, I had a fight on my hands. If I disappeared on her, she'd get Marshall or Fluke or someone else in the crew to go find me in the wee hours of the morning and coax me back to bed. If I'd been up for days until I'd finally had the sense to take a handful of sleeping pills and crash—there was always an instinct telling me when to do that, pointing to the line between "almost" and "fatal"—I'd wake up from a sleep like death to find that my drugs, no matter how ingeniously I'd hidden them, were gone.

She only gave up once, in the mid-'60s in the Four Seasons Hotel in Toronto. By that time I was totally reduced—I hate the term "wasted"—and it's incomprehensible to me how I kept walking around, how my brain continued to function. I was nothing but leather and bone; there was nothing in my blood but amphetamines; there was nothing in my heart but loneliness; there was nothing between me and my God but distance.

I don't know what exactly brought her to the point of leaving me. I'd been up for three or four days and I'd been giving her a really hard time, but that wasn't unusual. I guess there'd just been too much of it for her. She'd set out to save me and she thought she'd failed. We had adjoining rooms; she came into mine and said, "I'm going. I can't handle this anymore. I'm going to tell Saul that I can't work with you anymore. It's over."

I knew immediately that she wasn't kidding. I really didn't want her to go, so I went straight out of my room and into hers, gathered up her suitcase and all her clothes—everything, her shoes included (she was barefoot)—and took them back into my room. Then I pushed her out and locked my door. *That should do it*, I thought. All she had on was a towel.

I could hear her crying in her room for a long rime, but eventually she came knocking on my door. She promised not to leave if I gave back her clothes, and I believed her, so I did. And through all the trials to come, before and after she became my wife, she never tried to leave again.

✕

I just went on and on. I was taking amphetamines by the handful, literally, and barbiturates by the handful too, not to sleep but just to stop the shaking from the amphetamines. I was canceling shows and recording dates, and when I did manage to show up, I couldn't sing because my throat was too dried out from the pills. My weight was down to 155 pounds on a six-foot, one-and-a-half-inch frame. I was in and out of jails, hospitals, car wrecks. I was a walking vision of death, and that's exactly how I felt. I was scraping the filthy bottom of the barrel of life.

By early October 1967, I'd had enough. I hadn't slept or eaten in days, and there was nothing left of me. J.R. was just a distant memory. Whatever I'd become in his place, it felt barely human. I never wanted to see another dawn. I had wasted my life. I had drifted so far away from God and every stabilizing force in my life that I felt there was no hope for me.

I knew what to do. I'd go into Nickajack Cave, on the Tennessee River just north of Chattanooga, and let God take me from this earth and put me wherever He puts people like me.

You can't go into Nickajack Cave anymore. The Army Corps of Engineers put a dam in, which closed off the entrance we used. It was an amazing place, an opening, 150 feet wide and 50 feet high into a system of caves, some of them bigger than two or three football stadiums, that ran under the mountains all the way down into Alabama. I'd been there before with friends, Bob Johnston once, Hank Williams Jr. another time, exploring and looking for Civil War and Indian artifacts. Andrew Jackson and his army had slaughtered the Nickajack Indians there, men, women, and children, and soldiers from both sides of the War Between the States had taken shelter in the caves at various times during the conflict. The Indians left their bones in mounds. The soldiers left their names and affiliations and sometimes a message carved into the limestone of a chamber close to the entrance: *John Fox, C.S.A.; Reuben Matthews, Union; Jeff Davis, Burn in Hell.* The remains of the dead among them were joined by the bones of the many spelunkers and amateur adventurers who'd lost their lives in the caves over the years, usually by losing their way, and it was my hope and intention to join that company. If I crawled in far enough, I thought, I'd never be able to find my way back out, and nobody would be able to locate me until I was dead, if indeed they ever could. The dam would be going in soon.

I parked my Jeep and started crawling, and I crawled and crawled and crawled until, after two or three hours, the batteries in my flashlight wore out and I lay down to die in total darkness. The absolute lack of light was appropriate, for at that moment I was as far from God as I have ever been. My separation from Him, the deepest and most ravaging of the various kinds of loneliness I'd felt over the years, seemed finally complete.

It wasn't. I thought I'd left Him, but He hadn't left me. I felt something very powerful start to happen to me, a sensation of pure peace, clarity, and sobriety. I didn't believe it at first. I couldn't understand it. How, after being awake for so long and driving my body so hard and taking so many pills—dozens of them, scores, even hundreds—could I possibly feel *all right?* The feeling persisted, though, and then my mind started focusing on God. He didn't speak to me— He never has, and I'll be very surprised if he ever does—but I do believe that at times He has put feelings in my heart and perhaps even ideas in my head. There in Nickajack Cave I became conscious of a very clear, simple idea: I was not in charge of my destiny. I was not in charge of my own death. I was going to die at God's time, not mine. I hadn't prayed over my decision to seek death in the cave, but that hadn't stopped God from intervening.

I struggled, feeling defeated by the practicalities of the matter. There I was, after all, in total darkness, with no idea of which way was up, down, in, or out of that incredible complexity of passages and chambers so deep inside the earth that no scent or light or sensation from the outside could possibly reach me. How *could* I escape the death I'd willed?

No answer came, but an urging did: I had to move. So I did. I started crawling in whatever direction suggested itself, feeling ahead with my hands to guard against plunging over some precipice, just moving slowly and calmly, crablike. I have no idea how long it took, but at a certain point I felt a breath of wind on my back and knew that wherever the breath was blowing from, that was the way out. I followed it until I began to see light, and finally I saw the opening of the cave.

When I walked out, June was there with a basket of food and drink, and my mother. I was confused. I thought she was in California. I was right; she had been. "I knew there was something wrong," she said. I had to come and find you."

As we drove back toward Nashville I told my mother that God had saved me from killing myself. I told her I was ready to commit myself to Him, and do whatever it took to get off drugs. I wasn't lying.

During the following days I moved through withdrawal to recovery. I retreated to the house I'd just bought on Old Hickory Lake and at first lived in just one room, one of the big, circular rooms overlooking the lake. June and her mother and father formed a circle of faith around me, caring for me and insulating me from the outside world, particularly the people, some of them close friends, who'd been doing drugs with me. June contacted Dr. Nat Winston, the Commissioner of Mental Health of the State of Tennessee, on my behalf, and Nat came to the house every day, holding my feet to the fire and giving me vital support. At first it was very hard for me. To illustrate, in *Man in Black* I described a phenomenon that began on my third night home, when I was finally able to get to sleep at about three in the morning, and continued for about ten days.

It was the same nightmare every night, and it affected my stomach—I suppose because the stomach was where the pills had landed, exploded, and done their work. I'd be lying in bed on my back or curled up on my side. The cramps would come and go, and I'd roll over, doze off, and go to sleep. Then all of a sudden a glass ball would begin to expand in my stomach. My eyes were closed, but I could see it. It would grow to the size of a baseball, a volleyball, then a basketball. And about the time I felt that ball was twice the size of a basketball, it lifted me up off the bed. I was in a strange state, half-asleep and half-awake. I couldn't open my eyes, and I couldn't close them. It lifted me off the bed to the ceiling, and when it would go through the roof, the glass ball would explode and tiny, infinitesimal slivers of glass would go out into my bloodstream from my stomach. I could feel the pieces of glass being pumped through my heart into the veins of my arms, my legs, my feet, my neck, and my brain, and some of them would come out the pores of my skin. Then I'd float back down through the ceiling onto my bed and wake up. I'd turn over on my side for a while, unable to sleep. Then I'd lie on my back, doze off, get almost asleep—and the same nightmare would come again. I never imagined a hole in the roof. I just went right through it without an opening. . . . I wanted to scream, but I couldn't.

I also noted that as well as the glass coming out of my skin and the corners of my eyes, I had the old problem of splinters, briars, and thorns in my flesh, and sometimes worms.

Eventually—slowly, with relapses and setbacks—I regained my strength and sanity and I rebuilt my connection to God. By November 11, 1967, I was able to face an audience again, performing straight for the first time in more than a decade at the high school in Hendersonville, my new hometown. I was terrified before I went on, but surprised, almost shocked, to discover that the stage without drugs was not the frightening place I'd imagined it to be. I was relaxed that night. I joked with the audience between numbers. I amazed myself.

What happened then was even more startling. Vivian divorced me. June and I got married (on March 1, 1968). I went to Folsom Prison in California and recorded my *Live at Folsom Prison* album, which got me a huge hit (for the second time) with "Folsom Prison Blues" and lit a big fire under my career. The following year *The Johnny Cash Show* started up, putting me on ABC network television for an hour a week, coast to coast. Then, on March 3, 1970, John Carter Cash was born, and my happiness grew and grew. Sobriety suited me.

God had done more than speak to me. He had revealed His will to me through other people, family and friends. The greatest joy of my life was that I no longer felt separated from Him. Now He is my Counselor, my Rock of Ages to stand upon.

✕

My liberation from drug addiction wasn't permanent. Though I never regressed to spending years at a time on amphetamines, I've used mood-altering drugs for periods or varying length at various times since 1967: amphetamines, sleeping pills, and prescription painkillers.

One such spell, the most serious and protracted, began when I took painkillers after eye surgery in 1981, then kept taking them after I didn't need to. It escalated after I was almost killed by an ostrich.

Ostrich attacks are rare in Tennessee, it's true, but this one really happened, on the grounds of the exotic animal park I'd established behind the House of Cash offices near my house on Old Hickory Lake. It occurred during a particularly bitter winter, when below-zero temperatures had reduced our ostrich population by half; the hen of our pair wouldn't let herself be captured and taken inside the barn, so she froze to death. That, I guess, is what made her mate cranky. Before then he'd been perfectly pleasant with me, as had all the other birds and animals, when I walked through the compound.

That day, though, he was not happy to see me. I was walking through the woods in the compound when suddenly he jumped out onto the trail in front of me and crouched there with his wings spread out, hissing nastily.

Nothing came of that encounter. I just stood there until he laid his wings back, quit hissing, and moved off. Then I walked on. As I walked I plotted. He'd be waiting for me when I came back by there, ready to give me the same treatment, and I couldn't have that. I was the boss. It was my land.

The ostrich didn't care. When I came back I was carrying a good stout six-foot stick, and I was prepared to use it. And sure enough, there he was on the trail in front of me, doing his thing. When he started moving toward me I went on the offensive, making a good hard swipe at him.

I missed. He wasn't there. He was in the air, and a split second later he was on his way down again, with that big toe of his, larger than my size thirteen shoe, extended toward my stomach. He made contact—I'm sure there was never any question he wouldn't—and frankly, I got off lightly. All he did was break my two lower ribs and rip my stomach open down to my belt. If the belt hadn't been good and strong, with a solid buckle, he'd have spilled my guts exactly the way he meant to. As it was, he knocked me over onto my back and I broke three more ribs on a rock—but I had sense enough to keep swinging the stick, so he didn't get to finish me. I scored a good hit on one of his legs, and he ran off.

They cleaned my wounds, stitched me up, and sent me home, but I was nowhere near as good as new. Those five broken ribs *hurt.* That's what painkillers are for, though, so I felt perfectly justified in taking lots of them. Justification ceased to be relevant after that; once the pain subsided completely I knew I was taking them because I liked the way they made me feel. And while that troubled my conscience, it didn't trouble it enough to keep me from going down that old addictive road again. Soon I was going around to different doctors to keep those pills coming in the kind of quantities I needed, and when they started upsetting my digestive system, I started drinking wine to settle my stomach, which worked reasonably well. The wine also took the sharper, more uncomfortable edges off the amphetamines I'd begun adding to the mix because—well, because I was still looking for that euphoria.

So there I was, up and running, strung out, slowed down, sped up, turned around, hung on the hook, having a ball, living in hell. Before long I began to get the impression that I was in trouble—I had bleeding ulcers, for one thing—but I kept going anyway. The idea of taking things to their logical conclusion, just drugging and drinking until I slipped all the way out of this world, began to dance quietly around the back of my mind. That was weirdly comforting.

I went low. On tour in England in 1983 I got into the habit of going into John Carter's room to sleep in the early morning, thus avoiding June's dawn rising. John Carter was twelve. One morning he looked under the bed and said, "Daddy, where did all those wine bottles come from?"

I had to tell him I'd got them out of the mini-bar and drunk them during the night.

"I didn't know you drank like that," he said. I told him I'd been in a lot of pain, so I'd *had* to drink like that.

I met my spider in England. Nottingham, to be precise, in the Midlands, a region hitherto unrecognized as a habitat of aggressive arachnids. Where there's a will, though, there's a way.

Nottingham was the last stop on our tour, and we'd checked into a hotel with beautiful old wooden paneling. I was in the room with June when I got the idea that there was a Murphy bed set into one of the walls.

"Look, June, I can pull this bed down and you can make it up and sleep on it."

"John, that's not a bed," she said. "There's no Murphy bed there."

I disagreed with her quite strongly—I was *convinced* it was there—so I proceeded to tear at that wall until the paneling started splitting, driving old dirt and splinters into my right hand. The hand was a bloody wreck by the time I understood that I'd hallucinated the Murphy bed.

I hallucinated the spider, too—saw it in the middle of the night, biting my hand, causing me intense pain. I told June about it in the morning, by which time my hand was twice its normal size. She believed me at first, just as I believed myself. I don't know what others thought when we made the story public: *Cash Bitten by Poisonous English Spider!!!* Perhaps they considered the possibility that a miracle had occurred in Nottingham, or that the spider had arrived in my baggage (or someone else's) from some likelier part of the world, Mozambique or Mombasa, Belize or Brazil, or that somebody nearby was running a game park for exotic arachnids, reptiles, and worms. Perhaps they thought I was on drugs again.

When I got home my hand was just a giant ball of infection, so I had to check into Baptist Hospital and have surgery on it. I knew I'd be in there a while, so I went prepared. I hid a survival stash of Percodans, amphetamines, and Valium—a fifty-dose card of Valium I'd acquired in Switzerland—in a tobacco sack tied to the back of the TV set in my room.

They did the surgery on my hand, but then they discovered a worse problem in my midsection: all that internal bleeding. So back into surgery I went, this time for removal of my duodenum, parts of my stomach and spleen, and several feet of intestine. That presented a pretty severe problem as far as maintaining my habit went, but I handled it—I had the whole card of Valium right there with me in the intensive care unit. I had a great hiding place for it, too: under the bandages over the freshly sutured incision in my belly. I managed to pull the dressing up and get it snugged in there, safe and sound. I thought I'd been really clever.

A couple of days later, they couldn't wake me up. They'd get a rise out of me for a moment or two, but I'd drift straight off again no matter what they did. That went on for a while—I don't really know how long—until, in a flash of life-saving brilliance, I understood the problem and managed, despite my slurring and blurring, to tell the doctor that he should investigate my dressing. He didn't get it at first—it looked fine, he said, he didn't need to take it off—but I insisted. When he peeled away what was left of the card of Valium, he found that about half the pills had already dissolved straight into my wound.

I don't know if it was the Valium's fault, but that was a horrible wound; it took months to heal properly.

As it happened, the Valium was superfluous, because they treated my post-surgical pain with such strong doses of morphine that I was just about as high as I could be anyway, lost in intensely vivid hallucinations. I half wrecked the ICU, upsetting IV poles and doing all kinds of damage, because I just *had* to make somebody understand about the commandos: they'd gotten into the hospital and were setting their charges all around the room.

Finally, someone got the message and told the flight crew. The copilot came on the intercom to put me at ease.

"We're going to fly this wing of the hospital away from here," he said. "Get you away from these people bothering you."

"Good," I said. "Let's take off."

No sooner said than done. I looked out the window and sure enough, our wing of the hospital had detached itself and was rolling on its takeoff run. Soon we were up, beginning our first turn over Nashville, and I could see the Cumberland River, then the green Tennessee countryside.

The pilot came on the speaker. "It looks like everything's all right now."

I didn't think it was. As I told the flight attendant—this was a full-service hallucination—"The charges still lead up here. They can still blow us up."

"No," she said, "you're wrong. There are no charges aboard."

The woman was crazy, I realized, or dense, or blind, or a member of the conspiracy against me: the charges were right there in plain sight.

"Look, you can *see* them!" I urged. "They're going to blow us up while we're still in the air!"

Somehow I got word to the pilot, and he did a good job, turning back immediately and beginning his landing approach without further ado. The hospital buildings swung into sight, then slid up toward us as we made a faultless landing and eased back into our place.

It was perfect, but pointless. The commandos came right back, moving grimly through the ICU and laying their charges all over again.

"We're gonna get you, Cash," said one.

That was bad enough, but suddenly I was out of the ICU and in a ward, and a commando was standing in the doorway with his gun to John Carter's head (this was post-robbery).

"We're going to kill you and your whole family!" he barked. I realized with horror that there wasn't any "if" or "unless" about it; they were just going to do it.

I started screaming . . .

When I hallucinated that intensely, the medics would respond by giving me even higher doses of morphine. They didn't know who they were dealing with, or what: more dope just made me more crazy.

The people closest to me had had enough. Unbeknownst to me, they got together with a wonderful doctor from the Betty Ford Clinic, a great man who will remain anonymous, and in the parlance of the trade they "ran an intervention" on me.

I knew the doctor was coming. I was semi-alert by that time, about twenty days after the surgery, so I'd understood fine when June told me that the doctor was in town with Gene Autry. Gene was in town to buy a baseball player, and while he had to get back to California posthaste, the doctor would be paying me a visit the next day.

That he did, along with June, Rosanne, my mother, John Carter, Cindy, Tara,

Rosie, half the people who worked for me, and all the members of my band—about twenty-five souls in all. Every one of them had written out something they wanted me to know about my behavior toward them. So lying right there, literally a captive audience (unless I wanted to rip out a couple of IVs and risk spilling my guts on the floor), I listened. I heard about betrayals and broken promises, lies and neglect, love used and abused and abandoned and refused, trust destroyed, care turned to pain and fear.

Everyone read, and all the letters had their effect on me. Again, though, it was John Carter who got through to me most clearly. His letter was about one night at the farm when I'd fallen, stumbled and staggered, and otherwise made a fool of myself in front of his friends, embarrassing him and them terribly. I had to hold him and hug him while he read it, to keep his tears back; he hadn't wanted to write that letter and he wanted even less to read it to me.

The letters weren't designed just to vent their writers' anger, shame, or disgust at my behavior. Their greater purpose was to show me the depth of the trouble I was in, to express love and concern for me, and to ask me to accept help to save myself. As the doctor put it after everyone had read to me, "We all want you to get some help. We want you to go to the Betty Ford Center."

Simple request, simple reply. "I'm ready to go," I croaked, barely able to get the words out. "I want to go. I want some help."

I wasn't conning anyone, even myself, at that moment. I knew how serious my situation was. I was wasted, weak, hallucinating on the morphine every day, very far out in the cold—just a degree or two away from the physical final end, to say nothing of madness, spiritual bankruptcy, and financial ruin. I also knew that I was so close to death that if I really wanted, I could give up and go there quite easily. All the way down at the doors of death, though, I'd discovered that I didn't really want to die; I just wanted the pain and trouble and heartbreak to end, and I was so tired that dying seemed like the only way to get that done. I wanted to stop hating myself, too. Mine wasn't soft-core, pop-psychology self-hatred; it was a profound, violent, daily holocaust of revulsion and shame, and one way or another it *had* to stop. I couldn't stand it any longer. So when the intervention came, it was welcome. As my friends and family spoke, I was telling myself, *This is it. This is my salvation. God has sent these people to show me a way out. I'm going to get a chance to live.*

I'm still absolutely convinced that the intervention was the hand of God working in my life, telling me that I still had a long way to go, a lot left to do. The amazing encouragement I got, the testimony of all those people, made me believe in myself again. But first I had to humble myself before God.

✕ ✕ ✕ ✕

CHAPTER SEVEN / SLASH
THE STIEFEL HOUSE

EXCERPT FROM
Slash

AUTHORS
Slash and Anthony Bozza

COPYRIGHT © 2007 by Dik Hayd International, LLC
REPRINTED BY PERMISSION OF ~ HarperCollins Publishers

Slash is a founding member and guitarist of Guns N' Roses.

*"Izzy and Danny and I proceeded to tear
the bedroom apart, then the rest of the house. I knew
that I had put it there and I knew that Danny was the
only one there with me when I did, but I was willing
to give him the benefit of the doubt."*

SO NOW WE HAD A MANAGER and now we had half an album of "live" tracks and Zutaut was happy. He believed the EP would attract eligible producers. It definitely got us noticed: I remember leaving Alan's house in Redondo Beach with Duff and hearing "Move to the City" played on KNEC, this great heavy metal station out of Long Beach. The EP was a clear indication of our aesthetic, not to mention our lifestyle, and as it had always been, there weren't too many easy-to-find like-minded souls. To say the least, it took a few dry runs to find the right guy.

It was agreed that playing a few gigs would keep us visible and keep us from losing momentum. I, for one, knew that if there wasn't any concrete work commitment on the horizon, it was likely that I'd treat every day like a vacation. We went back up to San Francisco to open for Jetboy at the Stone, followed by a gig two nights later opening for Ted Nugent at the Santa Monica Civic Center.

At the time we were still living at the Stiefel house officially, though once we chose Alan as our manager, we began to vacate in anticipation of letting Stiefel know the bad news. Axl moved back to Erin's, I don't know where Steven was staying, and Duff was where he'd always been, so Izzy and I became the only full-time residents, living in comfortable squalor in the downstairs back bedroom. It was a gypsylike scene; our friend Danny crashed there much of the time, too, amid the sparsely appointed rooms.

Finding dope in L.A. had become difficult suddenly, so Danny and I scoured the streets regularly looking to score. One of those nights we got lucky and managed to pick up a sizable amount. We were elated; we drove back to the house and stashed it all in a gun-shaped lighter of mine. We hid it in my drawer because the next morning we were off to San Francisco. I saw no reason to bring any along, because in San Francisco, I'd never had a problem scoring top-grade China White.

We packed all the gear in the van we'd rented; Danny and Izzy and I drove up in Danny's car, and when we got there, Izzy and I went straight to someone's apartment, where we planned to score our shit. The dealer didn't get there before the show, so we went and did the gig, which was a blur because all that I could think about was getting my smack afterward. The rest of the band packed up, Danny included, and headed back to L.A., while Izzy and I offered to drive Danny's car back ourselves because we wanted to score. We went back to the apartment and waited around for the shit to show up. We waited . . . we waited . . . we waited . . . *nothing*. At that point, we were getting jumpy, and when the dealer finally showed up it was crap—just useless. We looked at each other, both realizing that we were a fuck of a long way from home, and we didn't have much time before we turned into pumpkins.

It was well into the next morning when we hit the road, but we knew that, at the very least, I had a bunch of shit stashed back at the house. All was well, we were making good time . . . until we ran out of gas. We lost a good hour there what with hitching to the gas station and back. Once we got on our way again, speeding to make up for lost time, as the itchiness stalked us, we got a flat tire. Changing a tire is never fun, but when your internal clock is counting down the seconds to your demise, it's something else altogether.

We finally got home that night, thinking that we were cool and all was well. There's a dope camaraderie that kicks in between junkies who are about to get high together, and as Izzy and I headed into the house, we were the greatest friends, just as tight as can be; all arm in arm and laughing about everything we'd just been through getting there. We went into my room, I opened up my stash drawer . . . and discovered that all my shit was gone.

Then I called Danny.

"Hey," I said. "Didn't I stash my shit in my lighter?"

"Yeah," he said innocently.

"It's gone."

"No way."

"I can't find it."

"That really sucks."

"Get over here and help me!"

Izzy and Danny and I proceeded to tear the bedroom apart, then the rest of the house. I knew that I had put it there and I knew that Danny was the only one there with me when I did, but I was willing to give him the benefit of the doubt.

"Man, you know what?" Danny said after we'd exhausted every possible stash spot. He shook his head. "I hid it. I hid it when I was high. I'm going to try to remember where . . . let me think."

After Danny thought about it long and hard, he came up with a few corners we hadn't checked; a few wild goose chases. Then he went home again, leaving Izzy and me with the impossible task of trying to hook up with Sammy, our Persian dealer—our only dealer at the time. It was not looking good: we beeped Sammy every ten minutes and he never called back.

The next morning, Izzy's girlfriend Dezi came over and she could tell that the situation was dire: we'd been up all night, we'd driven from San Francisco, we'd been paging dealers unsuccessfully all day, and we had to open for Ted Nugent in a few hours. Izzy and I were tripping out, nothing was happening, we had no one else to call, and we were wrecked. We were starting to jones pretty hard; we were like vampires out of *Blackula*, just rolling around on the ground and going to the bathroom to puke every five minutes.

Our show with Ted Nugent was all the way down in Santa Monica, at seven-thirty PM. Sammy was not calling us back, so we had to figure out how we were going to get something in our system—anything at all—to make us human enough to make the show. We were in no condition to perform, let alone even drive ourselves to the gig. In desperation, Dezi called her friend Melissa, who lived up in Hollywood, in Izzy's old apartment. She had heard from Sammy and was going to meet him shortly.

That was enough to motivate us: we drove over there somehow and hung out waiting for Melissa to return with our drugs. It looked like we might have taken care of one problem, but at the same time, it was around five p.m. and we were about an hour from the gig. Finally, she returned, Izzy and I got our shit, we did all that, and *what a relief that was*. Fuck! We were once again functional. We had barely enough time to join our band, who were waiting for us so that we could play our first arena, to a sold-out crowd of three thousand.

We hightailed it over there. We had no artist or parking lot passes on us, and after the night we'd had, we looked like scabs off the street. We left Dezi to park the car and climbed the fence at the back of the arena for lack of a better plan. In the process I got caught on the chain links and the button of my jeans popped off, so I spent the rest of the night making sure my zipper didn't go all the way down leaving me hanging out there, because I've never been the type to wear underwear.

Izzy and I somehow snuck into the loading area and made it up to the backstage area, and as we started down the hallway toward the stage I saw Gene Simmons. He was standing at the other end giving us a foreboding stare, which is something he is very good at doing. I had no idea why he was there, but it added to the surreal quality of the last twenty-four hours. Izzy and I got to the dressing room with less than ten minutes to spare. The guys may have been annoyed at first, but they were soon relieved. Disaster averted . . . we took one look in the mirror and headed to the stage.

And that was the first time we ever played "Sweet Child o' Mine" live. I hadn't at all mastered the signature riff to the degree that I could execute it on a whim, but I pulled it off anyway and the band as a whole played it really well. The whole set was good, and we had a collection of friends there: Yvonne, Marc Canter, and a few more of my "normal" friends. Even better, right after we got offstage, Izzy got beeped back from Sammy, who was going to meet us at the Stiefel house. Yvonne and her friends were there backstage, and at the time she and I were together again and the whole intervention incident was bygones. She didn't know exactly where I was in terms of drugs—and I didn't feel the need to tell her.

She was just there being a very supportive girlfriend, cheering her boyfriend on at his first big gig at a live arena. All things considered, she was letting me do my thing. Of course she wanted to celebrate afterward, which was a problem. I couldn't wait to get out of there and get home to do drugs, but I didn't want her to know so I tried to tell her that I'd call her and we'd meet up after we dropped off our guitars, but she wasn't having it—she and her friends were going to meet us up at the house.

Izzy and Danny and I couldn't think of a better way to celebrate our show than with some smack, so we flew back toward Griffith Park to score. It was so early that it wasn't even dark out yet, so as we cruised up Fairfax and stopped for a red light at Fountain, it was easy to see our dealer Sammy's car in the lane beside us. It added to the elated, epic mood of the day and cut Sammy's commute in half. At this point, I felt like I stood a chance of getting high at the house before Yvonne arrived.

We scored from Sammy, sped up to the house, and ran inside like lunatics: Izzy ducked into our room and slammed the door and I locked myself in Steven's bathroom, which was lit by a red bulb he'd installed. I was in there trying to navigate my fix, all while shaking and huffing and puffing from nerves in this unnatural red light, when suddenly there's a knock at the door.

"Hey, babe," Yvonne said. "Are you in there?"

"Oh, yeah, I am!" I said. . . . "Yes I am. But I'm taking a shower. I'm all sweaty from the show." Then I turned on the water.

"Let me in, babe," she said.

"I'm in the shower," I said. "I'll be right out."

I finished what I needed to do, I threw some water on myself and I went outside. I'm pretty sure she knew about it. Yvonne didn't want to stay over at our house—I can't imagine why—so I agreed to go back to her place with her. And that was the night that I decided fuck it, I'll just kick. I'd fixed in the early evening, so it wore off at about one a.m. and for the next few days I did a cold turkey there in Yvonne's bed. It wasn't the last time I'd do so before we all got it together to record *Appetite*, but each time I did, I never told her what was really going on. I acted like I had the flu and played down how terrible I felt. Yvonne was busy; she was in school, so most of those days I was on my own in bed, in hell. The truth was, she was happy enough that when she left I was there and when she came back I was there, even if I was just a shadow of myself on my back, in her bed.

I kicked at Yvonne's that time for a whole week, and despite the potential fiasco surrounding the gig, no one knew about it for better or for worse. Everyone in the band was on such a high after that show; I only regret that I didn't meet Ted Nugent that night, because he'd been such a huge influence on me when I was young.

Danny eventually admitted to Izzy and me that he'd done all of that dope I'd stashed, and I've never forgiven him for it. It was a cold-blooded thing to do that nearly ruined Izzy and me in the eyes of our bandmates. If it had all gone wrong, it would have caused our band untold professional embarrassment at a very crucial point for us. But that's the thing about smack—it's the devil. It is so alluring and seductive that it turns you into a dishonest, backstabbing demon. Being a junkie is akin to what we imagine vampires are: it has an enticing aura at first but it becomes a hunger that must be fed at all costs. It completely takes over, and it reels you in. It starts with a taste here and a taste there and then you're doing it all the time. You think it's your choice, but it's not that way—soon you *need* to do it all the time. Then you're hooked into a really vicious cycle before you're even aware that you've become just another statistic.

××××

CHAPTER EIGHT / STEVEN ADLER
TEARING IT UP ON THE ROAD

EXCERPT FROM
My Appetite For Destruction

- -

AUTHORS
Steven Adler and Lawrence J. Spagnola

- -

COPYRIGHT © 2010 by Steven Adler
REPRINTED BY PERMISSION OF ~ HarperCollins Publishers

- -

Steven Adler was the drummer for Guns N' Roses from 1985 to 1990.

✕ ✕ ✕ ✕

"He'd barely started plunging the syringe,
and some red flag popped up in my head."

WHAT'S NEXT?

IDEAS FOR TOURS began floating around. Originally the plan was to do a Midwest tour with Stryper, the Christian band I had dug on so much when I saw them play locally. They would throw Bibles out to the audience during their set, so me and Duff joked around about passing a couple of bottles out to the fans during ours. Another thought was to go up the East Coast with Y&T, another band that I saw often when I was younger. Those ideas, however, fell through. The very first tour to support our album was as the opening act for the Cult.

I remembered that a couple years before, Slash and I would dance at these clubs where they would play the Cult's videos on a big screen. In the early eighties, they called themselves the Southern Death Cult. They dressed all in black and wore white makeup, very gothic. Ian Astbury was the vocalist, a statuesque man with long black hair. He was so great. He would always let me go onstage, play tambourine, and sing in his mike. He just was the nicest, sweetest, most down-to-earth person. No wonder he had a beautiful, loving girlfriend.

You could talk to him, you could ask him anything, and he'd do anything for you. He made you feel good, and it was very comfortable to be around him. He was also a great performer. I didn't really hang out with their guitarist, Billy Duffy much. He seemed distant, maybe a bit egotistical. Les was the drummer and "Haggis" the bass player, whose nickname was inspired by the Scottish goat-stomach dish. Gross.

The Cult and GNR got along phenomenally well, and we had a great time together. They always had catering at sound check, great food that positively spoiled us. During our set, Axl made it a point to announce to the crowd how great the Cult was to us. As we would discover later, a lot of bands we opened up for would give us just half or even a quarter of the stage. The Cult was not like that at all; they gave us more room, more lights, more everything, the sign of a very cool, very confident group. When their album *Electric* came out, I really became a huge fan.

It's sort of a rock 'n' roll ritual for the headlining act to play a practical joke on the opening band on the last night of the tour. I was definitely the people person of the band, so I was always in with the roadies and the bands we toured with. The Cult's crew, and the band themselves, were all in on this particular joke. In New Orleans, during one of the last songs in our set, the Cult's crew came out and took my drum set apart piece by piece. First, the cymbal, then the cymbal stand, finally the snare drum, until I was just sitting there looking like a dork. Izzy, Duff, Axl, and Slash were all pointing and laughing at me. Then the guys brought the drum set back one piece at a time.

Now, usually opening bands dare not play a practical joke back at the headliners, but we got along so well, we knew it'd be cool. We got naked, with only towels wrapped around our waists. Then the five of us, and a couple of our roadies, walked out onstage while the Cult was playing. I had mixed a disgusting concoction of eggs, mustard, and relish in a Styrofoam cup. I walked behind Ian holding it. He didn't see me, and I motioned to the crowd, "Should I?" holding it over his head, ready to pour, and they were like, "Yeah!" He turned around and started chasing me all over the stage. He grabbed at me and pulled the towel off of my waist. I was totally naked onstage in front of everyone. I didn't mind one bit. In fact, I ended up without my clothes on many times, backstage, on the tour bus, in the hotels, and at the bars. The band called me "naked boy," a playful moniker and dependable indicator of how far along I was with my partying for the evening. I'd just look down and laugh—hey, I'm naked! Fortunately usually someone would wrap a tablecloth or something around me before I could get into any serious trouble.

That evening I covered my cock (needing both hands of course), smiled, and bounded off the stage. It was a thrill being stark naked in front of thousands of people.

The fun didn't end there. Afterward, I went upstairs to the dressing room, where Slash was talking to this hot little girl named Toy. He was looking to score with her but I walked in and she took one look at me and said, "Oh, I want to be with *him*." Thoroughly amused, I grabbed her, smiled, and said, "Sorry, Slash, that's how it goes."

Toy and I smoked a fatty and went out on the town. When we were leaving the theater, another hot young girl got my attention by grabbing my ass. She laughed and explained that she was a friend of a girl I knew in L.A. named Taylor. Taylor was a cool chick who had dated Axl and had been around the band from the beginning. This girl was from Baton Rouge and heard from Taylor that we were playing and came down. So I hit the town with a beautiful girl on each arm.

We went out on Bourbon Street. It was such a cool scene there. In one of the gift shops, I purchased a novelty cap that held a beer can, one on each side of your head. It had tubes attached so you could suck the beers dry. Wearing my new party hat, we entered a nightclub where we got drunk on Hurricane drinks. Toy had a couple hits of Ecstasy and since this was years before the drug caught on, I had never done it. It was mellow and pretty damn cool, a real body trip, like magic mushrooms. We were dancing, enjoying the lights and sounds like never before. All of us in the band had our own key to the bus, and the three of us went back to the bus and fucked and fucked and fucked. It felt incredible.

The tour dates for our shows started getting paced farther apart, and to pass the time we did what anyone who was bored shitless would do: we drank a lot. I also smoked a lot of weed while the other guys supplemented their booze intake with blow. Alan would pop up from time to time. And Dougie was with us all the time. He really made good on his pledge to take care of us. He had proved to be a real asset, particularly with his most important task: making sure that Axl got onstage on time.

Dougie ran everything. He was mom, wingman, and butler all rolled into one. He knew as long as Axl had hot tea with lemon, Izzy had his vino, and Duff and Slash had a steady supply of vodka, the boys were happy.

In late September 1987, we began a small tour of Europe again, this time with our good buds Faster Pussycat from L.A. The guys in FP were great. Of course, we knew Taime from years of partying at the Cathouse. Izzy and I really liked Brent, the band's guitarist. Me and Duff were hanging out with FP's drummer, a very nice guy, and after a night of hard drinking, he passed out in Duff's bed.

I couldn't understand it, but this made Duff super-pissed. Duff's the mellowest guy, but the booze could turn him into one mean mother. "Fuck this shit," he said. He wanted to play a practical joke on the guy, so he had me help him grab and tie the drummer's legs and wrists with duct tape. We taped all around his mouth and head too, and we carried him to the hotel elevator. It was one of those really old lifts with the gate that you have to pull open. We threw him in, and at that point, I thought at was funny as hell.

Then Duff pressed all the buttons in the elevator, closed the door, and let him go. The next day at the show, Duff and I saw him, bruised and very hungover. He avoided us completely, never uttering a word about the previous night.

When we got to Amsterdam, we went to the red-light district, where we met many stunning ladies. During that Euro tour, we hooked up with chicks everywhere. The girls were always there, always all over us. We were young, our dreams were coming true, and we reveled in it. Slash, Duff, and I would have contests to see who could get the most blow jobs in a single day. I won every time.

Slash and I would have orgies with five or more chicks. If I didn't like the way a chick looked, I'd send her over to the crew. Axl and Izzy weren't into that scene, however. They were more conservative; no orgies, no ménage à whatever, and I respected that.

AMSTERDAM GOOD TIME

Amsterdam is the greatest place I've ever been. Slash and Izzy were into heroin, and when they checked in, they couldn't wait to score some pure, quality shit. As soon as we got there, we all went our own ways in search of drugs.

For years, all I heard about from other rock musicians who had been to Amsterdam was how great the Bulldog was. The Bulldog's a popular bar in Amsterdam and I couldn't wait to hit it up. It was the first place I scoped out, and I was immediately directed to the Bulldog's pot bar downstairs. It was just a room full of thick sweet smoke.

On the wall were two menus; one had about fifteen different kinds of marijuana, and the other listed about nine different varieties of hashish. I was positively salivating over the prospects. Finally I said, "Give me the California Purple Indigo Bud" (I know, fly all the way from L.A. to Holland just to order some California bud). There were rolling papers on the bar in cups, much like napkin dispensers in a regular restaurant. They were huge cigarette papers, Cheech and Chong's Big Bambú style all the way.

The Bulldog also had a drinking bar that was located upstairs. I stayed in the smoking area for the most part. It was amazing. Everybody's dancing, the lights are flashing, and I'm drinking beers and smoking bud, definitely feeling right at home.

The venue we performed at, the Paradiso, was located directly across the street from the Bulldog. At the end of the show, I walked to the front of the stage and said, "You rock my world. Thank you very much." I threw my sticks out to the people and jumped into the crowd. They gently set me down so I could walk right out the door back over to the Bulldog. That's how much I loved the place. I never wanted to leave.

Of course Slash and Izzy continued with their fix-ation. All they could talk about was scoring heroin. That was *all they talked about.* When they finally scored they were horrified to discover that the shit they got was fake. They got screwed and they were depressed, because heroin was supposed to be good and plentiful. The truth was that smack actually was there in abundance; they just had shit luck.

Ronnie and I were walking down the street, and we saw this derelict wandering aimlessly. Two police officers walked up to him, sat him down, searched him, and found used syringes on him. I just assumed he was busted. But no, they broke the needles, disposed of them, and handed him new ones. They also gave him a box that contained a syringe, a rubber, and an alcohol swab. Then they sent him on his way. I thought that was so great, so *enlightened.*

Later that night, Ronnie and I walked out of the Bulldog. We stood there for a bit enjoying the night, and then this guy came up to us and asked, "Hey, you wanna party?" I smiled. He said, "Well, a friend of mine has a little flat." He explained that he was a big fan of the band, so I figured he was totally cool.

We followed him into a dark alley behind a Holiday Inn. He told us to wait for him a minute, and he ran inside. We were standing in this alley for about twenty-five minutes and started getting impatient. Right when we were about to say "Fuck this" he finally came out and told us, "Okay, guys, it's cool, come on up." We entered the structure and it was pitch-black; I couldn't see a thing. We were walking up a long, spiral staircase. Someone had their ten-speed bike locked up in there, just where you couldn't see, and I tripped right the fuck over it. "Oh, watch out for the bike," he said. Yeah, thanks.

We entered into this cool little den, which was illuminated with red, yellow, and green lights. Heavy, flowing beads hung in the doorways, very retro-psychedelic. He introduced us to his friend Sven, a scruffy-looking fellow in his early thirties. Sure enough, he had heroin and coke laid out before him. I'd done heroin twice before, but I never shot it up. We were in Amsterdam, smoking buds, feelin' great, and we said, "Okay. Fuck it, let's party."

GO SPEED RACER

He had this brown powder heroin and a little pile of clean white cocaine. I asked the guy if he wanted some money for us to party, but he refused, saying we didn't have to pay. The guy reached underneath the couch he was sitting on and pulled out a spoon. To the right of him was a brown paper bag full of factory-fresh syringes. He took the spoon and dipped it into the pile of coke, and then repeated with the heroin. He was mixing up a speedball. I never did this; both times I smoked the shit I got so sick. I don't know why I was going to do it again, but I was just there, and that was reason enough.

He held the spoon over a candle and cooked it up. He dipped the point of the needle into the hot liquid and filled the syringe with the concoction. They wrapped a piece of cloth around my arm and tied it up nice and tight. I guess being in the presence of a pro lowered my fear of needles, because I just relaxed and stared at all of the colorful lights in the room.

He'd barely started plunging the syringe, and some red flag popped up in my head. I screamed: "Take it out, take it out, take it out!" I instinctively pulled away from him as he quickly removed the needle from my arm. I could see that I had gotten about a quarter of the intended dose. I was instantly in a dazed euphoric state, but I was barely able to hang on.

I swear, if he had shot the whole thing in, I would have been in dire straits. The rest of the evening he just poured us drinks and played great tunes. I settled down pretty quickly, and we went on to have an incredibly fun night.

Early the next morning we went back to the hotel. The sun was barely coming up and there's Slash and Izzy sitting inside, still completely bummed. I boasted, "Yeah, we partied all night. We were doing coke and heroin, we were fucked up." They were so pissed. "Why didn't you come get us? You asshole!"

That night, Ronnie and I went back to the Bulldog. After getting nicely lit, we left to go exploring and check out the local culture a little more. We walked down the red-light district, where hookers and sexual decadence abounded. Just like window-shopping, you could view all kinds of girls literally on display. They were dancing, gyrating, trying to sell themselves. Whatever you wanted, tall, short, black, white, stacked, you picked her out for an hour or half hour, whatever.

I didn't need that shit; I did just fine for myself. We passed by this one porn shop where this Middle Eastern guy waved us over. "I want to show you something." He pointed up to a TV monitor in a corner of the place and we were mesmerized. A man and a woman were fucking and sucking off every farm animal you could think of. We couldn't stop staring. We stood there for forty-five minutes, mouths wide open. The guy tried to sell us videotapes of the action we were watching, but no thanks; I could go a long time before seeing that woman with Mr. Ed again.

We finally decided to visit our local friends from the night before. We did the right thing and collected Slash and Izzy, then proceeded to the den of euphoria that had so rocked my world the prior night. After a small search, we found the site and knocked on the door. The same guy answered. He smiled and said that he had an idea we might be back. It became my second time ever shooting up. We were higher than high. This time they knew to give me a smaller dose, but Izzy and Slash said "fill 'er up" and it was speedballs for all as we raged all night.

After Holland we went to Germany to play Hamburg and Düsseldorf. All of our shows were practically sold out. The audiences loved us. The Germans were insanely into the show, singing along. They knew every word and it threw me for a loop. A lot of Germans spoke English perfectly. I remember hearing the band on the radio in Hamburg and jumping for joy.

The German cities were immaculate, like they had cleaning ladies come out and scrub them at dawn every morning. While in Germany, I couldn't help but think about my family, the Jews, and the Holocaust. My grandma barely escaped to the United States just days ahead of the Nazi invasion of Poland. I shudder to think about all the innocent people packed into trains and shipped off to the gas chambers.

The next day we were to return to England, but I still had some weed from the Bulldog. On our ferry trip back, everyone was all worried and freaking out because I was bringing pot across and that was illegal. I wasn't concerned; I would just throw the shit overboard if I had to.

The weather was overcast, foggy, and cold. As we were crossing the English Channel, all I could think about was World War II and the invasion that was staged from those frigid waters. The whole turning point of the war took place there, massive maneuvers that brought tens of thousands of courageous troops from England into occupied France. Because of their bravery and sacrifice, I could play my music in a free world.

We continued our tour with stops in Newcastle, Nottingham, Bristol, and London. The shows started to meld together, but I distinctly remember the British crowds were a little more reserved than the Germans, although they clapped very enthusiastically.

Our last show in England was at the Hammersmith Odeon on October 8, 1987. We opened with "It's So Easy" and rocked that place, closing with "Sweet Child O' Mine" into "Whole Lona Rosie." Playing there cemented our popularity, which had grown during the tour. The Odeon seated over thirty-five hundred, five thousand standing room only. From Cream to Van Halen, a lot of the biggest, most legendary bands played there, and it felt amazing when I looked out over the crowd. It was nearly packed, and those Brits caught one hell of a show. GNR was moving up over hallowed ground to the big time.

When we got back from Europe, we were scheduled to have some time off. It was our first break from the road in a long time. We had been touring nonstop since our show at the Whiskey back in March. We arrived at LAX with a shuttle bus sitting there to pick us up. They dropped me off at the corner of Franklin and Highland and just took off. I had nowhere to go and nothing to do.

Before this, they had put us up at the Franklin Plaza suites. A lot of bands stay there. I never thought it was anything special, so rather than check in there again, I got an apartment down the street from where I grew up with my grandparents on Hayworth. My new place was across the street from the elementary school where I met Slash for the first time. I went to see my grandma, and as always she was very happy to see me and this time, so proud. I wasn't in touch with Mom at this point, and it really wasn't for any particular reason. I just didn't think to call. I wasn't being mean or unloving; it just honestly never occurred to me to ring her up. Anyone who knows me should understand that it's not something I do to hurt someone deliberately. That's the way I am, and I've never really dwelled on it.

It really felt great to be back home. I looked forward to hitting the Strip, checking out the clubs, and catching up with everyone. It was time to kick back and enjoy L.A. again.

✕ ✕ ✕ ✕

CHAPTER NINE / MARIANNE FAITHFULL
COURTFIELD ROAD

EXCERPT FROM
Faithfull: An Autobiography

AUTHORS
Marianne Faithfull with David Dalton

Marianne Faithfull is an English singer, songwriter and actress. Her first hit, "As Tears Go By," (1964) was written for her by Mick Jagger, Keith Richards, and Andrew Loog Oldham when she was just 17 years old.

✕ ✕ ✕ ✕

"You might reasonably ask why we were sharing our honeymoon suite with a bunch of drug-addled beatnik poets, but I didn't."

I BEGAN GOING ROUND to Courtfield Road a year after Nicholas was born. I had developed an irresistible need to get out of the flat. I was bored. I felt trapped and I was exhausted. In the three years between Adrienne Posta's party where I met Andrew Oldham until I ran off with Mick Jagger, I made four singles and two albums, went on three tours, did six weeks in Paris at the Olympia, not to mention countless interviews, *Top of the Pops* and on and on.

Before I started working in pop music I was seventeen and having a good time, going to parties, hanging about in coffee bars, the usual seventeen-year-old stuff. And nice as it was to be "discovered" and become a pop star, I couldn't shake the feeling that I had missed something. My marriage to John had been a shotgun wedding, naturally. In 1964, if you got pregnant you got married. Our honeymoon, although spent in Paris, was anything but conventional. The only people we saw during our week in Paris were Allen Ginsberg, Lawrence Ferlinghetti, and Gregory Corso. Great slangy, mantra-slathering beatniks careening around our hotel room, throwing up, spilling cheap rosé all over the place and ranting on about the Rosenbergs, Rimbaud, Tangier and buggery. Gregory's idea of breakfast was to mix up a Brompton Cocktail—half morphine and half cocaine—and pass out on the floor of the Hotel Louisiana.

You might reasonably ask why we were sharing our honeymoon suite with a bunch of drug-addled beatnik poets, but I didn't. Mostly we were doing it because it was what John wanted to do, and of course it *was* wonderful. But life back home at Lennox Gardens was more of the same. John's idea of a normal routine was to put liquid methedrine in his coffee in the morning before going off to work at Indica Bookstore with Miles. The bookstore was on the ground floor and John's gallery was in the basement.

My exquisitely decorated nest had turned into a crash pad for talented layabouts. American junkies, actually. This was when you could still get British pharmaceutical heroin legally, and that was the principle reason all these guys came to London. Mad types like Mason Hoffenberg would show up at our house and end up staying for months at time. Mason had popped in to see John for a few days around Christmastime the previous year and the following May he was *still there*, draped about the house and conked out in various states of stupefaction. He was a wicked mimic with an undepletable store of salty anecdotes. An enormously funny man—he had written *Candy* with Terry Southern—and wonderfully good company. I might have found it all a lot more amusing if I had been allowed to join in, but that's not the way John liked it. Life was quietly becoming nightmarish.

I would get up in the morning. There'd be no heat, I'd have to step over several people crashed in the living room. I'd go into the kitchen to warm up a bottle for Nicholas and find the draining board strewn with bloody needles. One morning I went round the whole flat and collected all these jacks, these little heroin pills, hidden all over the place—there were hundreds of them—and I flushed them down the toilet. I just couldn't take it anymore. But I stuck it out for two years, trying to lead my normal middle-class life as best I could for as long as I could. In this bohemian/druggie household I had been badly miscast as mother-angel-girlfriend-wife and blessed Virgin Mary. An insufferable role that I finally began to hate with a passion. I was bored, I was lonely, I had begun to find John and his cerebral junkies tiresome. And all around me was the centrifugal whirl of the sixties. I wanted to see what all the fuss was about.

I've always liked going out on my own—you can maneuver better—and that's just what I started to do. I'd leave John at home with Nicholas and the nanny and his drugs and his friends, and I'd go off to *my* drugs and *my* friends. I loved getting dressed up and putting on my makeup with John quietly fuming. He knew he couldn't really stop me going out, but that didn't stop him from trying. One night he threw all my jars of makeup against the wall. That was actually one of the reasons I left him!

Jealousy played little part in all this. His main objection was my extravagance. Every time I left the house I would spend an absolute fortune. Sure, I kept the house going but everything else I made—and I made a lot of money—I spent on myself. I was mean and I was petty when it came to money. John was running an art gallery and when it went bust, I didn't lift a finger to help. I didn't behave like a human at all. I was a shopping addict. My first really serious addiction.

My first stop of the evening was always Brian and Anita's. Keith Richards practically lived there, too; he and Brian were fast friends in those days. Every day Keith would walk all the way from his flat in St. John's Wood, about four miles, into Gloucester Road. After he broke with Linda Keith, his girlfriend at the time, he took to spending even more time there. Supposedly he no longer had a place to stay, but I always suspected it was to get closer to Anita. Keith just exuded lonely bachelorhood, and naturally Brian and Anita always let him crash there.

The Courtfield Road flat itself was a grungy place. Mattress on the floor, sink piled high with dirty dishes, posters half falling down. But Christopher had insisted Anita buy it. "You simply *have* to get it, darling. With a little tarting up it could be absolutely ravishing." And of course it *could* have been. It was your classic artist's studio. Very high ceilings, skylights, huge windows and one very large room with a winding staircase up to a minstrels' gallery.

The place had definite possibilities, but we all knew that absolutely *nothing* was ever going to be done. During the entire time Brian and Anita lived there it remained exactly as it was the day they moved in, with the exception of a few sticks of furniture and a couple of bizarre, moth-eaten stuffed animals from a movie Anita had done in Germany.

Brian would sit on the floor, very high, and tell you what it was going to look like when he got it together. Anita and Brian were like two beautiful children who had inherited a decrepit palazzo. Every day they would dress up in their furs and satins and velvets and parade about and invite people over, and we would all sit on the floor and talk about the fantastic things we would do with the kingdom if only we could.

There were two secret rooms, which added to the flat's play quality. A room below the kitchen that you got to through a hatch in the floor and an attic that you reached by means of a metal ladder you could pull down. This attic was a wonderful gothic-looking storage space where books and clothes and Brian's train magazines were stored.

A couple of times I dropped by Courtfield Road and found Brian there all by himself. He invited me in with a courtly flourish. Brian had lovely manners and a little whispery voice. He was so intelligent and would become very animated when the subject interested him. Trains, Ingmar Bergman movies, anything magical. Like a lot of people al time, myself included, he was convinced there was a mystic link tween Druidic monuments and flying saucers. Extraterrestrials were going to read these signs from their spaceship windows and get the message. It was the local credo: Glastonbury, ley lines and intelligent life in outer space. I've forgotten exactly *what* it was we believed, but we believed it fiercely! And if little green men were going to contact *anybody* on the planet it would have to be us wouldn't it?

In the middle of one of these conversations, Brian began coming on to me out of the clear blue. I had the oddest feeling he was simply being polite. I was in his flat, I was a pretty girl . . . and he was a Rolling Stone, making it almost *de rigueur* that he make a pass at me. It was the new sexual politeness. And I for my part thought, "Oh, he's making a play for me. I really should let him." I figured that was what a flower child did. Hippie etiquette. You just sort of went along, didn't you?

I didn't really fancy Brian, and I was truly terrified of Anita. But Anita unfortunately was out of town and Brian and I, needless to say, were both very high. So after several large spliffs and what I gathered was courtship patter (involving the *Flying Scotsman*, Mary Wells, William Morris wallpaper and Tantric art) Brian led me up the little staircase to the minstrels' gallery. We lay down on a mattress and he unbuttoned my blouse. But after a bit of groping about, it just fizzled out. He was a wonderfully feeble guy, quite incapable of real sex. And of course he was doing a lot of Mandrax, which rendered him even more wobbly than he already was. Brian only had so much energy.

Every once in a while, Mick would drop in at Courtfield Road. Very fastidious always, with an absolute *horror* of bohemian living. The sink full of dirty dishes so appalled him he could never stay long. Mick's visits were of an almost proprietal nature. He'd come by sort of to inspect everything, see that all was going well with the Firm, smoke a joint and split.

Mick and Brian were always far more interested in the power shifts in the group than Keith. But of course it was whoever allied himself with Keith who had the power. The balance in the group was completely different from what it was later to become. The guitar players, Brian and Keith, were inseparable, with Mick and Andrew Oldham off in the corner. They were all quite far from Their Satanic Majesties or whatever they were supposed to have become. Their personae were gradually forming out of a blend of blues mythology and Kings Road *noblesse oblige*. Like boys, playing in suits of armor shortly before a voice out of the clouds comes and tells them, "Thou shalt be Princes of Darkness."

One of the great attractions of Courtfield Road for me was getting high. I'd only recently started smoking hash but I couldn't smoke at home because John— an incredible piece of drug chauvinism this—wouldn't permit me to. People shooting up all over the house and I wasn't allowed to roll a joint! I never actually went to John and said, "Let me try what you're doing, let me have a joint," because I knew damn well John would never go for it. It was a men's club that I couldn't join. I was the wife and the mother and the golden goose. I was doing three gigs a night in Manchester and coming back with thousands of pounds—in cash. John was not one to screw *that* up.

The entertaining at Courtfield Road was the most basic kind. Joint-rolling, mainly. *Endless* joint-rolling. It was still quite a novelty and we would smoke until we were obliterated. Really fascinating stuff when you're eighteen. Every thought twined about itself so many times there was no way of articulating it, consequently very little was ever said.

At about ten o'clock at night everyone would be famished and we'd stagger out to Alvaro's for some wonderful pasta. But once we got there we'd be so stoned we could barely manage more than a mouthful. I'd stare the exquisite china and watch the tiny dragons crawl over the fettuccine while Anita and Robert talked about shoes and art in Italian.

One of the best things about visiting Anita and Brian was watching them get ready to go out. What a scene! They were both dauntless shoppers and excessively vain. Hours and hours were spent putting on clothes and taking them off again. Heaps of scarves, hats, shirts and boots flew out of drawers and trunks. Unending trying on of outfits, primping and sashaying. They were beautiful, they were the spitting image of each other and not an ounce of modesty existed between the two of them. I would sit mesmerized for hours, watching them preening in the mirror trying on each other's clothes. All roles and gender would evaporate in these narcissistic performances where Anita would turn Brian into the Sun King, Françoise Hardy or the mirror image of herself.

She loved him very much, but there was some ugly stuff going on between them. There were often bruises on her arms. No one said anything. What would there be to say? We all knew it was Brian. Anita is not the sort of feminine, confiding person who invites speculation into her private life. It would have been a point of honor on her part *not* to say anything. Anita wanted at all costs to be considered invincible. And she always seemed to know exactly what she was doing.

I think I knew very clearly how to detach even then. We were all doing so many drugs you had to be a bit careful what you focused on or you would become completely obsessed. It sounds a bit brutal, but as long as I wasn't the one being beaten up I didn't care. I was very, very self-involved, and I was walking a fucking tightrope myself.

When I first met Brian he was on one of his brief upswings, but even during this manic phase a doomed look began to set in his face. Inner demons had begun eating away at that Renaissance angel's head.

Whatever was wrong with Brian began a long time before; you have only to look at childhood pictures of Mick, Keith and Brian to see it. After looking at snapshots of a little cheerful Mick and a strong, very tough little Keith, to suddenly come upon Brian's baby picture is quite startling. A jowly, miserable child is looking up at you with exactly that expression of helpless victimization he gave off in the last year of his life.

Brian was a mess. Neurasthenic and hypersensitive. Twitchy. The slightest thing would set him off. He would let things gnaw at him and he would *brood*. This paranoiac-condition worsened, naturally, on acid. Everybody would be laughing and looning about, and Brian would be over in the corner all crumpled up. It's Anita's belief that Brian never recovered from his first trip. But he *embraced* his horrors, as if on acid he was finally able to confront his afflictions in palpable form.

Drowning voices in the pipes, traffic noises turning into sinister conversations. We've *all* heard these things on acid, God knows. Nevertheless, it's not too cool to announce that your appliances are plotting against you. For Brian these thoughts were so incessant that he couldn't help himself. Brian simply verbalized what everyone else was thinking. Things I, for one, was thinking! But these outbursts left him open to ridicule. And they *all* taunted him.

Keith would ask: "It's the snakes again, is it, Brian?" Then to us in a stage whisper: "The snakes in the wiring, they're talking to Brian." Gales of laughter.

Poor Brian was just somewhat uncool. He could summon coolness up, but fundamentally he wasn't cool at all. His was a false cool. Keith, on the other hand, really *was* cool, ice cool, always. And he hasn't changed at all. He's gotten more and more strange looking and developed this grand desperado carapace, but inside Keith is not unlike his twenty-two-year-old self. He has a wickedly twisted sense of humor that on acid would become quite diabolical. We'd be out on the balcony and he'd whisper to Anita: "Go on, darling, jump why don't you?" But she would turn with that wonderful smile of hers and tell him: "You little fucker, what are you trying to do?"

Keith was gorgeous in those days. When I think how he looked then, how beautiful he was—and pure. Long before I got to know him, I had a huge crush on him. For years. He was the epitome of my ideal of the tortured Byronic soul. It was quite clear even then that he was a genius. He isn't a bit shy now, but when I first met him he was agonizingly shy and painfully introverted. He didn't talk at all. I mean all that stuff that Mick did, like trying to make me sit on his lap, Keith would rather have died than do anything like that.

Mick and Keith both developed their tabloid personas while they were on the road. Mick became the grand seigneur and the great gentleman. And Keith developed this bravado. The pirate who sailed with Captain Kidd. Arrr!

✕

One of the things Brian liked to do when he was high was to make tapes. He'd record all night long and then in the morning erase everything.

Out of all the frenetic activity that went on, only one song, as far as I know, resulted during the entire time I was at Courtfield Road that was "Ruby Tuesday." It was Brian's swan song. Jekyll and Hyde. At one point he began to paint a mural of a graveyard on the wall behind the bed. Just above the pillows was a large headstone. He never got around to writing his name on it, but you knew that the headstone was for him.

Today you would put anybody in Brian's shaky condition into a hospital. But I don't honestly think it crossed anybody's mind to "seek professional help." And he, of course, would never have accepted it. We saw ourselves as the vanguard of the new era. The admission that one of the elite was mentally unbalanced might have endangered the whole Children's Crusade before it had even got started. And the fact that Brian was a self-indulgent and brittle monster didn't help in eliciting sympathy when he began to unravel.

I remember one particularly harrowing scene. There was no bell at Courtfield Road, so in order to get into the flat you had to shout up. Brian or Anita would throw the keys down or go down and open the door. One day we were all at the flat, Keith, Brian, Anita, myself and one or two other people. We were all quite stoned and suddenly we heard people outside on the pavement calling up. But it wasn't the usual hippie growl, "Brian, open the fuckin' door, man!" It was two troubled-sounding voices, a man's and a woman's, calling up. We all went out on the balcony to see who it was.

There down below was Brian's old girlfriend with her two-year-old baby, Julian, and her father. She was raising the baby up in the air in a classic gesture of supplication, asking Brian for help, begging him. She wanted child support and the baby was very obviously Brian's. "It's your kid, Brian, you know it is. We're really in a bad way, we need some help. Please!" All with the father chiming in: "You bloody do the right thing by her, boy, y'hear!"

And Brian and Anita just peered down on them as if they were some inferior species. Foppish aristocrats in their finery jeering at the *sans culottes* below. Upstairs everyone was *laughing* about it. It was so appalling, like something out of a Mexican folktale. But Anita and Brian seemed to enjoy every minute of it.

× × × ×

CHAPTER TEN / TONY SANCHEZ
HOOF AND BLOOD

EXCERPT FROM
Up And Down With The Rolling Stones: My Rollercoaster Ride With Keith Richards

- -

AUTHOR
Tony Sanchez

- -

COPYRIGHT © 2010 by John Blake Publishing, Ltd
REPRINTED BY PERMISSION OF ~ John Blake Publishing, Ltd

- -

Tony Sanchez worked as Keith Richards's assistant for eight years. He died in 2000.

*"I got hold of half an ounce of heroin
and a similar quantity of cocaine. I offered Johnny,
a friend of mine, £500 to carry it to Switzerland.
Everything was going smoothly."*

1968

MICK AND KEITH AND I dreamed up the idea of the Vesuvio Club after we
received a huge bill at the Speakeasy. Keith was furious at the way nightclubs
consistently overcharged him and Mick because they knew they wouldn't want
to be seen arguing over money.

He grudgingly slammed a dozen five-pound notes on top of the bill, turned
to me and said, "It's about time we had our own club, man, instead of being
ripped off everywhere we go." It had long been a dream of mine to have a place
of my own because I was well aware that fortunes can be made more quickly
in the nightclub business than in any other; besides, I now had so many rich,
famous friends that I felt the club couldn't fail to be a huge success. Within a
month I'd arranged a partnership with an old friend, and we found the perfect
place on Tottenham Court Road. It was a basement in an appalling condition,
with paper peeling from the walls and bare wires hanging from the ceiling. We
set out to modernize it ourselves.

Keith and Mick came down a couple of times to tell me how they wanted it
to look and to ask me if I could score any dope for them, but I'd just give them a
paint brush or scraper, and that ensured they didn't come back too often. Once
I asked them to paint an old honky-tonk piano I'd found, and they sat down at
it and started bashing out a new song they had dreamed up. It was an amazing,
thundering great number even though it didn't have any words at that time.
Much later the tune became "Honky Tonk Woman," which is probably the best

record the Stones have ever made.

It took only two months to transform that dingy cellar into one of the best clubs London has ever seen. The Vesuvio was designed to look like an exotic Arab tent. There were a dozen cubicles, each shielded by huge Moroccan tapestries. Inside each there were heaps of big cushions together with a small, ornate table and a bubble-bubble opium pipe. I gave a brilliant young artist friend of Robert's all the grass he could smoke to decorate the walls with Inca sunbursts and beautiful designs that went wild under black lights. These were interspersed with blow-ups of the Stones, which Michael Cooper had taken in Morocco. There was a silverfoil airship filled with helium that floated around at body level.

While I was busy with my paintbrush, the Stones put out a humdinger of a single called "Jumpin' Jack Flash" that more than made up for the *Satanic Majesties* debacle. Now they flew to Los Angeles for the final mix of their follow-up album *Beggars Banquet*. They were all due to return on Mick's twenty-fifth birthday, July 26, 1968, so I phoned all of the Stones' friends and arranged to combine Mick's party with the opening night of the Vesuvio. Mick flew in dramatically at the last minute, with the first advance pressing of *Beggars Banquet*, the album the whole world was waiting to hear, for this was a record on which the band's entire future hung. If they can't make a good album by now, the music business was saying, they never will.

Everything was perfect for the party. The club looked beautiful with huge silver bowls of Mescaline spiked punch, plus plates full of hash cakes, which had become a craze, and little dishes with hash for people to smoke beside every hubble-bubble pipe.

My only fear was our proximity to Tottenham Court Road police station. It was only three hundred yards away, and a couple of inquisitive cops would have been able to arrest just about every superstar in Britain if they had decided on a raid that night. I kept my fears to myself and put three huge Spanish boys on the door with instructions that no one was to be allowed through the locked entrance until I had vetted him. (At least then, I thought, I could flush most of the drugs down a toilet before the police could break the door down.) Among the first to arrive was Paul Getty II with his stunning young wife, Talitha, who wore a dress as sheer as gossamer, without a stitch underneath. The couple lived in Cheyne Walk, a few doors away from Mick, and they had become firm friends. Mick arrived, then Charlie Watts and John Lennon drifted in, and last of all came Paul McCartney.

As Paul walked in, everyone was leaping around to *Beggars Banquet*, which—with tracks like "Sympathy for the Devil" and "Street Fighting Man"—was far and away the best album of the Stones' career.

Paul discreetly handed me a record and told me, "See what you think of it, Tony. It's our new one." I stuck the record on the sound system, and the slow thundering build up of "Hey, Jude" shook the club. I turned the record over, and we all heard John Lennon's nasal voice pumping out "Revolution." When it was over, I noticed that Mick looked peeved. The Beatles had upstaged him.

Eventually John Lennon staggered across to me, looking as though his eyes were going to pop out of his head, and asked me if I could arrange a taxi to take him and Yoko home. I had warned all the people working for me not to drink the punch or eat the cakes, but they had been so excited by the sight of all these rock stars that they had started munching away at the extremely potent hash cakes and knocking back glasses of the punch. I asked the doorman, who looked the least mindblown, to dash out for a cab. He just said, "Yes," and wandered off into the night. Half-an-hour later he hadn't returned, and John came back to ask me where his taxi was. I explained that my man had gone half-an-hour before to find one, and John muttered, "What kind of doorman takes half-an-hour to find a taxi in Tottenham Court Road?"

I dashed up to the reception area to send another of my boys out for a cab. Twenty minutes later he hadn't come back either. I ran back up and sent the only man I had left, warning him, "Look, those other two idiots have vanished and John is freaking out. For Christ's sake, get a cab within five minutes—it can't be that difficult."

Of course, he didn't come back either, and John and Yoko were becoming angry by then. "What do you mean they've all vanished?" John was yelling. "What kind of a club is this?" I was getting scared by then; were the cops hauling everyone off to Scotland Yard as soon as they walked out of the door? Later I discovered that they all had gone completely gaga when the fresh air combined with the mescaline and hash they had taken. One of the fellows didn't come down for twelve hours, and then he had found himself lying in the middle of a rose bed in St. James's Park.

Mick asked why John was shouting. When he heard the disappearing waiter saga, he laughed and handed me the keys to his car, a beautiful midnight blue, black windowed Aston Martin DB6. I went to my cousin, who was a guest at the party, and asked him to drive John and Yoko home in the car. An ardent Beatles fan, he leapt at the opportunity. John and Yoko got in the back of the car while he climbed into the driving seat. Then his problems really began. The 160 mph Aston Martin was such a sophisticated, advanced piece of machinery that my cousin couldn't even locate the ignition keyhole, much less the interior light switch. To make matters worse, the car was parked on a yellow line, which was against the law.

Suddenly there was a tap on the window, and a huge policeman peered in. John was doing a lot of cocaine at that time, and he was convinced he was about to be busted, so he discreetly dropped a little bottle of the stuff on the floor of the car. All three of them were totally stoned anyway, so they just stared at the policeman in terror.

The cop smiled helpfully and said, "Good evening, sir, good evening, madam. What seems to be the trouble, young man?"

My cousin spluttered out his story of being unable to start the Aston because he was borrowing it from a friend and hadn't driven it before. The policeman climbed in, started the car and wished them all a pleasant drive home. John sighed with relief, then started searching for his cocaine, but he couldn't find it anywhere. He became agitated. "This is Mick Jagger's car, and the police are liable to search it at any time," he said. "I can't just leave my coke rolling around the floor of his car; it isn't fair."

As John poked around on the carpet, my cousin was experimenting with the power of the Aston, and at one point he accelerated so hard that John lost his balance and fell off his seat. By then they had travelled to Warren Street tube station—less than a quarter of a mile from the club. "Stop the car!" shouted John. "We're getting out. I'll walk home if I have to. You find the coke and keep it."

My cousin came back a few minutes later, and I asked him where John had wanted to go. When he told me he'd only gone to Warren Street, I felt really upset.

"You mean," I said, "that he made me send out three people for cabs, then he borrowed Mick's Aston Martin, to travel less than a quarter of a mile?"

"No, no," said my cousin. "He wanted to go further, but he lost his nerve." My cousin never was a very good driver.

Everyone at the party laughed hysterically when they heard the full story.

By one in the morning the entire staff seemed to have vanished. The barman had gone; there was no cloakroom girl and no one left on the door. When Paul McCartney wished me good night, I apologized and explained that he and Linda would have to find their own coats.

"Righto, Tone," he said, "don't worry . . . great party."

As Paul walked into the darkened cloakroom, his feet kicked against someone lying on the floor. His first thought was that a couple of the less inhibited guests were making love on the thickly carpeted floor, but then he looked down into the gloom and realized that there appeared to be only one body—not two. And that one body seemed ominously still. "Tony, come here quick," he called nervously, "I think you've got bad trouble."

I fumbled for the light switch and walked around behind the black Formica counter of the cloakroom. There, lying flat on her back, was my cloakroom girl with her blonde head pillowed on somebody's £1,000 wolfskin coat, with a beatific smile playing across her face.

"Looks like another hash cake casualty," Paul laughed.

Later there were just four of us left: Mick, Marianne, Robert and I. We sat cross-legged on the floor cushions inside one of the tents around the low Oriental table. Robert slipped a small polythene bag from the pocket of his velvet jacket. "Pure opium, all the way from Thailand," he whispered.

The thick oil was placed into the pipe on the table; and with some difficulty, we set light to it. "You first," Robert said to Mick, "it's your birthday."

Mick drew deeply, then lay back on the cushions with a contented sigh. The pipe was passed around the table until it was in front of me. I had never tried opium before, so I had little idea what to expect. As I sucked deeply, I could feel the acrid fumes burning their way into my lungs. I began to splutter and cough, but then my head seemed to become as light as a helium-filled balloon; I could see Robert grinning at me from the other side of the table, and then I could feel myself floating, like a feather, backwards on the cushions.

A moment later I was conscious again. Marianne's beautiful face was smiling down at me. "Come with me, Tony," she whispered, and grabbed my hand. Robert and Mick were so dazed that they didn't even look in our direction as we walked together across the darkened club hand in hand." Something marvelous has happened," she said when we reached the other side of the room. "I think I'm going to have Mick's baby."

"Christ," I said, genuinely pleased, "that's fantastic. But what does Mick say? Isn't he afraid of being tied down?"

"Not at all," she replied. "But he keeps on and on at me to divorce John and marry him. He can't seem to understand that I never want to marry anyone. I have learned my lesson; people who are really in love don't need to be handcuffed together by legal contracts. Oh, Tony, I've never been so happy in my life. I wish the world could stop now."

When I crawled into bed at my flat in Maida Vale the room swayed gently from side to side, and it was like being in a yacht anchored in some balmy bay. "It's really all going to work out," I thought euphorically. "I'm going to be really rich, really independent at last."

The phone shrilled me into reluctant consciousness shortly before ten the next morning. I picked up the receiver to hear the New York voice of Linda Eastman, the blonde who was now living with Paul McCartney. "Where's the acetate of Paul's record? We want it right away. We must have it now . . ." she was saying, as I tried to clear my head and work out what she was babbling about.

"Okay," I said. "Your place in St. John's Wood is just around the corner from here, so I was going to bring it to you this afternoon."

"Oh, no, you don't, we want it right now," she said, sounding more and more hostile.

Hell, I thought, she's talking as though she's Paul's old lady or something. "Let me speak to Paul then," I said wearily.

"What the hell's the matter with her?" I asked Paul. "I told her I'd bring the record. As far as I'm concerned, you lent me the acetate and I don't need her shrieking at me first thing in the morning as though I'm going to run off and steal it."

Paul, as always, was the perfect diplomat. "Don't worry, Tony," he said. "Linda just takes a keen interest in my affairs. Do me a favor, and bring the record over to keep her happy."

I drove to their big psychedelic painted house on Cavendish Avenue that afternoon. As always there were a dozen girls hanging around in the street outside for the moment when they would be able to see the most beautiful Beatle of all.

I rang the bell beside the high green painted wooden gates, then shouted out who I was over the crackling answerphone. The gates opened with a buzz, and I slipped inside.

"Thanks, Tony," said Paul. "I'm sorry about the fuss, but Linda had the idea you'd make pirate copies of the record—silly, isn't it? Still, she's a very special kind of lady, and she's the only person I know who really genuinely cares about what happens to me."

✕

1975

"When I'm five months pregnant, I'll give it up," Anita promised, and in fairness to her, she did stick out withdrawal symptoms for nearly three days. Her retching, fever and delusions became so chronic that she feared for the safety of her unborn child, and she took "just one little snort" to see her through. That, of course, was the end of that cure. She tried the same thing at seven months, but again it was useless. Perhaps if she had gone into Bowden House, she could have actually stuck out her cold turkey, but the place was linked in her mind with death and pain; she would never go back there again.

Her gynecologist warned her that the life of the baby was being severely endangered by her recklessness, but the more she worried about it, the more she sought solace in heroin like an alcoholic drinking to forget cirrhosis of the liver. In the final days a specialist recommended an exclusive private clinic in Montreux, Switzerland, a place where doctors specialized in discreet handling of delicate situations.

She flew there with Keith and two-year-old Marlon. The stewardesses commented on what a beautiful family they were. When Anita settled in the clinic, Keith took Marlon to a lavish suite in the historic Montreaux Metropole Hotel on the shore of Lake Geneva. The doctors were patient and sympathetic, for which they were well paid at £50 a day. Anita, they explained, would be given the minimum possible dosage of methadone until the child was born. Dandelion Richard arrived in the world red-faced and squawking on April 17, 1972.

Keith phoned me in London to tell me of the birth. Before I could finish congratulating him, he brusquely interrupted me. "Look, Anita's coming out of hospital tomorrow, and she's going to be screaming. I want you to fly out here with all the stuff you can get."

"You're the best mate I've got, and you know I'd do anything for you and Anita," I said. "But as I've told you before, I will never sell drugs and I'll certainly never smuggle them."

"Okay, okay," he said, riled. "Get someone else to carry the dope for you, and you come out as well. I'll pay whatever it costs."

I got hold of half an ounce of heroin and a similar quantity of cocaine. I offered Johnny, a friend of mine, £500 to carry it to Switzerland. Everything was going smoothly. Johnny sat four seats in front of me on the flight to Montreaux and we didn't acknowledge in any way that we knew each other. Keith was waiting for me at the airport in his big limousine. As arranged, Johnny proceeded alone to the taxi stand to take the short ride to the Montreaux Metropole.

We followed in the limo. I waited until Johnny checked in before I went to his room to collect the stash and take it up to Keith and Anita's suite. They both took deep, grateful snorts, called me their lifesaver and passed out. By the next morning their euphoria had worn off, and they got obstreperous when I told them I had promised Johnny £500 for his trouble, and he was eager to take his money and return to London. "I'm sorry, Tony," Keith lied. "I've only got £250. He'll have to take it or leave it."

Justifiably this boy, who had risked a hefty jail sentence, was displeased. "Don't ever ask me to do anything like that for you again," he said. The look of contempt in his eyes made me so guilty that I gave him another £100 from my own pocket. "Look," I said, "Keith's very worried about the baby. He's not usually as mean as this."

In five days' time, Keith and Anita had used up the cocaine and heroin, and asked me to arrange for Johnny to bring more drugs. "You must be joking," I said. "After the way you refused to pay him what you owed him last time."

"Go on," pleaded Keith. "I'll give him £500 this time plus the other £150 from last time."

Johnny reluctantly accepted the commission and flew over with a little more heroin and a bag of grass. Keith and Anita devoured it greedily and arranged for Johnny to bring dope every ten days or so.

Anita, meanwhile, had become introspective and reclusive, refusing to leave the suite. Keith and I would take the children out for walks, joyfully breathing the Champagne air blowing down from the mountains, but Anita languished in solitary splendor, smoking her joints, jabbing needles in her bottom and musing.

Whenever the maids came to clean the rooms, she'd snarl at them from behind locked doors, sending them away. After three weeks, the place stank of dirty socks and stale cigarette smoke. There were empty bottles everywhere, cigarette burns on most of the mock Louis XIV furniture and the sheets were an uninviting shade of grey. "We can't go on living in this pigsty," Keith announced at last. He buzzed the manager to ask for another suite on a different floor. The maids stuck with the onerous task of cleaning out the abandoned suite insisted on fumigation, I discovered later.

It was almost time for the Stones to begin their first tour of the States in three years—their first since Altamont. Jagger was afraid; he'd quietly visited America several times to discuss plans for the tour, and he came back critical and afraid of the place.

"Where is it?" he asked Robert Greenfield from *Rolling Stone*, referring to the radical political zeal of the young that had made the States such an exciting place to be only three years before. "It's nowhere. It's just a lot of people dopin' up now. All the doping has got to stop before anything else. All that smack and everything. If that's their thing, if they wanna take smack and downers and two gallons of some chemical wine, okay; you're never gonna do what I thought people were gonna do.

"I don't blame people for wanting to get fucked up. Everyone likes to get fucked up once in a while, but you can't go through life like that. You can't blot it out. It keeps coming back, man, and in the end you just kill yourself trying to blot it out.

"People say all the dope on the street has stopped people from being active . . . and I wonder . . . which is the best thing to do? Whether it's better . . . aw, fuckit, I just wanna be naïve about it. I think you have to make your country a better place to live and bring kids up in and think in, and sitting at home taking smack and listening to records just ain't gonna do it. That's old-fashioned, maybe, but you got to take the bull by the horns, and it's a huge fuckin' bull, America . . . and the horns are very nasty."

Many believed Jagger's propounded fears for the United States masked far greater fears for himself. "His nerve has gone," went the whispers. "He's afraid this is going to be the tour where one of those hordes of crazy assassins finally gets to him." Jagger spent hours dwelling on security and finally decided that the Stones would play only small theaters—no arenas—where he could communicate with the audience, so things wouldn't get out of control. The economic realities of taking the Stones to the States dashed such fantasies. After a series of stormy meetings with Marshall Chess and Prince Rupert it was reluctantly agreed—the band would spend fifty-four days touring the biggest stadiums in the United States.

"But this time it's got to be right," Jagger said solemnly. "There are a lot of people who are still bitter about the last tour. I don't want high-priced tickets, delays, riots or any of that crap. We're going out there to make a lot of money and win a lot of friends."

Peter Rudge, a soft-spoken university graduate who organized perfect American tours for the Who, was hired to ensure that Mick's decree was carried out. Every detail of the tour was calculated with the precision of a military campaign. Canadian film maker Robert Frank would make a movie of the tour, while writer Robert Greenfield would turn it into a book. This time there would be no mistakes.

Rehearsals started in an atmosphere of secrecy more appropriate to a CIA operation. They were held in a small cinema in Montreaux, the Stones having discovered that it was easier to go to Keith than to get Keith to come to them. In May they flew to Los Angeles, tour headquarters. Within days Governor George Wallace was shot down and crippled for life by a gun-toting maniac in a Maryland shopping center. Mick's hands shook uncontrollably when they told him about it; it seemed portentous of his own doom. Again and again people would blurt out to him the question that was on the tip of all our tongues: "But aren't you afraid of getting shot, Mick?"

"Sure," he would reply. "Yeah, of course I am. But what else can I do? Stay at home and get fat and write? The risk is worth taking."

The first gig was at the Pacific Coliseum in Vancouver. From the first chords of "Brown Sugar"—the title refers to crude heroin—the audience went berserk. Outside, two thousand kids who had been unable to buy tickets fought it out with the police. By the end of the evening the critics and the audience were mumbling phrases like 'the greatest rock 'n' roll band in the world.' Meanwhile, thirty injured policemen were being stitched, anointed and bandaged in the local hospital.

Tequila was the Stones' drink on this tour; poppers and coke, their drugs. The Stones were trendsetters as always, and now that everyone else was snorting coke they were looking for a new kick. Drugs were everywhere on this tour—jars of cocaine, uppers and downers. Jagger snorted quantities of coke before every show; he felt he couldn't get up there to dance and scream without the high of the drug tearing through his body. Keith fixed so much heroin that on stage he was an eerie, shambling wreck—everyone's idea of a freaked out, druggie rock superstar—and the kids loved him for it. He turned the people in his circle on to the euphoric oblivion of smack. One friend had always resisted the idea of fixing, but Keith talked him into it as a novel way to celebrate July 4 in Washington, D.C. The friend woke up one morning soon afterwards to the realization that he was a heroin addict.

Mick still managed to resist the lure of heroin. With his strength of will he was able to obtain all the benefits of coke without having to pay the price in needing the comedown of smack. He disapproved vehemently when Keith and several other session men playing with the band came to work stoned. "I think it's completely wrong to get totally fucked up and go out and play," he said.

After a month the tour started to take on a drug-induced ethereal quality. Mick and Keith both had become so paranoid about being murdered that they carried .38 police special revolvers. In Chicago they stayed at Hugh Hefner's vulgar mansion. They were using each other—Hugh Hefner wanted to polish up his image with some of the Stones' hip prestige, and the Stones were happy enough to fuck his bunnies, use his dope and smash up his furniture. They left after a few days and everybody was pleased with the way the reciprocally beneficial arrangement had worked out. Even Hef.

He wasn't the only one hoping that some of the Stones' sparkle would rub off. Just about every aging youth seeker in the States is scratching to get close to this elixir of youth, and a few of them made it. People like Princess Lee Radziwill, who was mostly famous for being famous, and writers Truman Capote and Terry Southern. Insiders knew they didn't really fit in. Only Andy Warhol, who was slightly mad, was accepted, and that was mainly because he was Bianca's favorite artist.

On stage and off the show was getting wilder. At the International Sports Arena in San Diego fifteen people went to the hospital, and sixty to jail. In Tucson tear-gas grenades were thrown at vociferous fans. In Washington there were sixty-one arrests. In Montreal maniacs blew up the Stones' equipment van with dynamite and three thousand fans who had been sold forged tickets rioted. In Boston the Stones were arrested after a fight with a photographer.

Some of this insanity was getting to the road crew. Their pranks began to show it. After "Street Fighting Man," Jagger always sprinkled a bucket of rose petals over the audience like a priest spreading holy water. Chip Monck, who was in charge of special effects, decided it would be fun to hide a chicken leg among the rose petals to see what would happen. Jagger didn't even notice it, and he hurled it straight into the crowd, hitting a singularly ecstatic girl on the head. That was in Detroit.

By Philadelphia, Chip had plucked up courage to hide a raw pig's liver in the bucket, and Jagger, still too rapt to realize what was happening, hurled it in a graceful arc into the crowd. Seconds later it arched back again, hung suspended momentarily in the glare of the spotlights and then splattered, bloodily, on the immaculate white stage. In Pittsburgh, Chip decided to go all the way and bought a pig's leg complete with hoof and blood and stuck that in the bucket. Fortunately for Pittsburgh, Jagger found the thing before the show started and hurled it at Chip instead.

By the time this circus rolled into New York for the last three shows of the tour at Madison Square Garden they were slick and perfect. Far from destroying them, their fifty days of drugs and debauchery on the road had brought the Stones to the peak of their career.

The tour climaxed on July 26, Mick's twenty-ninth birthday, with a final show at the Garden. Chip, determined to make the event unforgettable, hired a circus elephant to walk up to the stage to present Mick with a single rose from its trunk at the end of the show. "No," said the men who run the Garden, no doubt envisaging a maddened pachyderm running amok and squashing teenyboppers. Chip compromised by buying five hundred live chickens, which he planned to flutter gently on the heads of the audience. The management sealed off the roof. In desperation he settled for a routine custard-pie fight. But even that was out of line, decided the grey men, and they confiscated Chip's crates of pies. They didn't realize; however, that Chip had hidden reserve supplies backstage.

The last show was the best of the tour. After "Street Fighting Man," Chip wheeled a trolley with a birthday cake and champagne onto the stage. Bianca danced out to hand Mick a huge panda and kiss him. Chip stealthily crept up, pie in hand, and wopped the superstar in the face. Jagger grabbed a pie to throw at Charlie Watts, and suddenly the whole stage was transformed into something out of a Laurel and Hardy movie. The crowd started to roar out "Happy Birthday" with Charlie banging out the rhythm for them. Ian Stewart crept up behind Watts and gently screwed a pie on each of his ears, where they hung suspended for a moment like giant headphones.

The end-of-tour party was held at the St. Regis Hotel. Bob Dylan had his picture taken with Zsa Zsa Gabor, Woody Allen with Carly Simon. Other guests included Lord Hesketh, Sylvia Miles, Dick Cavett and Tennessee Williams drawn as much by the lure of Ahmet Ertegun, head of Atlantic Records and much else besides, as by the Stones. A nude girl climbed out of a huge birthday cake swinging the tassels on her nipples in opposite directions at the same time. But the party wasn't fun. Just another cold celebrity bash, a far cry from marching with revolutionaries. The Stones were now officially just a great vaudeville act.

Robert Frank, at forty-seven, was the oldest person on the tour. His films were not intended for mass consumption—they starred people like Allen Ginsberg and Gregory Corso—and the Stones had seen none of them. They had seen Frank's haunting book of black-and-white photographs called *The Americans*, which captured the feeling of the country's broken dream. The book had inspired Jack Kerouac to write: "To Robert Frank, I now give this message: You got eyes."

The Stones allowed Frank total freedom. This would be the first honest rock film. Image and mystique were to be thrown out the window; and he was given access to bedrooms, 'planes and dressing rooms. For Robert Frank there were no boundaries. His only brief was to tell it like it was.

It was with a tingle of anticipation that the Stones and I settled down in our plush seats in a Soho preview theater to watch the rough cut of Frank's movie. Since many Stones had screwed many women on the road, all their wives had been excluded from the screening.

As soon as the title flashed on the screen, I knew it wasn't going to work out: *Cocksucker Blues*. How could a film with a title like that stand a chance of being released?

After the credits we were in a jam session with the Stones building "Can't Always Get What You Want" into a thundering number with ten times the power of the recorded version. Then Marshall was introducing a song called "Cocksucker Blues," the number the Stones had recorded as a gratuitous insult to Decca years ago.

Jagger snarled away at a grand piano, and it was a great, tough number. But even Keith cringed each time Jagger sang the chorus about getting your cock sucked and getting your ass fucked. Then it was Keith's turn to play piano while Jagger wandered around a swimming pool with his hand inside the front of his brief trunks, unsubtly fondling himself. A quick couple of shifts of scene, and we were treated to the ludicrous spectacle of the very straight, very brash disc jockey, Emperor Rosko, attempting to interview Mick and Keith while they calmly rolled joints and mumbled incoherently in reply to his inane questioning.

More everyday scenes, and then the Stones thundered through "Brown Sugar" on stage like a flat out Ferrari. A shift back to the everyday world, and they climbed into their private jet which carried them around on the tour. Three busty groupies—Margot, Mary and Renee —trailed along, behind them.

With the 'plane twenty thousand feet above America one of the road crew lifted Mary off the floor and pulled off her tight sweater and jeans. She was wearing nothing underneath. Then Margot was stripped, protesting and giggling at the same time. As the roadies prepared to enjoy themselves, Jagger and Richard danced down from the front of the 'plane like evil dervishes. Mick playing tom-toms, Keith a tambourine, their heads bopping in time to the action. Someone turned Mary upside down and thrust his face into her crotch. Bobby Keyes poured orange juice over both girls as Mick and Keith speeded up the rhythms. It was voodoo time again. The Stones at their most unattractive and perverse. Renee, the other girl, screamed and struggled away. She was frightened and obviously wanted out.

Then it was gone, and the movie flashed to a black guy in a cocaine T-shirt selling black-market Stones tickets. In the dressing room now: Keith, wearing a Moroccan prayer rug around his neck, is having his make-up applied and eye drops administered by Janice, a black woman whose task it was to keep him looking human for the couple of hours a day he was on stage. Jagger, meanwhile, is snorting coke through a $100 bill, getting wired to give his all on stage.

They stroll off toward the arena, but at the last moment Jagger returns for more coke. Then they are in mid-performance with Jagger transformed into the demoniac "Midnight Rambler."

Backstage once more, and writer Terry Southern is snorting and mouthing banalities about coke. "If you had a million dollars a week to spend on coke," he propounds, "you could probably develop a habit. I mean coke is so expensive . . ."

In another bedroom are Keith and a scantily clad, good looking blonde. They are sieving and cooking up heroin. Slowly, with relish, she plunges a syringe filled with deadly nectar into his arm. Slowly, slowly he nods out.

Later Keith speaks thoughtfully about some young musicians he had met: "Those kids were saying if you really want to be a good band, get out of Switzerland and starve." Their words are demonstrably nonsensical, of course. Almost all the best bands nowadays consist exclusively of cosseted millionaires.

Then there is Ossie Clark, the designer, camping it up in a white suit with a red rose in his hand. He is helping Bianca try on a low-cut gown, and for a split second Bianca's breasts spill out much to her very obvious embarrassment. More domestic insight comes when she reminds Mick they have a dinner date. "I don't want to see that awful, awful woman," he whines petulantly. "And I don't want to eat her shitty food." Tantalizingly we are not told exactly who this awful lady is.

More mundane scenes as the Stones and their ladies drive around somewhere in the Deep South, bemoaning the shortage of decent places to eat, and then, suddenly, back to the flash of the stage show, with Stevie Wonder and the Stones roaring together through "Uptight" and then on into "Satisfaction."

Another hotel, and this time there is a new, completely naked girl lying on a bed with a couple of roadies. She is rubbing herself and murmuring about how she's just seen fireflies. The mind boggles.

A cut to Keith, who is playing poker while George Wallace screams out his message of hate from the television screen. And then back to the fireflies lady, who is now sharing a joint with an awkward Mick Taylor. "I've never seen a hotel room blessed with such limpid ecstasy," he jokes.

More strange scenes: Keith so stoned that he can't persuade room service to understand that he would like a bowl of fruit. The girl who fixed him last time is jabbing needles into some new people now; and then Keith and saxophonist Bobby Keyes are giggling inanely as they hurl a color television from the balcony of their umpteenth-floor hotel room.

The movie alternates the flamboyance of the stage with the inanity and de-bauchery of the road: another town, another hit, another fuck. The film closes with the Stones leaving the stage in slow motion as the malicious poetry of "Brown Sugar" is deliberately read in indictment.

"Whooee . . ." breathed Keith. "It certainly brings it all back to me. It's going to be the most amazing rock movie the world has ever seen."

"I don't think so," said Jagger. "We'd be busted from here to Timbuctoo the minute that movie hit the cinemas. It'd cause a public outcry, and the law would be after us again just like they were before.

"No, we'll have to leave it five years at least to cool down before we can even think about releasing it. And even then it could still be dangerous. Maybe we'll never be able to release it while we are still a working band."

Five years later he had completely lost interest. "Well, it wasn't much of a film anyway, was it?" was his only comment.

✕ ✕ ✕ ✕

CHAPTER ELEVEN / PHIL SPECTOR
LEONARD
I LOVE YOU

EXCERPT FROM
Tearing Down The Wall Of Sound: The Rise And Fall Of Phil Spector

---

AUTHOR
Mick Brown

Phil Spector is an American record producer, musician and songwriter best known for creating the famous Wall of Sound. He is currently serving a life sentence for the murder of Lana Clarkson.

✕ ✕ ✕ ✕

*"People were armed to the teeth ... everybody was drunk,
or intoxicated on other items, so you were slipping over
bullets, and you were biting into revolvers
in your hamburger. There were guns everywhere."*

[PHIL] SPECTOR HAD NOT BEEN IN THE STUDIO in almost a year, and in an attempt to keep some momentum going in his career, Marty Machat now proposed that he should produce another of his clients—Leonard Cohen. On paper, it seemed the most unlikely of partnerships. Cohen was a Canadian poet and author who had become a singer almost as an afterthought—he was thirty-three when he released his debut album, *Songs of Leonard Cohen*, in 1967. His reputation rested on a body of thoughtful, introspective and highly literary songs— bleak and melancholic meditations on love, sex and mortality, leavened with a dry, fatalistic humor. He sang in a flat, nasal monotone, framed either by his own acoustic guitar or discreet chamber arrangements. Nobody seemed more surprised by his success than Cohen himself.

But Cohen's life and career were now in need of restoration. It had been almost three years since his last album, *New Skin for the Old Ceremony*, and his record company, Columbia, had taken the step of issuing a *Best of* album—a sure sign that their patience was wearing thin. His family was breaking up and he was drinking heavily; in an attempt to find some equilibrium in his life he had been cultivating an interest in Zen Buddhism and spending time at a Zen retreat, Mount Baldy, in California.

One night Machat brought Cohen to a small gathering at the mansion. Cohen would later recall that he found the occasion "tedious" the mansion "dark, cold and dreary." When the other guests departed, and Spector locked the door and refused to let Cohen leave, Cohen was nonplussed. "To salvage the evening, I said, 'Rather than watch you shout at your servants, let's do something more interesting,'" he later recalled. "And so we sat down at the piano and started writing songs."

Over the next three weeks, they composed fifteen numbers, the writing sessions fueled by copious amounts of wine and liquor. Doc Pomus who was visiting from New York, would remember them as "like two drunks staggerin' around." Alarmed, Cohen's friends tried to warn him off the project. Joni Mitchell was particularly insistent; she had been recording her album *Court and Spark* at A&M studios at the time Spector had been recording the rock and roll album with Lennon and was aware of the turbulence around those session. Spector, she warned Cohen, was past his prime and "difficult." Her words were to prove prophetic in a way no one could imagine.

In June 1977 recording began at the Whitney Studios in Glendale. Larry Levine was now back in the fold, engineering the sessions. The studio had a pipe organ that Spector wanted to use on a couple of songs, but on the playbacks Spector had the volume so loud that he blew out the studio's speakers. The recording moved to Gold Star.

After eighteen months, Spector's sporadic love affair with Devra Robitaille had finally come to an end in an abrupt fashion, but she continued to work as his personal assistant. "There was never a discussion. We were just lovers, and then we weren't. But I think he still trusted me, still relied on me, and we still had a rapport. And I was still very loyal, always did what I was supposed to do with his best interests at heart."

But the Cohen sessions were trying even Devra's patience and loyalty. Going into the studio with Spector was "like a crapshoot. He could be in a great mood, or he could be a raving lunatic. He could go and make magic, or he'd be throwing things around and it would just be this debacle. A lot of it was the drinking. Someone would say something, or he'd just get in a mood and stalk off. Everybody would be hanging around, and then tempers would start to build, and I'd be the pivot point; people would be coming up saying, 'What's going on with Phil? Jesus Christ, when are we going to get out of here, when are we going to get a take?' And Phil would be joking around, getting drunk, walking up and down in the hall, disappearing into the bathroom for hours at a time, fixing his hair. Just prevarication. And it's five o'clock in the morning and everyone's exhausted and our prospective wives and husbands are furious with us, and he hasn't gotten a take yet. And you'd just want to shake him. 'Get on with it!' There were a couple of times when he'd pass out drunk, and Larry and I would have to haul him back into his chair and revive him. And sometimes he'd somehow rally and that would be the brilliant take, the moment of genius."

The boozy camaraderie between Spector and Cohen had quickly degenerated into fractious arguments—about song tempos, structures, arrangements, everything. "They didn't see eye-to-eye at all," Devra says, "and there were a lot of creative differences. It was always very tense, very uncomfortable."

Effectively relegated to the role of sideman, Cohen was doing his best to keep an even temper in the midst of the growing chaos. "Phil was pretty wacky on those sessions—animated," David Kessel remembers. "But what I dug about that was that you had Phil with all of his stuff going on, and then Leonard being like Dean Martin—just cool. It gave Leonard a chance to perfect his Shaolin priesthood stuff and become one with the universe."

Cohen recognized what Spector himself, and few around him, were prepared to acknowledge or admit—that Spector was not simply *eccentric* but seriously disturbed. "In the state that he found himself, which was post-Wagnerian, I would say Hitlerian, the atmosphere was one of guns," Cohen would later reflect. "I mean that's what was really going on, guns. The music was subsidiary, an enterprise. People were armed to the teeth, [and] everybody was drunk, or intoxicated on other items, so you were slipping over bullets, and you were biting into revolvers in your hamburger. There were guns everywhere."

Cohen would later recall how on one occasion in the studio Spector approached him with a bottle of Manischewitz in one hand and a pistol in the other, placed his am around Cohen's shoulder, shoved the gun in his neck and said, "Leonard, I love you." Cohen, with admirable aplomb, simply moved the barrel away, saying, "I hope you do, Phil."

On another evening Spector pulled a gun on the violin player Bobby Bruce and held it to his head, after Bruce had made some remarks to which Spector took exception. Larry Levine quickly stepped in to quiet things down. "Phil wasn't angry at Bobby; he was just showing off. But Bobby's gotta be scared shitless. And I said, 'Phil, I know you don't mean anything, but accidents happen. Put it down.' And he wasn't willing to do that. It was like 'Hey, I can handle my life.' So finally I said, 'I'm turning off the equipment and going home unless you put that down right now.' And that's when he finally realized I was serious and put the gun away. I loved Phil, and when you love somebody, you do what you can do to bring it back to the rational. I'd seen him both ways, so I knew that wasn't the real Phil."

The sessions finally ground to a conclusion in a bitter mood, with Spector refusing to allow Cohen to be present for the mixes, or to hear the finished album. Cohen would later claim Spector did not even properly complete his vocals, instead using 'guide vocals' which Cohen had intended to redo later.

Spector was equivocal about the result, scribbling a note to Larry Levine on the master tapes: "I'll tell you something, Larry—we've done worse with better, and better with worse!" For Devra Robitaille, the album was to prove the last straw. Spector would thank her on the album's liner notes for her "grave concern in the face of overwhelming odds." But her sympathies had been exhausted. "I came to the conclusion that I had no business putting myself in a position where I was behaving like a groupie. I disrespected myself. I was an accomplished musician; I was bright and able, and I let myself get trashed." She resigned from her job, and went back to working for Warner Bros.

On its release in 1978, the critics savaged *Death of a Ladies' Man*. Spector was accused of assassinating Cohen's poetic sensibility with grotesquely inappropriate arrangements and an overwrought production. But the critics were wrong. Out of the fog of alcohol and recrimination, Spector had somehow fashioned a series of almost vaudevillian settings that were perfectly pitched to Cohen's unsparing depiction of himself as a weary boulevardier, desperately seeking spiritual consolation in the pleasures of the flesh, in the face of advancing years and diminishing opportunities. A melancholy waltz for "True Love Leaves No Traces"; bump-and-grind burlesque for "Iodine." "Paper Thin Hotel," a minor-key, bittersweet rumination on infidelity, was dressed with choirs, pedal steel guitars and pianos, with a melody that recalled the work of Jimmy Webb at his most wistfully romantic. In this context even the hokey country hoedown arrangement of "Fingerprints" made a bizarre kind of sense.

Death of a Ladies' Man may not have been Phil Spector's greatest production, but it was certainly the oddest, and in many was the most compelling.

Cohen attempted to distance himself from the record, describing it to *Rolling Stone* as "an experiment that failed," while acknowledging it had real energizing capacities." In the final moment, he said, Spector "couldn't resist annihilating me. I don't think he can tolerate any other shadows in his own darkness. I say these things not to hurt him. Incidentally, beyond all this, I liked him. Just man to man he's delightful, and with children he's very kind."

The album would be the worst-selling of Cohen's career. Spector laconically told a friend that he had "got hate mail from all eight of Leonard's fans" and would never miss an opportunity thereafter to make a joke at the poet's expense. In 1993 he was approached by an academic seeking a contribution for a proposed volume of tributes to mark Cohen's sixtieth birthday.

Spector replied by sending a copy of a letter he had recently written to another correspondent, who had seemingly written to Spector seeking his opinion of—of all things—the Partridge Family. While Spector made clear that he regarded the Partridge Family as "an obscene joke," there was one distinguished artist of his acquaintance, he wrote, who had confessed to being "extremely influenced" by them. "And that artist is Leonard Cohen. Underneath that brooding, moody, de-pressed soul which Leonard possesses lies an out-and-out Partridge Family freak." Spector suggested that his correspondent might even wish to contact Cohen to discuss the Partridge Family further.

Signing the letter, "Cordially, Phil Spector," he helpfully appended Cohen's telephone and fax numbers, just in case his correspondent wanted to get in touch.

✕ ✕ ✕ ✕

Turn On, Tune In, Pass Out

CHAPTER TWELVE / AL JOURGENSEN
THE PSYCHEDELIC EVOLUTION OF LEARY

EXCERPT FROM
Ministry: The Lost Gospels According To Al Jourgensen

AUTHORS
Al Jourgensen and Jon Wiederhorn

COPYRIGHT © 2013 by Al Jourgensen
REPRINTED BY PERMISSION OF ~ Da Capo Press, a member of The Perseus Books Group.

Al Jourgensen is a six-time Grammy-nominated producer, composer, and musician. After getting clean in 2002, he produced another five Ministry discs and launched his own label, 13th Planet.

✕ ✕ ✕ ✕

"I'd have these horrific visions of hell and the apocalypse: naked people with blood spouting from every orifice; skies that turned black, then silver, then white again; winged beasts with razor-sharp talons; and, most of all, spiders of all shapes and sizes. They'd fall from the sky."

I LIVED WITH TIM FOR TWO YEARS, during which time I traveled back and forth on tour and to the studio. Back at Chicago Trax! we were putting the final touches on *Filth Pig*. Scratch Acid's Rey Washam's plundering drums matched the sluggish tone of the music, which gave the whole thing a depraved, depressing vibe. Former M.O.D. guitarist Louis Svitek came on to finish the guitars with Mikey. *Filth Pig* finally came out on January 30, 1996, and everyone hated it. They all wanted *Psalm 70*, and I gave them an electronic-free record full of gun-in-mouth dirges of nothing but pain. Aside from the cover art, the humor was gone. All that was left was misery. And I still had to tour the fucking thing—which went down in history as the interminable, intolerable, absolutely depraved "Sphinctour."

The bus had so many needles that it looked like a blood bank. Rey and I were shooting up all day, every day. By that point all the hot groupies had learned to steer clear of us, so we'd get all these mentally deranged or deformed girls hanging out on the bus. One night I fucked a paraplegic chick in a wheelchair. I think she had Parkinson's. So she's blowing a guy in our crew and I'm fucking her. She's wearing a colostomy bag, and I was naturally curious. I stopped fucking her for a second and I started squeezing the bag back into her." I asked, "Does this hurt Do you feel that?" She moans, "Noooooo." I'm squeezing her shit bag back up into her while I'm fucking her. Afterward I helped her back into her wheelchair and felt really kind of bad because that was the sickest thing I'd ever done. I've never been into degrading or humiliating women. If they want to get into some kinky shit, fine, but to do something to make them feel ashamed is just cruel. I may be an asshole, but I wasn't a cruel asshole.

We toured that album forever, and by that time I was just going through the motions. We did a few new songs, but mostly it was a greatest-hits cavalcade. We'd do "N.W.O.," "Thieves," "So What," "The Missing," "Deity," "So What," and then close with "Stigmata." Alternative music was on the decline, so we were drawing more of a metal crowd and playing smaller places, like the Electric Factory in Philadelphia and Roseland Ballroom in New York. That's why we stayed on the road for four months straight—I was too depressed and strung out to cause much trouble, except for the time I was caught on camera fucking a rotisserie chicken in our dressing room as a joke.

Oh, and in Norway we got fucked by the Cure and fucked with Slayer at a festival. It was a weird bill that featured a bunch of really big, totally diverse bands. At the Scandinavian festivals it's light until 3AM so they have what amounts to a headliner after the headliner. Ministry was opening for the Cure at that show, but the Cure went on first. We showed up before the show and the Cure's vocalist, Robert Smith, heard that I was a maniac and told security he didn't want me back there. They had a fjord that went around the stage; you could only get to it by boat. Since we weren't allowed backstage before the Cure played, I had to go out into the audience and wound up surrounded by all these skinheads. Maybe they were there for Slayer; I don't think they were Cure fans. These guys had purple moonshine that they had made in their bathtub. I'm sitting there with my luggage, waiting to go backstage, hanging with these degenerates. They gave me this shot of moonshine, and it instantly made me blind—not drunk blind, but literally blind, like I can't see my dick hanging out of my pants. I don't know what was in that stuff, but it fucked me up. When my sight came back twenty minutes later they got me to sing Swedish national songs with them. They didn't know who I was or if I was in a band; they just thought I was some weird freak carrying around my luggage. I did a second shot . . . and went blind again! I have no idea what substance on earth makes you go blind for twenty minutes, but forty minutes of sporadic blindness was enough for me. I stumbled around and met this boat captain who ferried me to the backstage area. I had to climb down this mountain to get to the stage. By this point the Cure were on, so I was able to get back there and drop off my stuff. That's where I met Fear Factory vocalist Burton Bell and guitarist Dino Cazares, who were also on the bill. The festival was at an open-air venue like Red Rocks in Morrison, Colorado. There's no dressing rooms; they just have these trailers. When we got there Slayer were in the trailer. We wanted in, and they had been offstage for a while. We said, "C'mon, man. Get out of the trailer!" They told us, "Fuck you!" So my crew and I tipped the trailer with Slayer in it over into the fjord. They scrambled out of the lake like spiders, cursing at us, but they should have known better than to start a fight with us. We didn't talk for years. Then I became friends with all those guys except Kerry King—he's not a nice person. He's got a chip on his shoulder, and he hated Mikey, which means I hate him. If you hate my little brother, I'll stick up for him.

In addition, Patty, now my ex-wife, caused a real commotion on that tour because she went to Florida to visit her mom and, while she was there, met some kid from a band in Atlanta who sold her a pound of coke for $20,000, which is really cheap. But there was a caveat. The kid figured she would get his band to open for Ministry in exchange for the cheap coke. I didn't know about any of this. Patty was banging him and getting coke from him and then she comes back to visit me and says, "Hey, give this CD a listen, will you?" I put it on and it was horrible. She said, "Well, you've got to let them open for you because I promised this guy." I said, "No fucking way. These people are not going to tour with us. They suck and they look weird."

When she told them they couldn't open for us after all, the guy went crazy. He figured this was his big chance. He had already given her a bunch of coke and she had promised, so he thought it was a done deal. I was in no mood to help her out because I was still pissed at her. The guy lost it. I found out later he was a rich kid dying of cancer. This was going to be his last hurrah; he was supposed to be dead within a year. And I dashed his dream, so he vowed to get back at me. He followed our bus in his Jaguar and threatened me at all the shows. He called me every night and said, "I'm going to kill you tonight."

It was creepy shit, and Barker and some of the other members thought I was delusional and making this shit up because I was on drugs, but it was the real deal. It got to the point where I started having to stay at different hotels than the band did and I used fake names so this guy couldn't track me down—yet somehow he still did. One night he called my hotel and said again, "Tonight is the night you're going to die."

I informed the FBI and told my management. I alerted local police officers all to no avail. This fucker followed us through twelve states, and kept making death threats. He was using a cell and hanging up right away, so the police couldn't trace his calls. I started wearing a bullet-proof vest, which was uncomfortable and made me feel like a pussy. But I decided I'd rather be a live pussy than a dead hero. After I wore the vest for a few shows, though, I started getting mad. I was like, "Fuck you for making me protect myself! I already hate myself and have a death wish." So I started to dare him. In Dallas he found me at my hotel and said again, "Definitely tonight. You're going down." At the show I wore a shirt that had a gun target on it and I took off the bullet-proof vest. I thought, "Fuck it. If I'm going down, I'm going down hard." I kept pointing to my chest like, "Fuck you! Do it!" Nothing happened. So I stopped wearing the vest altogether.

That didn't stop the craziness. This guy was so delusional that he became convinced I'd broken into his house and stolen some heroin or coke from him. I'm like, "I don't break into people's houses" (well, that is, at least not intentionally). But he was sure it was me. He threatened to kill me, my daughter, and Patty. He even took a shot through our front window in Chicago when I was visiting them. That's when I said, "Okay, this thing has gone far enough." Because I've never had much luck with the police, I called my good friend Danny Wirtz. I said, "Dude, I have this problem. I don't know what this guy's talking about. I didn't do anything. He's convinced and fixated that I stole his heroin. He threatened me and my family and shot my window."

It was embarrassing to admit all this to him, but I didn't have anywhere else to turn. The day after that one phone call, the cops showed up, formed a perimeter around my house, did a sweep, and arrested the guy. This all happened within twelve hours of Danny getting on the phone. I'd never seen that kind of power before. It was like, "Hey, I have a problem." "Don't worry about it. It's not a problem." The cops were like his security guards. And that psycho who threatened my family will never be back. I heard he passed away a few years ago from cancer.

Back at Tim's, life was both chaotic and fascinating. In addition to taking me in, Tim let Gibby Haynes stay at his house for a while. Tim encouraged us to take whatever drugs we wanted—he was the guru of LSD, after all. But as an academic and a researcher, he wanted to see what effects different hallucinogens had when they were coupled with different substances—coke, heroin, Nyquil, Hungry Man dinners. He would get all this hallucinogenic shit mailed to him from all these companies and universities and then test it on us every couple weeks. Actually, it was mostly on me. He kicked Gibby out of the house after he peed in the drawer of an antique desk in Tim's office when he was off his head. So Gibby went and I stayed. Tim would get me to shoot up all these laboratory drugs that were based out of MDA—ecstasy and Ayahuasca, an Amazonian concoction made from shrubs, leaves and Virola, a South American drug that you grind into a powder and cook down. Tim had me shooting up all this shit. He would be all excited and say, "Hey, I got a new package." And I would groan, "Okay, fuck. Let's do it." I would shoot it up, and he would scribble down notes on how the drugs affected me. I don't know what he was writing because to me the hallucinations were always the same.

I'd have these horrific visions of hell and the apocalypse: naked people with blood spouting from every orifice; skies that turned black, then silver, then white again; winged beasts with razor-sharp talons; and, most of all, spiders of all shapes and sizes. They'd fall from the sky. They'd come up from the ground. They'd creep around corners and crawl all over me. I'd be screaming and trying to brush off the bugs. And I'd always end up staggering over to Tim's blind dog, a sweet golden retriever, Mr. Bodies, that Lemmy, my dog, is probably related to. I'd grab his collar, and he would take me outside so I could breathe without spiders scurrying in my mouth and down my throat. Talk about the blind leading the blind. After an hour or so Tim would come out and stare at me. Then he'd take more notes and ask me some questions about how I was feeling and what I was seeing. He'd measure the diameter of my pupils and see if I could track his fingers with my eyes. I don't know if I passed or failed; I just know I saw spiders. The stuff he gave me was so strong that it took effect in less than twenty minutes. The visions were instantaneous, and they were never enjoyable. But I'd subject myself to it because it helped him out somehow, and I knew if I did my job, my rent was paid and I had a place to stay.

Some people have asked me why I'm not angry at Tim for using me as a human guinea pig. Man, I could *never* be mad at Tim. I was a willing subject, and he was a good friend—a father figure, actually. I was this rock junkie, but he didn't treat me like a degenerate. He was patient and understanding. We had long talks about everything: quantum mechanics, esoterics, philosophy, psychology, the occult, psychedelic science and the opening of the third eye, even pop culture. He was a knowledgeable figure who had credentials, and we had a strong bond with one another. Tim would recite baseball statistics to me of every batting champion since 1967. He was encyclopedic.

Hall of Fame left fielder and first basemen Carl Yastrzemski was his favorite. He knew everything that guy was involved with. And his passion didn't stop with sports. He was involved on a day-to-day basis with the growth of society and culture, whether it was through entertainment, acting, or music. He taught me how to be a Renaissance man—Tim was a Renaissance man, but he wasn't an elitist. He got his world views by dealing with students who taught him there's more to the world than your little brain. Tim was gregarious and wanted to know everything about every aspect of life. Nothing bored him, and no one was too stupid to talk to. In the mid-90s he watched *Entertainment Tonight* and the E! Channel and was very serious about following what they covered. At the same time he was extremely well read and could recite Shakespeare, the Bible, and Burroughs, to name a few.

I was a part of pop culture and wanted nothing to do with it, but Tim taught me to pay attention to what the masses were consuming. That was really important to him. He used to throw dinner parties once a week and invite billionaire businessmen, politicians, athletes, astronauts, journalists, actors, and industrialists, and then he would sprinkle the table with some assorted rockers, whether it was me or Trent Reznor, who lived a few hundred yards up the canyon. It was the original *Dinner for Five* long before there was ever a TV show.

I hung out with people with all kinds of views and all sorts of experiences at these things, and I learned a lot about human behavior. Some of the people I thought would be arrogant and condescending were the nicest folks I could ever hope to meet, and some of the guys who had accomplished the least in their life acted like their shit didn't stink. I hung out with oil barons. I sat next to Frank Borman, who is an ex-astronaut and the CEO and chairman of the board of Eastern Airlines. This guy was the commander of the *Apollo 8* and was one of the first guys to fly around the moon. He was on the NASA review board that investigated the fire on *Apollo 1*. And I was just sitting next to him, sipping wine and cutting prime rib or filet mignon like we were colleagues. I'm sure half of these people thought I was a crazy homeless person, but it was something I looked forward to every week—one of the few things.

Tim was a beacon of hope for me. He had acquired so much wisdom in life; it was contagious. He once told me, "You haven't made it until you get people to pay you for just being you! No particular skills or services required." Winona Ryder's dad, a famous plastic surgeon in Beverly Hills, bought him his house. Tim's her godfather. He had people who were interested in him who broke him out of prison in Texas, people who got him out of Switzerland and got him asylum in this country. He interacted with all sorts of important people, and he'd say, "It is not that I have sold out to them, because I am still Tim, but a lot of these people put a lot of money and stock into my ides."

While I was with Tim he would pick up girls even though he was in his late sixties or seventies. He'd sometimes have two at a time. He had Viagra and would try to get hard, but he really wasn't interested in sex anymore. So he would give up and send the girls over to my corner. Faithful Al would be stiffy in a jiffy and fuck every girl that came through the place—all these hot, young college chicks. That lasted for a while until he started dating Aileen Getty; he fell head over heels for her. Getty is the granddaughter of billionaire oil baron J. Paul Getty, but she's not into money, capitalism, and the hoity-toity lifestyle. She had given millions of dollars to homeless organizations in Hollywood. She was a heroin and cocaine addict most of her life, and, while I was lucky and only caught hepatitis C, Aileen was diagnosed as HIV positive more than twenty years ago. But Tim didn't care. He loved her. I hung out with them a bunch of times when I wasn't busy being his hallucinogen guinea pig.

One of Tim's greatest disappointments in life was that Aileen turned down his marriage proposal. He proposed to her in Vegas, and I went along. He was hoping it would be this big, happy event to celebrate forever, and I was there for him. We flew to Vegas, he got down on one knee and popped the question. She said no, which crushed him. She was sick at the time. He said, "I don't want your money." She said, "I will be your friend. I will be your lover, whatever you want. But I'm not going to do this. I've got my money, you've got your money. Just relax."

We were stuck in Vegas, and there isn't going to be a wedding, so what were we going to do? Get wasted and gamble, of course. I'm not a gambling pro. I kinda suck, actually. So I'm losing, as usual, and I hit this one table, where I just had a good feeling. I have a theory—and this may sound racist, but it's not. I have really bad luck with Asian dealers; I have really bad luck with sourpuss people. I always go for a gay guy, who is flamboyantly gay, or a lady with a beehive, like Marge Simpson. We were at some cheap hotel. It wasn't a Trump casino, I'll put it that way. I was losing all fucking day with this Asian dude, and then I found this beehive lady at a blackjack table. I had fifteen and she had a king out. It was the end of the night, and we had to get to a *Hustler* party I had been invited to. So I was like, "I'm going to hold on this—fuck it—because you're going to bust." She loved it. That's why you go to the old beehive ladies: because they have been in Vegas since the '60s and hate the casinos. They hate the corporations, so they want you to win. I think the Asian dealers are trying to prove themselves, so they are very meticulous. They are very good, and they kick your ass and smile. It's a bad vibe. I want the vibe of some old lady hating Vegas who wants me to win; after all, it doesn't come out of their pocket. So I held on fifteen and she busted. I don't know if she did it on purpose or what, but you don't hold on fifteen. I did and won $24,000. On my way out the door I put half the money on black on the roulette wheel and I won that. Lucky night.

We flew from Vegas back to Los Angeles, and I had $36,000 in my pocket when we got to this 25TH Anniversary *Hustler* party at the Beverly Hilton Hotel. For some reason Tim wasn't on the guest list nor was Aileen Getty. It was just me and my girlfriend at the time, Lydia. Can you imagine that? Timothy Leary, one of the most legendary figures of the counterculture, and Aileen Getty, who belongs to one of the richest families in the world, are left off the list. So I said to the guy at the door, "Fuck you. I'm not going to leave Timothy Leary outside. That's lunacy." At the time I didn't realize he and Larry had a feud once so they didn't like each other. But after a lot of arguing and threatening to piss in the entranceway, I got Tim in. We went inside and my girlfriend started freaking out because there were all these naked chicks, with fake tits running around.

I guess she had reason to be paranoid: I had been drinking all day and was wasted. We all sat down for dinner and were at a table with the Nelson twins, Frank Stallone and his wife, and Ron Jeremy. They served us lobsters that were undercooked, so Tim and I threw them as hard as we could; they thudded off a table about fifty feet away and landed on the ground. No one said anything or seemed any the wiser. The waiter brought me another lobster, and it was also almost raw. It tasted horrible. So I threw that one too. We were throwing lobsters all over the place, and people started to throw them back. I guess they didn't like undercooked lobsters either.

In the middle of this food fight Ron Jeremy turned to me and said, "Hey man, I thought I recognized you. You're Trent Reznor. I'm a big fan."

That was the last straw. I laid down on the table, dropped my trousers, threw my legs over my head, and started blowing myself right in front of Ron. I said, "Fuck you! I'm not Trent Reznor. I can do this. Trent can't blow himself." That was one advantage to heroin and other painkillers: They dull the receptors in your back and spine, so an act I usually couldn't perform, like self-fellatio, was no problem.

Ron laughed it off. He'd certainly seen stranger things on the set. But this porn star Savannah, who went out with Slash for a while, was impressed. The situation calmed down for a bit, and everybody was drinking wine and talking again. Then Savannah came over and whispered in my ear that my big "fuck you" to Ron Jeremy turned her on. I don't know if it was because she liked seeing me stand up to Ron, who had probably blown gallons of sperm in her face over the years, or if she was such a horny piece of ass that she wanted my cock. Whatever. We started making out while my girlfriend was in the ladies' room. But then she came back and saw us, and those two got into a knock-down, drag-out cat fight. It was pretty exciting to see hot chicks fighting over me, but I broke up the fight. My girlfriend stormed out, and I went to the bathroom to do some coke to clear my head. That was the last time I saw Savannah. She eventually committed suicide by shooting herself in the head after injuring her face and breaking her nose in a car accident. But I had nothing to do with that.

While I was cleaning up in the bathroom, this guy asked me who I was, and I told him. He said he was with the FBI, so I put away my coke, punched him in the face, and ran out. It turned out he was one of the Copeland Brothers, who runs the FBI Booking agency. I thought he was trying to arrest me, because he was part of the Federal Bureau of Investigation and I didn't need any more trouble with the government. As I was running out, a big entourage came in with Robert Williams, the artist who did the first Guns N' Roses album cover. I was so freaked out about the whole FBI thing that I puked all over his brand-new blue suede shoes. He had just bought them that day, and there was vomit everywhere. He was cool about it, though. He wiped up the vomit, autographed some napkins with vomit on them, and handed them back to me. I thought that was pretty classy. I stayed there for another hour, and everything kept going downhill. Someone from Mötley Crüe was there with a member of Guns N' Roses. I was too fucked up to know which ones they were, but one of them pissed me off. So I took a swing at him, and then the security caught up to me. But they didn't want to drag me out, get puke on them, and have me cause a scene. So they tied a bottle of wine to a stick and lured me out of the place, dangling the bottle in front of me. I'd go to grab it, and it would hop away and roll down the hallway, which I couldn't figure out. I was like a cat going after a catnip toy. They lured me outside with this bottle and closed and locked the door behind me.

When I realized I was duped, I got pissed. The hotel had a three-tiered fountain in front of it. Because I couldn't get back into the party, I climbed the fountain. I had to take a shit, so I clambered up to the second tier, dropped my pants for the second time that night, took a dump in the fountain, and wiped myself with the water. Then I saw Tim, Aileen, and Lydia running out after me. Tim said, "I think we ought to get out of here." He called a cab, and as we got in and pulled away from the party, multiple police cars with flashers on pulled into the hotel. I narrowly escaped being arrested.

That was the last big adventure I had with Tim. I went on tour with Ministry and we talked on the phone a lot, but when the band got to Europe in 1995 Tim was sick with prostate cancer. He sounded awful. We had to do a couple more shows in the States, so I told him, "Tim, hang on for me. I am coming back. I want to see you. Just hold tight."

He was still alive when we played the Palladium in L.A. and Tim came to both shows with Aileen. That was a couple weeks before he died. We hung out with Joe Strummer and Captain Sensible, and the four of us did more cocaine than you can fit onto a picnic table. Tim had a good time, and I gave him a big hug at the end of the night. Something told me it was his way of saying goodbye. I went back on tour, and the day we got off the road I got the call that Tim was dead. It was a dark, dark day for me. I felt like I lost my best friend and my father at the same time. Before he died Tim arranged for seven grams of his ashes to be buried out in space on a rocket that also had the remains of *Star Trek* creator Gene Roddenberry, a space physicist named Gerard O'Neil, and rocket scientist Krafft Ehricke. The ashes went onboard a Pegasus rocket on April 21, 1997. The spaceship was in orbit for six years before it burned up in the Earth's atmosphere. What's even cooler is that Tim told me he put a clause in his will saying an ounce of *my* ashes will go up in space on a future rocket after I die. It's already paid for, which is totally an honor. He was a special, special man.

There weren't many bands that could get me to leave my house in 1996, but Anthrax were one of them. They were playing San Antonio, so I drove my Supra twin-turbo to the show. By then Anthrax were no longer sober, so Lydia and

I partied with them all night. I was wasted by the time we left to go back to Austin. I got lost somewhere in San Antonio and was thinking, "I'm really too drunk to drive all the way home." So we decided to find a hotel and crash for the night. I was doing 105 down a side street and Lydia screamed, "There's a hotel the other way!" I tried to spin the car around and hit this giant curb. The car rocketed into the air, flipped, and went directly into a light pole, which took out half the city's electricity. We careened off of that, back across the road and into a concrete bus stop park bench, which further crunched up my car. Then we pinballed directly across the street again. By now the car was right side up again, the airbags were deployed, there were pieces of glass, metal, and plastic everywhere, plus the stuff we had in the car. We went over another curb, which sent us airborne again. I landed and realized I was in this empty parking lot. Then I saw an eighteen-wheeler gas tanker in front of us. There were no brakes left; the front of the car was gone. Impulsively, I was slamming on the brakes anyway because we kept getting closer and closer to this parked eighteen-wheeler. We stopped right in the nick of time, six inches from the truck. If I had piled onto it, the gas tank would have exploded and we both would have been dead.

After we stopped I took a deep breath and then took inventory. Lydia had a fucked up wrist. I had crushed my chest and broken a bunch of ribs—again. Miraculously we were still alive. I kicked the car door open, and the police were there immediately. This cop came over to us and said, "I saw the first two of your hits. I was right behind you." For once I was happy to see a cop. We were so shaken up that I seemed absolutely sober. I didn't even have to do the alphabet backward. Then I did something really stupid: I peed on the road right in front of the cop. He just figured I was in shock and he was so freaked out that we survived that crash that he refused to put on the accident report the fact that we had eighteen empty beer bottles in the back. He just went, "Well, I'm not gonna make your night worse." I didn't go to the hospital because I know they can't do anything for ribs. I had already broken my rib cage a few times previously; they just put me in plaster or some debilitating bandage and said, "Here are some pain pills. Just deal with it." I already had pain medication—lots of it. Even with all the accidents and debilitating situations I was in, I played almost every single show that was scheduled.

Tons of bands scrap a week or two of dates every time the singer comes down with a sore throat or whenever someone gets hurt. I have to be literally incapacitated not to play because I know it's my job and people have paid money to see me. I guess it's that work ethic thing I got from my dad. The first show I ever canceled in my career was the Peoria, Illinois, Sphinctour date. That's the only show I canceled in thirty years before Paris 2012 on the European Ministry tour. In Peoria I got laryngitis and lost my voice. I didn't give up so easily either. I had a doctor give me a steroid injection through my neck and into my esophagus just as a short-term fix to get me through the night. On the 2003 Ministry tour, I also lost my voice before a Paris show, but that time the steroid shot worked. By the way—it hurts like hell. But this time the doctor shot me up. Nothing. Mudvayne was supposed to open for us, and it was their first show ever. They were completely psyched. They were in high school and right out of rehearsing in mom and dad's basement, and they went from going, "Really!! We get to play with Ministry?" to having to tell the crowd that Ministry canceled. No one had heard of them, and their singer, Chad Gray, went up to the mic and announced, "Uhh, Ministry's not gonna be able to play. We're sorry. But we're gonna do an extra long set." BOOOOOOOOO! They got pelted. Angry fans slashed the tires on their van. They were heckled through their whole set. Poor bastards. They thought it would be the time of their lives; instead, they had to dodge debris and pay to get their tires fixed. Welcome to the crazy world of rock 'n' roll, kids.

Years later, after I had kicked drugs and married Angie (more on that later), we were in Europe on the 2003 Fornica Tour, and Mudvayne opened for us at a festival in Germany. Afterward Chad wound up on our bus and we were drinking and talking. He was shitfaced, and suddenly he said, "Uhh, I gotta go." He walked off, and I thought he left. So our bus left to get to Copenhagen for the next show. We were driving through Luxembourg, and I was in the back lounge with Angie. I was drinking, as usual. Then, Angie started getting all these calls from management, a promoter, and, finally, members of Mudvayne. They're all asking, "What happened to Chad?" I said, "Nothing. He was hanging out and then he left. He's probably passed out somewhere near the Mudvayne bus." By this time I was really drunk, and people from my team were coming up to me, asking, "Where's Chad? What did you do to him?" I got grilled about this about fifteen times in ninety minutes. I started to get mad. Finally, I said, "Look, this is not my problem. He's not here." At nine o'clock the next morning we started hearing these weird rumbling noises that sounded like a sasquatch coming from one of the bunks that we didn't use; we just threw our gear there. So these noises continue, and Chad crawled out from between these road cases, where he had passed out the night before without anyone knowing.

We were in Luxembourg. Fortunately, Mudvayne was scheduled to perform in Luxembourg that night, and we had a day off. Chad was still wasted, completely incoherent, and on our bus, so Angie and I walked over to the venue where Mudvayne was scheduled to perform and hung out in their dressing room before the band even arrived. I drank all their wine.

× × × ×

CHAPTER THIRTEEN / REX BROWN
TRENDKILL OUT ON THE TILES

EXCERPT FROM
Official Truth, 101 Proof: The Inside Story Of Pantera

AUTHORS
Rex Brown and Mark Eglinton

Rex Brown was the bassist for Pantera. He's also played with Down and Kill Devil Hill.

✕ ✕ ✕ ✕

"I was in the hospital before the show, got up, played the show, and went straight into an ambulance back to the hospital; that's how sick I was and still we only cut the show short by fifteen minutes."

WE STARTED TOURING TRENDKILL after it came out in May of '96, and we were all hitting it extremely hard. When you're partying like that you really can't tell what the next guy's doing, so it wasn't as if we were watching Phil and wondering what he was getting into, because it was full-on debauchery for all of us in our own way.

The boys had built "The Clubhouse," a full-beaver strip club in Dallas with a loose, 19TH hole golf-like theme. The place had all our records hanging on the wall and became a stopping point for almost every band that came through town. For Vinnie it was the culmination of his obsession—he now had his very own titty bar. I invested in it, too, and I'm glad I did because the return was three hundred percent. But apart from dealing with all the legal aspects in the planning process, I probably went in there only a handful of times. This was Vinnie and Dime's deal and not the kind of place in which I ever wanted to hang, though I'm happy to have made money from it.

Part of the reason they wanted the place was to entertain their friends. At home, they had a completely different set of people who wanted to be around them all the time. You can't criticize the brothers for it. That's what they did. You can't question what anyone's doing when they do what they want to do. They had this other family that I wanted no part of, and that was their choice. To a degree I would allow people to hang around me, even use me, but it got to a certain point where I'd rather knock somebody out than sit and listen to their bullshit. And I did many times.

We were playing a show in Dallas, one of the first shows on that tour, in July.

It should have been a raucous homecoming but it turned into something else. I remember the night well, not because of anything particular other than there was something weird going on in Phil's dressing room, which was next door. I recall that all these crazy people showed up out of the woodwork and I just thought, "Well, this is kind of trippy." There was always weed being smoked in Phil's dressing room, heavily at times, so much that you'd get a contact buzz as soon as you walked in the door, but I wasn't really smoking and drinking at this time. At that point I was kind of tired of it, so my memory of that night is as vivid as if it were yesterday.

I remember this one dude in particular hanging around—someone I knew from back in the Joe's Garage days—and he's looking at me with these red, glassy eyes saying, "Yeah man, what's going awwwwwwwn . . ." doing this fucking bead-shuffle thing and I remember thinking, "Okay, let's see what this is all about." In my mind, I knew there was something amiss so I said, "Look, what the fuck are *you* on?" I asked him straight out.

"Oh, nothing. man," he said, but it turned out that he was the guy who brought it—heroin—in that night.

Now in those days I had a personal car and driver for me, my sister, and the rest of my family, and they would take anyone wherever they wanted to go. We were making the kind of money that we could afford to have limousines drive us wherever the fuck we wanted to.

So after the show, just as my sister is heading home, it suddenly hits the radio wire: "Philip Anselmo, singer with the rock band Pantera, has overdosed on heroin," and all I could think was, "Who the hell had *that* scoop?" It seemed that somebody knew quicker than they should have. Something about the whole night just didn't seem right to me.

When I went into the dressing room, it was a scene of total chaos: Phil was fucking blue because he had shot up after the show. Paramedics were called in and there was nothing I could do, although what I really wanted to do was beat the living shit out of Phil. As a compromise I took my rage out on the dressing room. I started throwing bowls of chips and chili around to release my anger. It was sickening and I was fucking furious. How the fuck could he have done this? How could he put all of our livelihoods at risk like this?

The three of us met that night while Phil recovered in the hospital. Then the next morning, the boys picked me up in Dime's Cadillac, and we all went over to the hotel to confront the dude. He'd gotten out of the hospital already and had this girl with him who would die of an overdose shortly afterwards. It began to feel like there was some kind of dope plague going around.

We said to him, "What the fuck is this? What's going to happen? This could be the very fucking end of everything."

Walter was there with the other main management guy, Andy Gould, but neither of them did or said anything constructive. Because Walter had seen drug overdoses before, he'd just say; "Fuck you." That was his way of dealing. Management was no help at all. The best thing they could have done would have been to immediately put Phil in goddamn rehab, cancel the tour until he was clean, and then we could have all continued with what we were doing.

But that didn't happen.

Of course, when he was in front of us, Phil simply said, "I'm sorry, dudes. I really fucked up." What else could he say? But his response to the fact that the overdose was now public knowledge was more of a problem.

For some reason Phil wrote a confessional letter about his near-death experience, a public statement saying, "I saw no shining lights" or whatever the fuck he said—it's all well-documented—and that was the dumbest thing he could have done, as far as I was concerned, because the moment he did that, he was labeled a junkie. Why would you do something like that? And why would management let him do it? They should have covered that shit up and that's all there is to it.

"Dude, why? We're *flying*," I said. "Money's through the fucking roof. What are you doing?"

Of course, Phil said it would never happen again, and we gave him the benefit of the doubt because when we examined the situation in the cold light of day, it wasn't like he was in a coma every fucking day. Even we would have noticed that. In fact, I suspect he actually hadn't been using very long and had just been dabbling a little, but just happened to be unlucky and overdosed. Nobody's perfect, and there certainly aren't any saints in the business of rock 'n' roll, so of course people are occasionally going to have problems.

✕

Despite the fact that we were willing to move forward after the fiasco that night in Dallas, I'd be lying if I said that the thought of getting rid of Phil didn't cross our minds. But it only did so briefly and probably only as a knee-jerk response to what had happened, driven by our lack of understanding of and experience with what was actually going on.

Deep down, we knew that kicking out Phil would have been like ripping your heart out of your chest, or siphoning all the gas out of your car so that you can save the fucking car. There's no gasoline to make that car run, so you're keeping it for what? Totally pointless. We knew that to carry on without Phil would have been pointless, too. Even then and to this day he is one of the best front men in metal. Nobody commands an audience like he does, so we did carry on and after only one day off and our singer almost dead, Pantera was back and ready to hit Oklahoma.

✕

We all improvised individually where we could and on the occasions when Dime decided to go off on one, it was always fucking awesome to behold from the other side of the stage. Me? I just laid down the low end and he could play anything he wanted to over the top, no matter what I had going on. Sometimes I'd get goose bumps from some of the stuff he did. Dime's playing never ceased to blow me away so much so that I'd occasionally go over and give him a kiss!

We'd usually critique right after the show. Ask questions like "What could have been better?," "Was the tempo of this or that song right?," or "Does this song fit in." By that time we had so much adrenaline going that we could sit in the dressing room for hours afterwards, drinking and getting loaded. In later years when we had more space, Phil was usually in another dressing room, but the three of us would analyze every fucking thing over and over and that's why we were always such a tight live band.

We refined our pre-show routine over the years, too. We'd have hospitality rooms, game rooms, all kinds of shit laid on for us, but apart from playing video games, reading a magazine, or watching football on TV, there isn't a whole lot to do on show days once you're at the venue. It would have been easy to get loaded, but for the most part, we started drinking usually an hour before the show. We'd have a few shots and the whole bit.

Then that hour turned into an hour and a half before the show, which eventually turned into two hours, and so on.

Then sometimes me and Dime would just get up in the morning, say "fuck it," and just start drinking. And then when it came to getting up onstage *those* nights we'd somehow fly by the seat of our asses. How we did it I have no idea, but we played some of the best shows of our career in that state. I was never so fucked up that I didn't know where I was or anything or was staggering around onstage, stumblin' and grumblin' as I like to call it, but there were a few nights where definitely I came off afterwards and thought, "How the fuck did I do that?" But there weren't that many nights like that and I never ever missed a show. Amazing statistics when you consider how many fucking dates we played. I'm not saying every night was the best night we ever played, that's not realistic, but Pantera at 80 percent was like another band's hundred and fifty percent.

✕

I remember many occasions when Dime and I used to get off the bus in the morning when we pulled into a new town. He and I would be fucking *green* from drinking all night but it never even entered our minds not to play that night. On those days, "Here we go again, buddy," was all I would say to him as we walked across the parking lot to the venue, arm in arm. We knew what had to be done.

I got really fucking sick one night in Atlanta touring *Far Beyond Driven*, but it had nothing to do with alcohol. I had strep throat with a hundred and four degree fever and we were playing a place that must have been a hundred and twenty degrees. It was all I could do to just stand up. I was in the hospital before the show, got up, played the show, and went straight into an ambulance back to the hospital; that's how sick I was and still we only cut the show short by fifteen minutes. That was the only stage time I ever missed.

✕

My drinks of choice were beer and whiskey—although in later years I took a liking to red wine—and there would be nights where my bass tech would have a trash can at my side of the stage, just in case. Sometimes, I'd think, "Fuck it, Goddamn, I've got to catch up," so I'd drink another beer real fast just before we went on and so the trash can was there so I could fucking chunk if I had to. And then I'd have another shot and be fine.

This was all Jeff's job, as well as changing all the strings on the basses, making sure that all my amps are powered, all the hook-ups set up and the whole bit. And of course he kept my mini-bar stocked. I usually took about six basses on stage at a time and all I had to do was take the guitar I was playing off my shoulder, he'd hand me another, switch the wireless packs over, and I was good to go. Depending on where you're playing, guitars and basses go out of tune a lot. If you're playing in a fucking hockey rink—and we played in a lot of them—where they just board up the ice, it could be really cold and Jeff would be tuning my basses all night long. And if the venue's really humid the bass necks would seem to bend.

×

We went to Australia in late '96 and the process of getting there was a complete nightmare. Vinnie, Dime, and the rest had already gone on before us, so I was scheduled to fly out with Phil, his assistant, and Big Val. So I get to LAX and in those days we had fans everywhere, so someone at the airport would always recognize me, shoot me into a little buggy, and say, "So, Mr. Brown, where would you like to go?"

On this occasion they put me and Big Val in a buggy and took us to one of these waiting lounges called something like the Admiral's Club. We walk in there and I see Phil sitting with the comedian Don Rickles. So for the next couple of hours before we fly, he sits and gets scotch-drunk with Don as our pre-flight entertainment. You can't even imagine the crazy shit that was coming out of his mouth. I wasn't drinking at the time, but Big Val had a shitload of Valium on him.

Predictably, by the time we got to our first class seats on Qantas Airlines, Phil was completely wasted. It was very high-end—champagne and caviar for the whole trip—and Phil's looking around, panicking that we're not sitting together and the whole bit. I asked some guy if he would move, but he just had to have his fucking window seat or something, so I just said, "No big deal, I'll just sit wherever I've been assigned." I was just trying to be nice, but this guy was being a real fucking asshole about it for whatever reason.

Then Phil says to him, "You know what, you're a fucking dick," and that just escalated things, and Phil started to become all paranoid thinking everyone was looking at him. "Fuck you, don't look at me, fuck you, don't look at me!" he'd say to everyone. Then he wanted to get his Walkman or something to use during the flight and they wouldn't let him get into his luggage. "Settle down, dude," I told him, "It's really not that big, of a deal."

Phil had a history of being a handful on flights. We'd fly places and he'd kind of nod out, face down in his food. That happened all the time. So, I'd grab his head. "What the fuck are you doing?" he'd say. "Dude, I'm tired of looking at you with your face in a plate," I'd tell him.

Meanwhile, downstairs in coach class, Big Val was throwing a fucking commotion about something—he couldn't find his headphones or his seat wasn't big enough, some stupid shit like that—so they ended up throwing us all off the plane. They got the cops in LAX to come and get us and the whole bit.

Back in the terminal we had to go all the way back through security. I had to put a call in to someone who could think of something fast that would get us out of this mess, but Sykes and them were already Down Under. I didn't know who I could call. So as we're going back through the security line, they find all this Valium on Big Val; they detained him and escorted us out of there. But Phil and I still had to find a way to get on another flight.

We had to get all the way across LAX—and it's a huge fucking airport. We could see the United Airlines terminal straight across from where we were dumped off, but it was going to take forever to get all the way over there in a cab.

So we just started hauling ass across this field in the middle of LAX—it was probably part of the goddamn runway, who knows, and Phil didn't have a suitcase either. He had everything in fucking boxes. For some reason that's how he liked to do it, and it should be said that Phil is pretty eccentric in that respect. And he always had problems with luggage. On what seemed like every trip, everybody else's bag would get through, but Phil's wouldn't show up. So he would just throw a fucking fit. I'm philosophical about that kind of thing, so I used to say to him, "Come on man, you're still breathing. It's not the end of the world." So from then on he started taking boxes and carry-on shit.

I didn't question it at this point either, I just thought, "You want to do your shit in boxes, do it in boxes. Fuck it."

So I'm trying to carry his shit as well as my bags, and by the time we get to the United desk we're both just covered with sweat. Not just that, I'd snapped a fingernail in half carrying Phil's stuff, but because it was my right hand, I could tape it up and it wouldn't be a problem for when I had to play a bass.

So we finally get booked on this plane in roach class but the problem was that it was going to fucking New Zealand and not Australia. When we get there, after too many hours of traveling, we find out that U.S. Customs had called New Zealand Customs, presumably to have us checked out for carrying drugs.

Now by this point I'm fucking pissed. I'd flown double-digit hours to the wrong country in coach class, when I could have been living in seventeen hours of luxury in a full-blown champagne and caviar wet dream that was pure intoxication.

That was a fantasy.

The reality was different. They took us into a room at the airport in New Zealand and stripped us fucking nude.

And it was a full strip search, rubber gloves up the ass and the whole bit. Phil and I weren't carrying, so there wasn't a problem for us. Big Val had all the Valium on him, and he was probably still detained at LAX!

After another short flight from New Zealand, we finally got to our hotel in Australia. I called Vince and said, "Fuck Val, he's fired, man."

I thought he should have handled the situation better—that's what we pay him to do—but Vinnie wanted him (a) because he hated confrontation of any kind and (b) because he needed a security guard. He was right about the second part, probably. We all needed a security guard when it came to controlling the crowd at shows, and Val was admittedly really good at that. Although he flew out a couple of days later, nobody really spoke to him and this was the beginning of the end for Big Val. He was starting to think he was a bigger rock star than us.

✕ ✕ ✕ ✕

CHAPTER FOURTEEN / NOFX
JUNKIE STUDIES

EXCERPT FROM
NOFX: The Hepatitis Bathtub And Other Stories

AUTHORS
NOFX and Jeff Alulis

COPYRIGHT © 2016 by NOFX
REPRINTED BY PERMISSION OF ~ Da Capo Press, a member of The Perseus Books Group.

NOFX formed in 1983 and has since released over a dozen albums, sold more than eight million records, toured 42 countries on six continents, founded one of the most successful indie labels in the world, and starred in their own reality TV show.

✗ ✗ ✗ ✗

"Sure, it's gross that you're swapping spit with random scumbags, but this is probably the LEAST disgusting element of your future as a heroin addict, so you should try to get over it quickly."

SMELLY: DJ WAS ONLY SIXTEEN when we met him, but he was so goofy and hilarious that he fit in with all the twenty-something punks he was living with in Baltimore, and he fit in even better with NOFX. He pitched in as a roadie and everyone in the band loved him, but DJ and I grew closer to each other than anyone else. Which is why I feel bad for kind of ruining his life.

I guess in the end I can't blame myself entirely for DJ's willingness to shoot heroin, but I was the one who first stuck in the needle. The first person I initiated into junkiedom was my friend Ming. He was one of the older punk kids who went with me to my first show. We went to MacArthur Park one night to go to an underground dub called the Scream, but it was dosed for some reason. Two chicks pulled up, also looking for the dub, so we chatted them up for a while. One of them seemed a little rough around the edges, so I asked if they knew where I could score some dope. They told me about a place nearby, so Ming gave me a ride to the Mexican neighborhood to get the drugs, and then a ride to the black neighborhood to get "outfits" (needles and other associated junkie tools). We drove up some side street and I shot up what turned out be really shitty Mexican junk. Ming was always open to new experiences, so when I asked him if he wanted to try it he said yes.

I cooked him up a shot and went to inject it in the top of his hand, but for some reason his blood coagulated in the needle and plugged it up. The standard procedure in such a case is to heat up the needle in order to liquefy the blood and clear the passage. Once the syringe was unclogged, I shot him up, but I didn't wipe the black residue from the flame off the needle, so Ming was left with a small, circular tattoo about the size of a BB pellet to commemorate his first fix.

It's still there. I cringe whenever I see it because I think about how I was partially responsible for his journey from being an aspiring artist going to college to being a substitute teacher who was shooting up between classes. Eventually I helped him get clean, but the drug took a lot from him during those years in between.

DJ was the only other junkie I ever mentored. Ming and I were shooting up in Ming's garage, and DJ wanted to be included. He put on a front like he had done heroin before but just forgot how to do it and needed a refresher course. He had just arrived in California; he was probably as eager to be accepted as I always was. I couldn't see that at the time, though. So I stuck in the needle and brought him down into the pit with me.

✕

My friend Johnny Sixpack started a gang called the Dog Patch Winos. Well, they weren't really a gang; they were more like a group of alcoholic misfits who liked to get as wasted as possible and wear matching jackets. I had been inducted before the tour, and DJ fit in with them immediately when he moved to California. They provided a modest network of people up and down the coast who could offer drugs and places to sleep. DJ and I became junkie hobos, couch surfing with friends and bouncing between crash pads in L.A. and San Francisco.

DJ was my junkie apprentice. Despite the fascination with heroin in our pop culture and the vast amounts of books and movies about the subject, there's so much more you learn when you actually start shooting up. I apprenticed under Raymond, but I earned my master's degree in Junkie Studies on my own, and now it was time to share my knowledge, I could teach a UCLA Extension course in that shit.

LESSON 1: RADAR

If you're not a junkie, you may not realize that heroin is being bought, sold, and shot all around you. The need for junk gives you a sixth sense. When you walk or drive through a neighborhood where heroin is available, you know. You can spot a dealer from a mile away, and you can predict when he's going to make his handoff down to the second. You can look at two nearly identical drunk gutter punks and tell which one is holding. Other junkies can outwardly appear as Mexican gangsters or high-powered businessmen in perfectly pressed suits, but, either way, you see through the disguise.

And they see through yours, too. You'll walk down the same street you've walked down a thousand times, but now that you're a junkie some random sketchy dude will walk up and say, "Hey man, I'm holding, you want some?" It's a subconscious subculture. And later when you're trying desperately to get clean you'll still be acutely aware of every dealer, every user, and every speck of heroin within reach. For the rest of your life.

LESSON 2: TRANSPORT

So now you know where the dealers are, and you want to buy some drugs. You think it's going to be sexy and cool—you'll shake hands with someone and exchange a palmed wad of cash for a discreet little baggie, using a sleight-of-hand move that would make Penn & Teller jealous.

Well, yes, you hand over the cash very deftly, but they don't hand you a baggie. They pull a small, tied-off balloon out of their mouth, and you quickly rake it and stick it inside your own cheek.

The concept is that if the cops stop either you or the dealer, you can quickly swallow the balloon and "retrieve" it later. Sure, it's gross that you're swapping spit with random scumbags, but this is probably the LEAST disgusting element of your future as a heroin addict, so you should try to get over it quickly.

Much more disgusting is what happens when you do have to swallow your stash. I bought four balloons (such was my tolerance at the time) from a dealer in Hollywood while hanging out with a girl I was dating. She didn't know I made the deal or that my cheeks were stuffed with heroin; we were just drunk and driving back to my mom's house where I'd been crashing while my folks were away.

I got pulled over. I was way too drunk to be driving, and I was ordered out of the car to perform a field sobriety test. As I was doing my best to walk a straight line and touch my fingers to my nose I gulped down all four balloons. And then I passed the fucking test! The girl I was with was probably confused about why I was so angry that I had just avoided a jail sentence.

I excused myself to the bathroom when we arrived at my mom's house and I stuck my fingers down my throat in order to throw up the balloons, but I couldn't get myself to puke, so I had to wait and let nature take its course.

The next day I went through my mom's cabinets and pulled out a spaghetti strainer. (I told you the spit-swapping wouldn't seem so bad after a while . . .) I put the strainer in the toilet and took a balloon-speckled dump. I went into the backyard and used the hose to melt away the poo while I panned for gold. After a full day of waiting to get high, watching my shit dissolve in that strainer was equivalent to being a kid on Christmas morning, running into the living room and seeing all those gleaming presents under the tree.

After I shot up, I washed off the strainer and put it back in the cabinet. It's probably still there. After all, when was the last time you replaced your spaghetti strainer?

LESSON 3: FUNDING

My circle of junkie friends had a racket going where we would steal high-end art books and sell them to some scummy guy we knew for 20 percent of the cover price. Snag a $200 book on architecture, make $40 cash. Enough to get high for the day. You'd walk into the store with a coat draped over your arm, shop around, and pile up the books that might be worth something, and then, on the way out, cover the pile with the coat and slip out the door. You could usually hit the same store several times, until one day you would walk in and they'd tell you to get the fuck out because they finally got wise.

DJ and I were hitting a store in the Valley that we had hit before. I had a car at the time, so I was the getaway driver and he was the thief. I parked at a gas station with easy access to an alley that would allow us a covert escape. While I was waiting for DJ, I got out to take a leak. I locked the car because we had probably a thousand bucks' worth of stolen books in the back. As I returned to the car after my pee break, I saw two big-ass dudes chasing DJ. They tackled him and started manhandling him. I grabbed my car's door handle: I had locked the keys inside.

The big dudes looked up at me while they roughed up DJ and could tell from our dreadlocks and matching Dog Patch Winos jackets that we were probably in cahoots, I ran down the alley, hid out for a couple hours, and watched the cops take DJ away. When the heat died down I borrowed a coat hanger from a nearby dry cleaner and retrieved my car. DJ ended up in county jail for thirty days. I kept stealing books and never got busted.

I guess the real lesson is that you shouldn't steal. But theft generally goes with the junkie territory, so you should at least try not to lock your keys in the car when you're the GODDAMNED GETAWAY DRIVER.

LESSON 4: OVERDOSING

My friend Jimmy Dread and I were shooting up at an apartment in San Francisco. I did my dope first, went to the bathroom, and came back to find Jimmy unconscious and not breathing. Everyone else in the apartment was too high to notice, so I dragged Jimmy to the shower and sprayed him with cold water, I guess current medical advice says you're not supposed to do that because it could send a person into shock, but that's what I was taught to do by other junkies. I assume you're not supposed to dump ice on a person's balls either, but I did that as well in my frantic attempt to wake him up.

He still wasn't breathing, so I called 911. Part of the junkie code is that if someone ODs you call the ambulance, wait until you hear the sirens, and then split. That way you're with them if they need you, but you also don't get busted. I could've gotten nailed for manslaughter if Jimmy died, since I was the one who copped the dope he was using. Best-case scenario I was getting arrested for possession. So I shouted at him and slapped him around until I heard sirens and then bailed.

Jimmy spent a few days in the hospital, but he lived. I ended up with a pretty bad rep in the San Francisco music scene, though, because the rumors were that I left him for dead. No one gave me credit for calling 911, much less icing down his balls.

You start to grow numb to the news of friends OD'ing because you can't possibly keep up emotionally. Susan, one of my roommates from San Francisco, OD'd on Christmas morning and died in a Taco Bell bathroom. As soon as one of our other roommates found out, she grabbed all of Susan's stuff—her clothes, her bike, everything—and sold it all to buy dope. It sounds like a cold and ghoulish thing to do, but the truth is Susan probably would've done the same thing if it had been one of us.

LESSON 5: SOCIAL STIGMA

If you've started shooting heroin in the first place, you're probably the type of person who already feels out of step with society, but heroin addiction will take you to an even lonelier place. It's not a party drug; it's something you do in dark alleys and bathroom stalls and places where you know no one's watching. Sure, you'll still spend time with your straight friends, but you'll spend more and more of your time with other junkies, or in pursuit of dope, or in pursuit of money to buy dope. It's a full-time job. But even if you manage your time effectively enough to hang out with your friends, your friends will stop wanting to hang out with you.

I moved into the basement of a party house in San Francisco, and a German girl named Suzy who I met on our European tour flew out and moved in with me. She OD'd the first night. I found her on the floor of the bathroom and, just like Jimmy, threw her in the shower and smacked her around. Again: you're not supposed to throw an overdose victim in the shower. But you're also not supposed to let them stay asleep. If I hadn't been there to wake her up, she most likely would have died.

After clearing that little hurdle we just lived in our basement world of fucking and shooting up and shooting up and fucking. Mike and Erin moved into the house a month or so after I did and were so grossed out by our behavior that a couple weeks later Suzy and I came home and found all of our shit on the porch and the sidewalk. (Bringing my Dog Patch Wino friends over and having Johnny Sixpack and Bob Lush spray paint the kitchen walls probably didn't make me an ideal roommate, either.)

Without a place to live, Suzy and I went our separate ways. She tried to go straight but couldn't. She hanged herself six months later.

LESSON 6: DOPE SICKNESS

It's the fucking worst. You're nauseous. You're agitated. You shiver and sweat. Your muscles ache, especially the ones in your legs for some reason. And you can't sleep because your brain tortures you, whispering devilishly over and over again, "If you just had a little bit of dope you'd feel fine . . ."

The first time I was dope sick was when I was still living in Santa Barbara. I went home to visit my family for Christmas and didn't realize I was already an addict. I just thought I had the flu. And I didn't connect the dots when my "flu" went away the minute I got back to Santa Barbara and got some junk in my system.I finally put two and two together on the next NOFX tour. I rarely scored on the road, so when I was hit with the same "flu" symptoms I slowly figured out the connection between the sickness and the distance from home.

I rode in the back of the van, shivering, sweating, cramping, and sleepless. DJ came out with us again, and I'm sure he was hurting just as bad. In the absence of heroin, the only way we could relax was by drinking to excess and then beyond. Our natural predilection for mischief coupled with our unbridled drinking and drug use gave birth to our new nickname: The Moron Brothers.

X X X X

CHAPTER FIFTEEN / DEE DEE RAMONE
CONNIE

EXCERPT FROM
Lobotomy: Surviving The Ramones

AUTHORS
Dee Dee Ramone with Veronica Kofman

Dee Dee Ramone (1951-2002) was the original bassist for the Ramones.

✕ ✕ ✕ ✕

"It was supposed to be good luck if someone had rocks. I must have had a lot of luck."

I GOT DRUNK AFTER OUR GIG at CBGB's and as I was leaving the club at four o'clock in the morning, I noticed this babe sitting by the Bowery on the hood of an old car, filing her nails. I liked her right away. She was wearing a black evening dress, spiked high-heeled shoes and had a bottle of blackberry brandy in her purse. She looked like an ancient vampire countess. Her name was Connie and her mission was to capture my soul, which she did. I spent the next few years depending on her, while the Ramones were getting famous but not making any money. We were both a lot alike—totally nuts. She was just as crazy as I was. We got kicked out of everywhere we lived because of our violent arguments.

Connie had an apartment on the first floor of a brownstone building on 16th Street. She was a little older and wiser than I was, and tried to look after me, but I was difficult. You couldn't trust me and I had to be checked up on. It must have been exhausting having me for a boyfriend. Connie put up with a lot from me, but she was also a well-known troublemaker. She was always starting fights.

Not long after I met Connie, she started up with one of my ex-girlfriends in CBGB's. Blondie had been playing, and it had been a fun night, but Connie had to ruin it. She and the other girl ended up ranking on each other and shouting terrible names at each other. I hate spectacles, so I made a quick exit out the back door, taking one of my other girlfriends, Elaine, with me. Elaine was used to battling with Connie. They had been doing it for years over Arthur Kane, the bass player for the New York Dolls, before I'd met either of them. Once, the two of them squared off on 11th Street, when Connie caught me sneaking around with Elaine. They were both tough girls and this looked like it might become more than a verbal row.

Elaine and her mother lived on a beautiful block on 11th Street, near St. Vincent's Hospital. Once in a while they let me crash there, but I was getting on their nerves already. I could tell. I drank too much beer and raided the liquor cabinet one too many times. Elaine's mom could only take so much and finally she had had enough of me. There was trouble in the air, so Elaine took me for a walk over to Smiler's, the deli on 13th Street, to get some Colt .45 beer, which was the strongest beer you could get in the States.

Connie stepped out of nowhere as we were leaving the deli. She was swinging her handbag around her head like Bruce Lee and she had put a brick in it for effect. She wasn't kidding around. Connie and Elaine went right at it, started maneuvering for the best position and were shouting at each other. This was at the end of the glitter period in New York. It was 6:30 in the morning and we were very dressed up. I had been at the Eighty-Two Club in the East Village and had been getting into hassles all night. It was quite dramatic. Then suddenly, Connie and Elaine both turned on me, Elaine grabbing me by the collar, saying "Dec Dec, do you want me or Connie?" Then, without waiting for an answer, she punched me really hard right on the side of my head. It sent me down the sidewalk and I busted open my chin when I hit the curb. Connie thought that this was very funny, so with her bloodlust satisfied, but still slightly annoyed, she took me back home.

It wasn't long before we were thrown out of our apartment on 16th Street and home was now in something called the Village Plaza. The walls in there were painted a creepy lime green like the paint jobs in mental institutions and police stations. It smelled like green roach spray and was much more horrible than the Chelsea Hotel. Even most of my lowlife friends wouldn't stay there. They would stay at The Earl, where Connie and I had already worn out our welcome.

It may be hard to believe but I had kept my job at the mailroom to be able to afford to go to school. My dream was to attend the Wilfred Academy of hairstyling. I had a part-time job at Bergdorf Goodman's and I was starting to do really good. I wanted to be a colorist and start over.

Then the guy I wanted to work for, Robert Kramer at Pierre Michelle's, died. And they told me: Forget it, you can't work here anymore.

I had no family to speak of. I had fallen totally out of touch with my sister, who had gotten married when she was seventeen. Beverly was going down the drain.

She could have had a great career, but my family was too rugged and everybody paid for it. She got married, stopped dancing, and that was that.

Johnny Ramone had gotten into a fight with her husband. He wanted to hang out with us. And I didn't want them to hang out. I didn't want them to be around me, or drugs, or bad people. But Beverly's husband had a condescending attitude. He was a college jock type, laughing in our faces, and calling us freaks, but then trying to imitate us and hang out. John tried to be as polite as he could. He offered to drive them home, things he would never offer anyone. Finally, he just let him have it. He pulled over and said, "That's it, I'm gonna put the boot to you."

When I went home, they got mad at me and threw me out for good.

I was trying to follow my working class dream and it just got interrupted. I wanted to be a hairstylist, get self-sufficient, have a roof over my head, get married, whatever.

But instead the band got popular and I fell right back into this aimless behavior with a license to do whatever l wanted. I was playing every night, and being in a band and eventually I quit working. With no job, and no family, I lived in a void of irresponsibility, nothing but more free time.

With all that free time, we were making our lives much worse than they had to be. Connie was dancing at the Metropole, the go-go place on 48th Street. She also turned the occasional trick when she could get a lot of money.

And I was her little protégé. She was about ten years older than me. I was twenty-one. She had a lot of experience. She was originally from Fort Worth, Texas. I think she had been traumatized way back. She also had lived with the GTOs, Pamela, and all those people, in California. She had been living with Jobriath at the Chelsea Hotel. He had all this money and just ended up a dope fiend: he never became the next David Bowie.

In her own way, Connie took care of me. She taught me all the tricks of the trade, but unintentionally, so I'd think it was normal: this is life and this is music. In a way she was like a soulmate or the mother I wished I would have had. She was like a friend. And she tried to be good to me, in her own way. She had a total idiot on her hands to raise.

My job was to get dope for us. It started like this: Either I was playing or I would go out all night. She was dancing. Whenever she came home, around five in the morning, we'd be together; we'd meet in a bar and get drunk. By noon. I would go cop for us. As soon as they were selling I'd be there. If they would have been selling earlier, I would have been there earlier.

I'd go to the B&H Dairy and try to eat something. I'd always throw up from anxiety, getting ready to cop. Sometimes you had to fight for it. The first time I went to cop we got held up and had to run for it. But this became the routine, every day, drinking all night at Max's or CBGB's, drinking horrible things like grasshoppers, blackberry brandy, and wine mixed together, then going to cop in the morning and shooting up. It was part of the thing we were all doing.

After I quit my hairdressing job I moved into the loft above Arturo's loft with Connie and Joey. I caught my first habit by the age of twenty-six. One day I thought to myself: I don't want to do dope today. I knew everybody would be doing some and I just wanted to lay off. God knows why.

Of course, I started getting sick; really sick. Jonesing bad. Dope sick for the first time. Hot-cold sweats. Weird sensations. Different states of mind. A complete physical breakdown, like pneumonia. You have only one thing that wants to live and that's the craving for dope.

Connie felt sorry for me and brought some dope over.

What chance did I have? What chance did she have with me? I wasn't supporting her. Prostitution is an addiction. I think hers had been a continuous lifestyle from day one.

✕

We would spend one hundred dollars a day on dope if we could. I'd go cop around Rivington, Suffolk, and Norfolk Streets—side streets around Houston in the East Village towards Delancey Street.

Sometimes Jerry Nolan, the former drummer for the New York Dolls, and I would go cop together. Jerry sometimes got dope for this weirdo called Dorian Zero, who lived uptown near where I used to live, near Third Avenue in the Eighties. He also always had a steady supply of Dioxin, a speed that you could shoot up and get with a prescription from a doctor. You put Dioxin in a little glass bottle with water and closed the lid, then you would put that in boiling water for a minute and let it cook up. Then it was ready to shoot into your vein.

Dorian could hit his parents up for money, so sometimes we would hop into a cab with him up to 48th Street to a restaurant that his father owned. That was the start of the insanity. Then, with the meter still ticking, we would head deep into New Jersey to complete the whole picture. We would end up in front of Dorian's parents' house in Cherry Hill. His parents were wealthy and connected. Their home was expensive and had seven acres of manicured lawn around it. It didn't exactly have a welcome sign outside, though, and it made me nervous. The whole deal made me nervous. Dorian would leave us outside and then go into the house to argue with his mother. We could hear him shouting terrible things at her. It would remind me of fighting with my mother, except that I never got any money from her.

For a while dope was called Chinese Rock in New York. When you would walk around the Lower East Side, people would smirk at one another on the sidewalk and let you know with hand signals that they had the Chinese Rocks. "The Rock." It was supposed to be good luck if someone had rocks. I must have had a lot of luck.

Jerry Nolan and Johnny Thunders used to call me quite frequently. Jerry would come over to my place to pick me up and then we would go cop some dope. The Heartbreakers were just getting together with John, Jerry, and Richard Hell. I guess those guys were all dope fiends then. It was not easy to cop dope. It was unreliable, it was annoying and there were rip-offs. People would buddy up and go cop. If you went and copped for someone, you were entitled to "tap" the bag. Richard Hell had mentioned to me that he was going to write a song better than Lou Reed's "Heroin," so I took his idea and wrote "Chinese Rocks" in Deborah Harry's apartment that night.

I wrote the song about Jerry calling me up to come over and go cop. The line "My girlfriend's crying in the shower stall" was about Connie, and the shower was at Arturo Vega's loft. The intro to the song was the same kind of stuff I had put in songs like "Commando" and the chorus of "53rd & 3rd" I wrote those songs before "Chinese Rocks" and The Ramones had already performed and recorded these tunes.

By the time I got the song finished I was living on 10th Street. Jerry Nolan would come over as usual. It was perfect because the dope spot had moved to 10th Street and Avenue D, so my new apartment became a meeting place because it was so close to the action.

When Jerry was over at my place one day, we did some dope and then I played him my song, and he took it with him to a Heartbreakers' rehearsal. When Leee Childers starred managing them, and got them a record deal, "Chinese Rocks" was their first single off *LAMF*. Leee was originally a photographer who took all the pictures that were on the wall of Max's Kansas City. He also managed Wayne County. The song did well too, and helped start a career for the Heartbreakers. It was dedicated to the boys on Norfolk Street. I can understand that, but the credits are false. Johnny Thunders ranked on me for fourteen years, trying to make out like he wrote the song. What a low-life maneuver by those guys! By then, I was really too fucked up to care.

Being a dope addict was the worst. It was never any fun. It gives a person every reason to be miserable so you have every excuse to do it again. Connie was only adding to my misery and I was starting to be glad when she wasn't at home and was at work, dancing at the Metropole.

A friend or mine then was Black Randy, one of the most hated punks in California. Randy would fly back and forth between Los Angeles and New York, in a Brooks Brothers three-piece suit. He was robbing these people for dope money and doing very well at it. He was a freak, a dope fiend, and a con man. The Wall Street image was a front. I would always get Randy some dope when he came by for a visit. Because he was overweight it was always hard for Randy to find a vein when he was shooting up, so it would be messy, and I would end up miserable every time he came by.

Once Randy came over to the Village Plaza with a big wad of cash. I went to Rivington Street on my bike to cop for him. All the Puerto Rican dealers were sitting on the stoop checking me out. I was a customer, so they left me alone. I felt all right around Rivington and Norfolk Streets, but it wasn't my neighborhood and I was risking it being there. But that's where the dope was.

These cop spots were store fronts that the dealers turned into social clubs. They were painted in blood red, Day-Glo orange and green colors. There were Day-Glo devil heads painted on the walls. They would glare at you from under the black lights. Somehow these places reminded me of the Café Wha. It made it weird to cop.

The dope was sort of going along with the decorations. It was cut with Procaine. The word was that it was from Mexico. It was brown rocks. Chinese Bock. But they were saying it was South American. Clever, but silly. It was just a delusion to make it easier to get the dope into America from Thailand or wherever. It wasn't as refined as the old dope. I wish whomever was manufacturing it would have kept the dope a little smoother. We had to take what they had, or be sick, so we took it. Shooting up the dope with Procaine was like shooting up heroin while you were rushing on glue. I knew that's what I would be in for, but I copped two bundles anyway. One for Randy and one for myself. Then I rode my bike back to the Village Plaza.

Soon Randy and I were really stoned. Then Randy seemed like he was over-dosing. I was very fucked up, in a heroin and Procaine daze. Randy could have died. I should have called the police, but instead I poured water over him. using the garbage can under the sink for a bucket. It worked, thank God, and soon he started coming to, but by then the whole room was flooded, which I knew would be a dead giveaway to Connie. When Randy woke up, he was pretty confused. The first thing he said was "Dee Dee, got any dope?" That's how it was.

Later, when Connie came home from dancing at the Metropole on Broadway she was pissed off.

"Dee Dee, what were you doing in here? You don't even have to tell me, you motherfucking bastard. You've been doing dope without me! This whole room is flooded. What the hell happened here?"

She didn't wait for my answer. In a flurry she picked up a wine bottle, broke it over the radiator, and slashed me with it. It was a deep wound. There was blood all over the place. I held a towel over the cut and somehow made it to St. Vincent's to get stitched up. I took the stitches out later by myself.

A couple of weeks later, I got a blade stuck in my chest. I was trying to get away from these two guys, but they pushed me into the hallway. I was walking away as fast as I could, being as cool about it as I could, but they overtook me. "Narcotics control!" they shouted in my face. That stunned me a little, but I reacted with caution and said to them, '"Show me your badges."

"What are you a wise guy?" one of them accused me. Then they shoved me into the hallway of a vacant building. Both of them had German cat knives. One of them said, "Should I stick him?" The creep he was with said, "Yeah!" There was nothing I could really do about it. I was just glad they didn't kill me.

A friend of mine had a loft at 6 East 2nd Street, around the corner from CBGB's, so it was very convenient for the Ramones. Mostly for Joey and me. There were three lofts in the building and a factory on the first floor. A crazy painter named Jimmy lived on the top floor. Below that was a loft that six drag queens from San Francisco called home. On the floor below that lived Arturo Vega. Arturo had had bricks thrown through his windows so many times because of bad dope deals and crazy love feuds that it's a wonder no one ever got conked in the head by one.

Behind the building was a graveyard that had been dug up by the city. Some of the corpses had been buried upright in the brick wall. Once I went down there to get a loose brick, and a dead person's hand fell out of the hole where the brick had been. The hand was all bone, but a gold and diamond ring was still stubbornly stuck on its finger. It was an old engagement ring that some sucker must have bought this broad. The diamond must have been at least two and a half carats and the money I got for it at the pawnshop kept me in dope and Hostess cupcakes for months. A lot better than the nickel bag I got twenty years later for my wedding ring on 10th Street after I left the Ramones.

So, I wasn't doing so well when the Ramones started. We were playing CBGB's over and over to survive. We kept saying we wouldn't go back but we had to.

To keep my spending on dope down, I tried to keep on the Flower and Fifth methadone program, a twenty-four-day program in New York. All my creepy friends autographed the cork bulletin board for the staff. Eventually everybody was on that program. Johnny Thunders, Sid Vicious, Nancy Spungen, me . . . Most of these people are dead now. I don't want to start counting or thinking about that. I don't know how I am still alive after all the drugs I used. I am glad they had that program then. For whatever it was worth, it made my miserable life a little bit better being on it. But this kind of lifestyle sucks.

Nancy Spungen was a go-go dancer and a groupie for The Heartbreakers. Everybody slept with Nancy once, and then dumped her. Then no one wanted her around at all. She could really get to you. Once, Connie tried to set me up with Sable Star, Johnny Thunder' girlfriend, while she was in Boston go-go dancing. But I went off with some other go-go dancer that I met at a Neon Leon show at Max's. Sable wasn't that hot.

I don't remember how well I really knew Nancy. Everything happened so fast. Connie knew Nancy first, because Connie was an ex-Dolls groupie and had been around more than everyone else. Everyone had a mutual fondness for drugs, sin, and violence. The sicker the better. Like one day we went to go cop some dope like we always did, but we got ripped off. We lost our dope and our money. We were all dressed up and made ourselves look too conspicuous. I was in full Bay

City Rollers gear, and Connie was in hot pants, platform boots, and a halter top. We almost started a riot on 10th Street. I was glad I had dumped my platforms a couple of months before in favor of Keds sneakers. The monster boots like Slade, the Dolls, and the Wombles wore, were impossible to run in. Connie was such a pro that she had no problem with wearing platforms—which for her could also double as weapons.

We ended up by the Gem Spa on St. Mark's Place, huffing and puffing, out of breath. As we were regaining our composure, Nancy Spungen walked up to Connie and me. She seemed very miserable and started trying to bullshit us and get our sympathy. What a laugh!

Everybody was screaming and soon we started to walk towards Chelsea. Nancy had an apartment on 23rd and Ninth Avenue. It was on the first floor. It might have been borrowed from a trick, I don't know for sure. Soon we were all stoned. Then Nancy gave Connie money, and Connie hopped a cab to 1st Street and Avenue C. I stayed with Nancy to case her apartment or whatever, and to get a free lunch out of it. When Connie came back from copping, we all got stoned again, and then we ended up in bed and tried to do some bad things. I don't think it ended up too special, though—it's all a blur.

Connie also stole Nancy's silver dollar collection. Connie was a clever dope fiend, always scheming to make more on the sneak. Nancy was younger and just learning then. She had a big crush on Jerry Nolan, but Jerry totally ignored her. He let Nancy buy him a few bags of dope, but that's about it. She was too much of a hassle. Also you could get a bad reputation hanging out with Nancy. On the bathroom wall in CBGB's there was some bad shit written about her by the other girls, who all hated Nancy.

Sometime around then I escaped from Connie with a girl that lived in the loft above Arturo Vega's loft. We both wanted to get away from 2nd Street and found an apartment in the *Village Voice* rental ads. I picked it out. It was on 10th Street, right in the dope area. Even though we were going out together and living together, I still didn't know much about her. She started going to some "job" every day. It was strange, but fine with me. When she was at work, Jerry Nolan started to come over to do dope and then he started bringing Johnny Thunders over.

One day my girlfriend stayed home. No matter—she was a big Johnny Thunders fan and was thrilled when John and Jerry came over. Thing is, though, she OD'd on us. We had to strip her and toss her in a bathtub filled with iced water.

Soon, we sort of just forgot about her. Later, when she came to, I was the only one there.

"What happened?" she muttered in a daze.

"Oh, I threw you in the bathtub," I answered her back.

"You didn't do this in front of Johnny Thunders, did you?"

"Yes. I did!" I shouted.

Later we were in bed and she rolled over and tried to hug me. I automatically jumped right off the mattress and that did it. She went crazy and started yelling, "Fuck you, Dee Dee! Fuck you! Fuck you, Dee Dee! You never let me kiss you! All you're interested in is dope!" She was right. We broke up soon after that and I went back to the loft on Second Street. Arturo took me in. I was really glad to be back at the loft. All the commotion on 10th Street was too much already.

✕ ✕ ✕ ✕

CHAPTER SIXTEEN / ANTHONY KIEDIS
GROUNDHOG YEAR

EXCERPT FROM
Scar Tissue

AUTHORS
Anthony Kiedis with Larry Sloman

Anthony Kiedis is the lead singer of the rock group the Red Hot Chili Peppers,
one of the most beloved bands in the world.

"There was no way a demo should cost that much. When I brought it up with Hillel and Keith, I found out that they'd earmarked two thousand dollars for drugs to make the tape."

WHEN HILLEL REJOINED THE BAND in 1985, it was a monumental feeling, like we were back on track. We finally had a guitarist who knew which songs worked for us and which songs I was capable of singing. Plus, Hillel was our brother. And, like a brother, he was worried about the amount of drugs I was doing. I was in and out of rehearsals; sometimes showing up late, sometimes not showing up. By then I had shown up at Jennifer's mom's two-bedroom apartment on Cahuenga, right at the Hollywood Freeway. God bless her mom, she accepted me, but I was a mess. I was the horrible, leeching boyfriend who had no money, lived under her roof, ate the Corn Pops out of the kitchen, and never replaced anything because I was strapped.

I would disappear for days on end behind my coke runs, then come back like a beaten puppy and try to quietly sneak in the house to get some rest. But Jennifer wasn't having it. She answered the door once holding a giant pair of leather clipping shears that she used for her clothing designing. I knew when she was bluffing and when she was out for blood and bone damage, and that particular time she would have gladly stuck those through my skull if I had gotten close enough.

"Where were you? Who were you sleeping with?" she screamed at me.

"Are you kidding me? I didn't sleep with anybody. I was trying to get high. You know how I am," I pleaded. Eventually, I sweet-talked my way back into the house.

The more Jennifer got into heroin, the easier it became for me to get into the house, because she needed a coconspirator to cop with, and I needed her money. She didn't mind me doing the dope, because when I'd do that, I was calm and we could actually be together and melt in each other's arms and nod out watching old black-and-white movies at four in the morning, enmeshed in the blissful, deadly euphoria of the opium. But she absolutely hated it when I was shooting the cocaine. Then I'd turn into a freak and disappear. Of course, I never wanted to shoot just heroin. So when we were shooting heroin in her room, I'd sneak out to do a hit of coke. But she was the total eagle eye. "No, you're not. Give me the coke. Give me the syringe. You're not shooting coke!"

I came up with these horrible and deceptive ways of getting high on coke. By then my hair was so long and matted that I'd slide syringes up into the undercarriage of my hairdo and consent to a full-body pat-down. I'd previously hidden the coke in a cereal box in the kitchen, so I'd rush downstairs and shoot up before Jennifer or her sister or her mom came in. I can't imagine the emotional terrorism that I inflicted on these people. I was lost in that addiction. And it was going to get a lot worse before it got any better.

I didn't have any idea how dependent on heroin I was becoming. It seemed like there was an endless supply. All these weird-ass dealers were popping up all over Hollywood. You had the Russian dealer who lived in a shitty apartment with his Russian wife and spoke hardly any English but had a nonstop supply of China White. You had the white-trash mullet-wearing Hollywood dealer on the corner of Sunset Boulevard. You had five or six different Frenchmen, from my old friend Fabrice to Dominique to Francois, and then five other people they knew.

If I was copping from Fab, I could go over to his house with fifty bucks and get a bindle that would last me a day—probably a tenth of a gram. But if I had to go to the Russian guy, who was a shyster, I'd give him fifty bucks and it would be good for one poke. Of course, I didn't go there with fifty bucks, I went with twenty-two, begging for the fifty-dollar bindle and offering to leave my shoes. Russians don't appreciate a negotiation, but that didn't stop me from hounding and begging and bickering and sleazing. I would sit there and wear that bitch out, make him feel the misery before I would.

The other French guys were pompous, arrogant, heartless dealers. Not a lot of fronting going on there. They were all dope fiends, too, so they knew what it was to need a little something to get well, but if you weren't a girl and you didn't have a lot of money, good luck. So I had to work every angle imaginable. I wasn't beneath showing up with a copy of our first record.

"I don't know if you've seen this record here, but this is my band. That's me there. I've got a manager who's holding a couple thousand dollars of mine right now. I'm going to reach him later. I don't know if you feel like coming to the show that we're having next week. Of course, you and your girlfriend would be welcome to attend." Any scam, any lie, any bullshit tactic whatsoever. It was a humiliating, god-awful place in which to find myself.

Somehow I was maintaining and still writing music and showing up to rehearsal more often than not. But without me really knowing it, my life was starting to leave me. I became broom-handle thin. Then the cops busted the old Fabster, which kiboshed his business. He went from dealing and being to able to inhale monster lines of smack, to having no smack, no cash flow, no customers, and a huge habit. Next thing I knew, Fab had aligned himself with a young Mexican guy. I called him Johnny Devil, because he was, quite obviously, *the* devil incarnate on Planet Earth—charming enough for you to want to hang out with him, and clever and conniving enough for you to see other faces that weren't his. But I liked him. He never burned me, and he was fair and generous and kind in his evil, devilish ways.

My habit was getting worse, and my money was diminishing rapidly, so I had to do the pawnshop thing. Every day I woke up as late as possible, because I knew I was about to get sick. I'd ask Jennifer for twenty dollars. There would be no twenty dollars.

"Do we have anything we can sell?" I'd plead.

"We've sold everything."

"Can we sell this picture? Can we sell the fire extinguisher? Can we sell this rug? Is there an old radio that no one uses around the house?"

I kept going down to the pawnshop with anything I could find to get twenty or thirty bucks. Then I'd go meet the man, whether it was the Russian, the Frenchman, or the white-trash guy; I'd cop the stuff and go to a little hill at Argyle and Franklin, overlooking the freeway, throw the dope into a spoon, hit it with water, and shoot up immediately. The minute that shit hit me, it was like pouring water on a withered sponge. I'd go from being sick and miserable and weak and devoid of life to frisky and conversational. As soon as I shot the dope, up came the leg of pork, and I'd want to have sex with Jennifer right away. But she'd be mad at me for this ordeal of getting and buying and selling and pawning and copping.

One day I woke up, and the cupboards were literally bare. I borrowed Jennifer's sister's bike. I had no intention of pawning it; I was just desperate to get something. I didn't have the time to take the conventional street route to downtown, where the Devil lived, so I hopped on this one-speed beach cruiser, rode it out of the apartment grounds, up the on-ramp to the Hollywood Freeway, into the right lane of traffic, and peddled my way from Hollywood to downtown Los Angeles.

I finally got to Johnny Devil's, but his cash was low, and he was down on his flow. First we tried melting some Tuinals in a spoon and shooting that, but the minute the powder inside the capsules hit the water, it foamed up. We tried to get the foam into the syringe just to get some relief, but it wasn't working.

"You and I are going to find something," he promised, and we jumped into his car and drove out to the San Bernardino Valley. We stopped in a neighborhood that looked like it could have been uprooted from the poorest section of Tijuana. The whole area was brimming with one-story shacks in dirt yards. On each plot there were fires burning in oil barrels. There were no windows or doors on the houses. It was like being in Beirut during wartime.

Johnny pulled up to the curb and got out of the car. "You wait here. Don't move," he said, and disappeared into this labyrinth of streets and houses. I was so weak that I couldn't move if I wanted to. I sat there certain somebody was going to walk up and fill me full of twenty-twos and take the car and leave. Finally, the Devil reappeared out of a shadow, far away from where he entered. He was walking that purposeful walk. He got back in the car.

"Did you get it? Did you get it? Did you get it?"

He shot me an agitated look. "Just chill. Everything's going to be okay. Don't ask me nothing." He was obviously in a bad mood. For all I knew, he went in there and killed a family for that shit, he was acting so weird. But as soon as we got out of the neighborhood, he pulled a huge baseball-sized object out of his coat. It was pure Black Tar heroin. He twisted off a Bazooka gum-sized piece of the stuff and handed it to me and pocketed the rest.

"Uh, are you going to keep all of that? That's a lot. Maybe I can hold on to some of that," I schemed.

"That's how much I need," he said. We drove to some girl's house in Hollywood, and be proceeded to melt that fucking baseball down, shot after shot, until most of it was gone, all the while never once passing out or OD'ing or even becoming incoherent. He just settled into his demonic wellness. A few days later, he disappeared, and I never saw him or heard about him again.

Despite all my drug use, the writing for the second album was going well. I would watch Hillel and Flea play together, and I'd realize that music was an act of telepathy, that if you were standing next to your soul mate with a guitar in your hand and he with a bass, you could know what the other guy was thinking and communicate that through playing. Hillel had definitely grown as a guitar player in his time away from us. He started off as a Kiss-influenced player with some progressive rock thrown in. Then he experimented with the early Red Hot Chili Peppers, and now he'd come back with a weird, sultry element to his style. It wasn't all syncopated manic funk, there was something smooth and fluid in his style also.

While we were in the EMI rehearsal space on Sunset, we got a call that the legendary impresario Malcolm McLaren wanted to talk to us. McLaren was the mystery man who had created the Sex Pistols and Bow Wow Wow. Now he was looking for the Next Big Thing, and if we were lucky, the Starmaker would sprinkle his dust on us. He came to a rehearsal with a few cronies, and we played him a couple of our crazy-assed, complicated songs—fast and chaotic and dense and layered, with no rhyme or reason but a lot of feeling and a lot of funk.

He clearly wasn't impressed. "All right, then, can we have a chat somewhere, mates?"

We walked to a tiny meeting room adjacent to the rehearsal space. Someone started passing around a spliff the size of a Havana cigar.

"Okay, all that stuff you're playing, that's great, but it makes no sense. No one's going to care about that type of music. What I'm envisioning . . . "

He started throwing out words like "cacophony" and "epiphany," and we were getting higher and higher, going, "What does he mean by a cacophony of sounds?"

At last he got to the point. By way of demonstration, he took out some pictures of surfers who were wearing hot pink punk rock colors.

"I want to take this band and simplify all of the music. Turn it into old fifties rock and roll, simple as can be, bass, rote notes, guitar, simple riffs, basic beats. And I want to make Anthony the star, the front man, so there's no confusion. The public can get their head around looking at one central character, and the rest of you will be in the background playing the most simple rock and roll known to man."

He paused to get our reaction, and I looked over at Flea.

Flea had passed out.

I guess Malcolm could tell that his message hadn't been well-received. I was kind of flattered that he thought I had the potential to be this front man, but everything else he said disavowed everything that we held near and dear to our hearts. It was like the Wizard of Oz had spoken, and what he said was too ludicrous to take seriously.

Now it was time for us to make our second record. EMI asked us who we wanted to produce it. Without hesitating, we said, "George Clinton," because after our first record, people came up to us and said, "You must be students of the P Funk," which was George's legendary funk group. We were latecomers to the Parliament/Funkadelic experience, and didn't know as much about George as we should have or later would, but we knew that if James Brown was considered the Godfather, then George was the Great God-Uncle of Funk.

So EMI got George on the phone, and we said. "George, we're the Red Hot Chili Peppers, we're from Hollywood, California, we're really hard-rocking motherfuckers, and we think you should produce our record." We sent him our record and our demo tape, and he liked them, and after Flea and Lindy went out to Detroit to meet him, he agreed to produce us. To this day, when people ask me how we got George Clinton, I tell them that we asked him on the phone, but Flea always says, "Twenty-five grand," which was the amount of money that EMI agreed to pay him. I don't believe he did it just for the money. I think he also saw something special and beautiful and remarkable about these four kids who were attempting to keep the spirit of hard-core funk music alive, not in a pretentious or a copycat way but by helping to invent a new genre of funk.

We went to Detroit with about 70 percent of the songs finished. We had "Jungle Man," my ode to Flea, this half-man, half-beast born in the belly of the volcano in Australia and coming to the world and using his thumb as the conductor of thunder on the bass. "American Ghost Dance," "Catholic School Girls Rule," and "Battleship" (whose chorus, "blow job park," was inspired by Cliff's true-life adventures fending off blow-job entreaties at Mulholland rest stops while he practiced his vocal lessons). "Nevermind" and "Sex Rap" were songs that we had on our original demo, and "30 Dirty Birds" was an old Hillel camp song. George's vision was that we would hang out in Detroit with him for about a month before we went into the studio, so there was always room to write more songs.

We would record in George's studio, called United Sound, which was a two-story brick building in the middle of the barren wasteland that inner-city Detroit had become in the mid-'80s. Sometime in the '70s, George had taken over the studio from Motown, and that was where he recorded all those classic Parliament/Funkadelic albums. It was a great studio, with big old analog boards, a beautiful drum room, and separate horn rooms.

First the plan was to move into George's house for about a week, until we rented a house for the band. (We found a house on Wabeek Lake, which was in the most affluent of all suburbs. So it was this whole triangle of opposites, staying with George in the country, rehearsing downtown, where the land couldn't have cost more than ten cents a square foot, and living with rich whiteys on a golf course.) George lived in a contemporary country house on fifty acres in a place called Brooklyn, which was about an hour outside of Detroit. Even though it wasn't the most attractive countryside around (you could hear the nearby Michigan 500 auto races from his property), it was his sanctuary. There were a fishing pond and nice hills, and his house was graced with the presence of George's beautiful wife. She was totally sweet and maternal, not the Vixen of the Funk Superfreak you might think George would be hooked up with, but instead an "Oh God, wish this was my mom" type of woman.

Hillel and I shared a room, Cliff and Flea did the same, Lindy got his own room, and George and his wife were in their master bedroom. The idea was to stay out of the city to get the ball rolling, because we didn't want the sessions to become drug-derailed right away. But as soon as I got there, I felt like I had a horrible case of food poisoning. I started throwing up, my skin turned a strange color, and I couldn't eat. I had no idea what was wrong with me, but Flea said, "You're fucking dope sick." I was so clueless that I didn't even realize I was going through a proper heroin withdrawal.

For some stupid reason, we sent out for five hundred dollars' worth of coke, and Lindy and Hillel and Flea and George and I hoofed it all up. That made me feel great for about a half an hour. Then it was back to no sleep and dope sickness. After a few days, it subsided, and we set shop in George's living room. Drums, guitars, bass, amps—we started playing and getting to know George.

To know George is to love him. He's a huge man with huge hair, but there's this other thing about him that's the size of an elephant—his aura. George is a guy who loves to tell stories, and he's not ashamed to admit to all kinds of weird and kooky and questionable behavior. We became the campfire kids listening to the grand master of psychedelic funk experience. "George, tell us another story

about Sly Stone," and he would be off and running. Besides being a great raconteur, George was teaching us the importance of being regular. He would walk
around the house with a bottle of prune juice, going, "You all know how old I
am. You know how I can go all day and all night. It's because of this, it's because
I'm regular."

George also had a stuffed-animal collection. Where there wasn't furniture, per
se, in the house, there were life-size stuffed animals everywhere, some very old.
I guess he had been a collector, and his fans and friends and family constantly
added pieces, so we were in the middle of this big circus of stuffed animals.

After about a week of living with George, we moved into our house on the
golf course. Then it was time to start making demos in a studio in downtown
Detroit that was owned by a guy called Navarro, who was a colorful but nefarious
old-school pimp/drug dealer/studio owner. He was an older gentleman, with the
lowest, grumbliest, deepest Isaac Hayes/Barry White voice. You couldn't understand a lot of what he said, but you sure could understand what he meant. When
he walked into the room, no matter who was there—girls, the crew, George—he
was the man to respect.

So we started doing the demos. And we also started doing the coke, which was
everywhere. We'd order the Popeye's chicken, and we'd order the cocaine. And if
you could eat the chicken before you got too high on the coke, you'd have dinner.
If not, you didn't care about dinner. Unlike us, George never acted like a weirdo
when he was high on coke. You wouldn't know whether he was on a ton of coke
or not; he just had a really strong constitution.

I'd get all tweaked out and try to finish these songs that I had started, and
sometimes it would work and sometimes I'd go in circles, coming up with these
complex word combinations. So I was writing, and George was listening to these
Hollywood kids playing eccentric hard-core funk music, and loving every minute
of it. I'd show him some lyrics and ask his opinion, and he'd go, "Wow, that's
some outside shit. I love it. Go write another one, we need another verse."

At one point during preproduction, Flea, who had been listening to a lot of
Meters, suggested that we do a cover of their song "Africa." George thought
about it and said, "What if you did the song 'Africa' but had Anthony do a rewrite so it's no longer 'Africa,' but it's your 'Africa,' which is Hollywood?" So I did
the rewrite, and George later fashioned one of his incredible vocal arrangements
behind it. I think he even sang one or two of the lines in that song.

"Freaky Styley" was another interesting George innovation. That was originally an instrumental overture to lead into another piece, but George was so into that swelling, riding groove that he was adamant it had to be its own song, even if the vocal was simple chanting. When we recorded that music, we were all in the control room, listening to that groove, which is still one of the best pieces of music that we ever wrote. George just started chanting, "Fuck 'em, just to see the look on their face. Fuck 'em, just to see the look on their face." We all joined in, and it was a spontaneous bit of musical combustion. The other vocal in that song, "Say it out loud, I'm Freaky Styley and I'm proud," was one of those born-in-the-moment colloquialisms. At that time we called everything that was cool "Freaky Styley." A dance, a girl, a drumbeat, anything. When this whole process was finished and we were sitting around the kitchen table going, "What should we call this album?" Cliff looked up and said, "Why don't we just call it what we call everything else? *Freaky Styley.*"

After a little while in Navarro's studio, we finalized the arrangements, and I had some new lyrics ready to go. George had a unique style of producing. It wasn't a lot of super-refined high-tuning, reacting to every kick-drum pattern. It was more from-the-heart producing. George was a master at hearing backup vocal parts, especially for esoteric parts of the song, where you wouldn't normally hear vocals. If you listen to the Funkadelic records or the Parliament records, the vocal arrangements within the body of music are masterpieces unto themselves. So he started hearing that stuff in our songs, and we were open to anything. If he said, "I want to do a five-person vocal at this part in the song," we jumped for joy.

We shifted over to United Sound and started recording the basic tracks. We always put down a scratch vocal, because that was the era when you'd record a scratch and then try to beat it. We didn't have comping vocals, where you'd sing a song twenty times and cut and paste the best syllables. George put me in the middle of the room; not off in some other room, so I felt like a part of the band, which was a wise thing to do, since everyone had always said, "Oh, the Chili Peppers are great live, but you'll never capture their zany onstage chemistry in the studio."

During the recording process, we started getting an unusual visitor. His name was Louie, and he was a pale and bald Middle Easterner. Turned out he was George's personal coke-delivery guy. After a few visits, it was clear that George was into this guy for a lot of money, but George was unflappable. Louie began showing up, with a couple of henchmen, and he'd say, in his slow thick accent,

"George, I'm real serious, man, you're going to have to make good before I can give you anything else. I'm running a business here."

George would go, "Louie, look around. Do you think I'm strapped for cash? In this business, you get paid when you get paid. When I get paid, you're the first motherfucker who gets paid after me."

Louie would look pained. "George, I've heard that before. I didn't bring these guys for show, and if they have to hurt somebody . . ."

George never blinked an eye, because he had a plan. He knew Louie was fascinated by the music business, so he intuited that making Louie a part of the whole process would ensure a steady flow of coke. Finally, George promised Louie that he could make his vocal debut on the album.

I was thinking, "Okay, I trust George, I know that everything's happening for a reason here, but I'll be damned if I'm going to let this motherfucker on my record. This shit is sacred." George told me, "Don't worry, everyone will be happy. He'll be on the record, and you will not mind." George was right. At the very beginning of "Yertle the Turtle," you hear a weird, out-of-context voice come in and say, "Look at the, turtle go, bro," and then the song goes into a syncopated funk beat. That was Louie's debut, and that was what made him happy enough not to hurt somebody. The longer the sessions went on, the more regularly he would show up with the blow, because he was wanting his fifteen minutes in the damn spotlight.

Right before it was time for me to go in and do the final vocals, I decided I wasn't going to do any cocaine for two weeks, which is like deciding to be celibate when you're living in a brothel. My decision had nothing to do with sobriety, because even though I was twenty-three, I was still an emotionally troubled youth. I just didn't want to get back to Hollywood and go, "What happened? I had my chance making a record with George Clinton, and I fucked up." The two-week period was the time that was allotted for my vocals. I guess I realized it was harder to sing when you've got coke dripping down the back of your throat.

One of the reasons I was so concerned about my vocals was that during the preproduction process, Flea started to play a Sly Stone song, "If You Want Me to Stay," on the bass. Hillel and Cliff got into it, and we decided to cover that song, which was daunting to me, because I can sing anything I write, but another man's tune is always a challenge—let alone one by Sly Stone, one of the most original vocalists in terms of phrasing.

George must have sensed my uneasiness. "You have this in the bag, don't even worry about it. I know what you're capable of," he reassured me. Then he invited me to his house for the weekend to work on the song. First I decided to visit my mom for a few days, and I took the tape of the song with me and practiced it over and over again. On the way back from Grand Rapids, I stopped at George's house. We talked about the song and we practiced it, then we took these long strolls through his property. I didn't even see it, but he was quietly schooling me. We'd be talking about anything under the sun, and he was subconsciously building my confidence and steering me toward getting comfortable and creating magic in the studio. I think he realized that Hillel was a tremendously talented guitar player, Flea knew exactly what he was doing on bass, and Cliff was an ace drummer, but I was this guy with a lyrical ability who wasn't so sure of his voice.

Early in the morning, we'd go out fishing in his pond. His whole demeanor changed when he fished. He was no longer the rabble-rousing toastmaster of the funk universe, but more of an introspective, quirky man who had some vast experience. Fishing was his meditation. And he didn't care what we caught, he was eating it. Bluegills, sunfish, catfish, whatever that lake was spitting out was going in the frying pan. We'd catch them and bring them back, and his wife would cook them for breakfast.

By the time I left his place, I felt good about the song. George mentored me even during the recording process. He had a mike set up inside his booth, and he'd send up shout-outs or sing along. We'd be out there recording the basic tracks and hear this great voice coming through the little transistorized speaker. When we set up the vocal booth and it was just me doing my vocals, George came into the studio, put on headphones, and sang and danced along with me while I was singing. He was like a big brother to me, thoughtful, totally sensitive, and understanding of the colorful and zany place where we were coming from: I wanted never to let him down.

We finished the record; and in our minds, it so far surpassed anything we thought we could have done that we were thinking we were on the road to enormity. Some EMI execs made a trip out to Detroit to hear some of the material. We played them a few tracks, and instead of them going, "You guys are going to be huge," they said nothing. I'm dancing and singing along, going nuts, and they're like "Well, we'll see what we can do with this." Of course; we're talking about a record company that did not have an inkling of the awareness necessary to take something different and original and recognize its worth and introduce it to the world. They were looking for another bank like Roxette.

We went back to L.A. feeling absolutely accomplished and more experienced, and then everyone jumped back into his madness. By this time, Jennifer's mother had moved from Cahuenga to an apartment complex in Pasadena. Right next door to that was an abandoned building, so Jennifer and I started squatting there. The hot and cold water still worked, and we ran an extension cord into the building so we could listen to music, and we set up a bed and some candles.

That's when I really started getting into heroin sex. I realized that if you were in love with somebody and you were sexually inspired to begin with, being high on heroin could amplify the experience tenfold, because you could have sex all night and not be able to come but still be interested. I remember having these marathon sex encounters with Jennifer on that bed, thinking, "Life doesn't get any better than this. I'm in a band, I've got a couple of dollars in my pocket. I've got a beautiful, sweet hot, sexy, crazy little girlfriend, a roof over my head, and some dope."

Those feelings would disappear, and the next day I'd be off on a run. Jennifer would do her best to deal with my insanity, as she was slowly working on her own. Around the time I got back from Detroit, I intensified my relationship with a girl named Kim Jones. My friend Bob Forest had this monstrous crush on Kim, but she had jilted him (he promptly wrote a song about her with the chorus "Why don't you blow me and the rest of the band?"). He was still obsessed with her, and he used to take me to her apartment in Echo Park, and we'd knock on her door to see if she was around.

Bob would recite her many virtues—she was brilliant and beautiful, she studied in China, she wrote for the *L.A. Weekly*, she was from Tennessee, plus, she was a lesbian, because she had left Bob for this really hot girl. Turns out she wasn't a lesbian, but all of her other virtues were true. As soon as I met her, I knew we'd be best friends. We were both Scorpios, and there was never any sexual tension between us.

In some ways, Kim was a female equivalent to Hillel, because there was no crime you could commit that she would not forgive you for, no heinous act of selfish behavior that she would not try to find the good side of you behind. Of course, she was also a complete mess. Intelligent but dizzy, a drug addict, codependent, an enabler and a caretaker, just a beautiful, warm kindred spirit to me. I started to become closer and closer to Kim, because she was a source of love and comfort and friendship and companionship and like-mindedness without any of the difficulties of a girlfriend. I never lost my sexual attraction to Jennifer; the longer I was with her, the better the sex got, but I was not a great boyfriend. If I said I'd be home in an hour, I might stroll in three days later. Today, if someone did that to me, I'd have a heart attack, but when you're a kid, you don't know any better.

Kim didn't care if I left for three days at a time, so there was no downside to hanging out with her. It was never like "You motherfucker, you looked at that girl, you didn't come home, you spent all the money." Kim *expected* me to spend all the money, look at all the other girls, and disappear. One time I went over to Kim's house, and she wasn't there. In a fit of desperation, I grabbed her toaster oven and traded it for a bag of dope. When she got home, she was unfazed. "That's okay, we'll get another one."

Before long, I moved in with Kim, and our daily mission became getting high. She was getting some cash inflow—disability checks because her dad had died, checks from the *L.A. Weekly*, or checks from her mom at home in Tennessee. We'd cash them and meet some French guy or some Russian guy on a corner in Hollywood and buy the heroin, and if we had any money left over, we'd score some coke. Soon we both had a habit. Hillel was also using, and he had a crazy girlfriend named Maggie, who was a friend of Kim's, so we'd have a lot of small drug parties.

From time to time the band would go on tours to San Francisco. We were still young enough and not so damaged that we could play well, even though we had these drug habits. In September 1985 we played two shows with Run-DMC, one in San Francisco and one in L.A. The LA. show was at the Palladium, and besides opening for Oingo Boingo, it was our biggest show to date. Sold out. Of course, the night before the show, I went on a drug binge, so I showed up for the gig hammered on coke and heroin. The band was furious at me, but somehow I managed to pull it together and made it onstage. That show was notable for two things. About halfway through the show, George Clinton came rocking onto the stage, and he and I started doing a full, funky ballroom dance to our jams. He injected a fat dose of color and love and energy and meaning into that show.

It was also memorable because shortly before George came out, I decided to interrupt the set and give a heartfelt, ten-minute long rambling discourse on the dangers of doing drugs. I certainly hadn't planned the speech, but something came over me as I was looking down at my black-and-blue arms, and I just started rapping.

"If you haven't ever put a needle in your arm, don't ever do it. Let me tell you from experience that you don't have to do this, that's where I am right now, and it's horrible, and I don't want anyone to ever have to feel like I'm feeling right now. Let me do the suffering for you, because this is something that no one needs to subject themselves to. If you're doing this, okay, just do it, but don't ever think that you're going to be the same once you've gone this far."

I proceeded to explain, in detail, why it was a big mistake to shoot drugs. I kept going, I couldn't hang up on it. Meanwhile, the band was shooting me looks like "Oh my God, this fucking idiot. " After the show, I was afraid to face the guys. I thought they'd hate my guts for saying that stuff and being a hypocritical moron. In the middle of everyone giving me dirty looks, my friend Pete Weiss, the drummer from Thelonious Monster, came backstage.

"Swan, I've heard you say a lot of stuff from the stage, but that was the coolest shit you ever said," he gushed. "That was riveting, you had every single ear in the place. They knew you were a fucked-up bastard but also that you cared and you were just trying to share some love. Don't let that band of yours fool you, you did the right thing tonight."

A month later, when it was time to tour the U.S. for *Freaky Styley*, my speechifying hadn't changed anything for us. Both Hillel and I were strung out, but for the first time, I noticed that he wasn't doing so well. He seemed weak, and while I was able to bounce right back from a run, he didn't seem to have that Israeli fire stoking like he always had in the past. It became evident when we started our usual on-tour wrestling diversion. Hillel and I had teamed up; I was his manager, and he was set to wrestle Flea. Even though Flea was real solid, Hillel was bigger, and he had massive tree-trunk legs, like a tall Pan. We had a two-week buildup to this match, and when they wrestled in a hotel room one night, Flea destroyed him in as long as it takes to grab somebody and hurl him to the ground and pin him mercilessly to his death—ten seconds. I could tell that Hillel had no inner core of strength; he had been robbed by his addiction of that life force that allows you to at least defend yourself. It was a sad moment.

Hillel and I didn't do heroin on the road, so we would drink bottles of Jagermeister, because that gave us the feeling closest to a heroin high. He'd always tease me that I was a sloppy drunk, because I'd get drunk and take off all my clothes in the motel and walk down the hall and knock on people's doors, whereas he'd get drunk and act suave.

Leaving to go on tour was an ordeal for me then, mainly because of my volatile relationship with Jennifer. Even though I was staying mainly at Kim's house, Jennifer was still my girlfriend. Jennifer became convinced that Kim and I were having sex. One day she came by Kim's house, and Kim and I were sound asleep, naked and cuddling up. I know it would look like a bad scene if you were the girlfriend of the boy in the bed, but we were just having a nice drug high. No romance, just friendship.

Jennifer didn't quite see it that way. Kim and I woke up to Jennifer shattering the bedroom window. She wouldn't come in with a good, old-fashioned baseball bat; she made her entrance with an elaborately carved and painted bird-head cane from the Mayan lands. After she broke through the window, she proceeded to try to kill me with the cane.

When it was time to leave on a tour, I'd avoid Jennifer for days before, because I knew some kind of hatchet was going to be thrown at me. One time I was early to the breakout place, which was the EMI parking lot on Sunset. I was with Kim, and we were both completely high on heroin, sitting in the front seat of some car.

I guess in my half-awake drug reverie, I had somehow unbuttoned Kim's blouse because I wanted to see her milky-white chest. I may even have been sucking on her nipple or holding her tit when, BAM, BAM, BAM, there was the loud sound of something rapping against the window. I looked up and it was Jennifer.

"You motherfucker, you've been gone for days, and I knew that this was going on," she screamed.

"Jennifer, believe me, I may have had her shirt open, but I've never had sex with this girl, she's just my friend," I protested,

"You said you were coming home three days ago, and you're leaving for three weeks, and by the way, I'm pregnant," she screamed.

Meanwhile, the dispute had escalated to the sidewalk, and Jennifer was trying to kill me or at least scratch my eyeballs out.

"Jennifer, you see, this is why I don't come home for three days before I leave, because I don't want to get hit and you're too hard to deal with and I know you're not pregnant, because you just had your period and I haven't had sex with you since you had your period, so don't try to tell me you're fucking pregnant," I tried to reason with her, but she was a bull. Not that I can blame her.

There was no stopping her, and Kim was getting caught in the crossfire, so I ducked inside the EMI building. Jennifer followed me in and proceeded to pull my hair and scratch at my face. I was still high out of my mind and trying not to lose an eyeball or a tuft of hair, so I started running through the halls.

Jennifer chased me. For some reason, I had a bag of cookies, so I started throwing the cookies at her, to keep her far enough away that she couldn't connect with any of her punches. She grabbed some blunt instrument, so I put my foot out to keep her from hitting me with it, and she went further nuts, if that was possible.

"Don't you try to kick me in my stomach just because I'm pregnant. I know you want to get rid of the baby," she screamed.

Thankfully, Lindy came to my rescue. "Jennifer, we're only going away for a couple of weeks. I know how much this boy loves you. You're all he ever talks about." Somehow we made it out on tour in one piece.

Despite our touring, EMI never got behind the album, and they wouldn't give us any money for a video. That didn't stop us. Lindy had one of the first home-video cameras, and he shot footage on our tours and took that footage and cut it into a BBC documentary that had filmed us lip-synching "Jungle Man" at the Club Lingerie in Hollywood. He attached two VCRs in some back room at EMI, did an edit, and we had a video for a hundred dollars. Later, our good friend Dick Rude shot a video for "Catholic School Girls Rule" that featured a shot of me singing from the cross, among other blasphemous things, so that video got played only in clubs.

When we weren't touring, I was pretty much staying high. It was like Ground-hog Day every single day, exactly the same. Kim and I would wake up and have to look out of her window to see which direction the freeway traffic was going to determine whether it was dusk or dawn. Then we'd hustle up some money, get the drugs, shoot up, and go for a walk around Echo Park Lake, holding hands, in a complete haze. If I was supposed to show up to rehearsal, I would probably miss it. If I did show up, I'd be too stoned to do anything, so I'd nod out in the corner of the room or pass out on the loading dock.

Every day Kim and I would get high, and right in the middle of the euphoria, we'd vow that tomorrow we were going to get off that stuff. The next day we'd start the whole process over again.

By now a lot of our friends were strung out on dope, and often the only time we'd see each other was when we were in our cars waiting to cop. We were each scoring from the same French guy, so we'd page him, and he'd call back and say, "Meet at Beverly and Sweezer in ten minutes." We'd drive down there, and on one corner we'd see Hillel and Maggie in their car and on another corner we'd see Bob Forest and his girlfriend. The dealer would go from car to car, and Kim and I would always get served last, because we were the most likely either to not have the right amount of money or to owe money; but we were patient and willing to take whatever we could get. Then we'd go back, and I'd be in charge of splitting the bag and loading the syringes. Because I knew I had a much greater tolerance to heroin than Kim, unbeknownst to her, I would always take 75 percent of the bag and give her the rest. Ironically, that practice almost killed her.

It happened at Hillel's one night. He had moved into an infamous Hollywood haunt called the Milagro Castle, right off Gower. Marilyn Monroe had once lived there, but now it was populated with drug dealers and punk rockers. One night after we scored some China White, Kim and Hillel and I went to his place to do the drugs. Hillel had his bindle, and Kim had our bindle, and for some reason Hillel offered to share his with Kim; so I could have a whole bindle to myself. I was in such a frenzy over doing my stuff that it didn't dawn on me that Hillel would actually split his bag fifty-fifty with Kim.

The high was amazing, and I remember Hillel and I going into the kitchen and sharing some Lucky Charms, dancing and talking and generally exuberant about how potent the drugs were. Then I realized that we hadn't heard a peep out of Kim for a while. It dawned on me that she'd taken much more than she ever had before.

I rushed into the living room and saw Kim sitting upright in the chair, basically dead. She was cold and white, and her lips were blue, and she wasn't breathing. Suddenly, I remembered all the techniques for reviving someone from a heroin overdose that Blackie had taught me when I was thirteen years old. I picked her up, dragged her into the shower, turned the cold water on her, and began giving her mouth-to-mouth resuscitation. I was frantically slapping her face and screaming, "Kim, don't fucking die on me. I don't want to have to call your mother and tell her that her daughter's gone. I don't want to have breakfast alone tomorrow."

She started going in and out of consciousness. I was shaking her like a rag doll, screaming, "Stay awake!" Hillel had called 911, and when the paramedics showed up, I jumped out the window and ran away because I had outstanding warrants out for my arrest for moving violations. Hillel went to the hospital with her, and they got her up and running. About twelve hours later, I called her room in the hospital.

"Come and get me. Those motherfuckers ruined my high," she said. "I'm sick. We need to go cop." Amazingly enough, it never occurred to me that there might have been a problem there.

From time to time, I'd make halfhearted attempts to get clean. One of them was at the urging of Flea, who suggested that I might want to get off the stuff for a while and reconnect with what we were doing as bandmates. He was living in this cute apartment on Carmen Street, and he proposed that I come and kick on his futon. I showed up with a couple of bottles of NyQuil and said, "Flea, this is going to be ugly. I'm not going to be able to sleep and I'm going to be in serious pain. Are you sure you want me in your house?"

He was willing, so we listened to music and I kicked. After a white, Flea said I should get an apartment in the building, so I did. Of course, Jennifer promptly moved in with me. Unfortunately, a new dope dealer named Dominique, who had usurped all the other French dealers, lived only about a block away.

Then it was time to go out on another tour leg. The night before, Jennifer and I were having one of those marathon sex/heroin sessions. We'd have sex for a couple of hours, and then we'd fight for an hour about me leaving the next day, and she'd be screaming as loudly during the sex as she was when she was yelling at me for going on tour. It was hard to distinguish when we were fighting and when we were having sex. So a neighbor who hated me called the cops on what he thought was a domestic violence thing.

"We got a domestic violence call here," the one cop announced,

"What are you talking about, domestic violence? It's me and my girlfriend, and that's that," I said.

"Can we come in and take a look around?" the cop asked.

I was saying no when Jennifer came to the door. She was obviously not abused, but she was hotheaded and still screaming at me. One cop was trying to poke his head in the door and shine his flashlight on Jennifer. In the meantime, the other cop had run a check on me and found the outstanding warrants, so they arrested me on the spot and dragged me out in handcuffs, half naked. All the neighbors were watching, convinced I was getting arrested for beating up a girl. Jennifer and I were screaming at each other as they took me away. It was just a bad episode of *COPS*. Thankfully, Lindy bailed me out, and we left on tour the next day, but during that period of my life, you had to plan on something like that happening before a tour.

Or when we got back from a tour. We were returning from a *Freaky Styley* tour leg when I ran into Bob Forest, who was waiting for us at the EMI parking lot. Bob was the classic shit stirrer of the day. If he could stir the pot, if he could drop a hint, if he could make drama and conflict, he would. He loved it because, God knows, he was falling apart at the seams, and I'm sure it took some of the attention away from him.

Bob knew about my indiscretions on the road, but I was surprised when he came up to me and said, "Okay, you're out there doing all that crazy stuff. Don't you ever worry about Jennifer?" That was the last thing I would have worried about. In my mind, she would never do anything to betray me, even though I was cheating on her right, left, and center.

He smirked. "I've got some bad news for you, buddy."

My heart started pounding in my chest.

My friend, the unusual hour is upon us when I'm going to share with you information you might not be too keen on," he continued. "Maybe a certain someone wasn't so loyal to you while you were away, either."

"You're crazy," I stammered. "Jennifer would rather cut her own wrists than take interest in another man. She loves me with every cell in her body. She's physiologically and emotionally incapable of giving herself to another man."

"No, it's possible. Because I have proof."

I threatened to crack his skull open on the pavement if he didn't tell me all he knew. Finally, he spilled the beans. Jennifer had slept with Chris Fish, the keyboard player of Fishbone, one of our brother L.A. groups, while I was out on tour. But it still didn't compute to me. I could have seen if she'd slept with Angelo Moore, who was the good-looking lead singer. What girl didn't want to fuck Angelo? But Chris Fish—a guy with bad dreadlocks and worse fashion sense?

I was mortified. It hadn't mattered that I'd slept with a hundred girls on the road in the last year. This killed me. The reality of my friend and my girlfriend doing this while I was away was incomprehensible demoralization to the tenth degree. I felt paralyzed. I probably gave myself cancer at that moment. But what could I do?

For some reason, I went to my father's house and formulated a plan. First I picked up the phone and called Chris. "Chris, did you fuck my girlfriend?"

There was a giant pause, and then a slow and stunned voice said, "Oh man, Bob spilled the beans."

I took a deep breath.

"You're not going to come after me, are you?"

"I'm not going to come after you, but you are not my friend, and stay the fuck away from me," I warned. End of conversation. He wasn't my problem. Jennifer was.

I called her. "Jennifer, I know what happened."

"Nothing happened," she protested.

"Nope, I know exactly what happened. I've spoken to Chris, and we are finished."

She started protesting, claiming Chris was lying, but I was adamant. "We're finished. Don't ever come around me, I hate your guts. Good-bye forever."

I hung up, and I meant it. It was time to move on. This sense of excitement came over me, and I called up Flea, and he and I and Pete Weiss went out driving. I stood on the top of the car as it was rolling down the streets of Hollywood, screaming, "I'm a free man. I'm a free man."

We had toured on and off till the spring of '86, and now it was time to start thinking about our next album. One of the producers we were considering was Keith Levene, who had been in Public Image Ltd. I knew Keith and thought he was a great guy, but I also knew he was a heroin addict, so we were in for a convoluted experience. But that sounded great to me, since I was a mess. The more convoluted the landscape was, the less obvious I would seem as a fuckup.

EMI had given us a budget of five grand for the demo, and that seemed pretty high to me. There was no way a demo should cost that much. When I brought it up with Hillel and Keith, I found out that they'd earmarked two thousand dollars for drugs to make the tape. I don't think Flea agreed to it, and I know Cliff had no idea; he was just caught up in the maelstrom of insanity.

I was late for the session, and as I pulled up at the studio, I wondered if they had been serious about putting aside funds to get high. The first thing I saw when I walked in that room was a mountain of cocaine and a small molehill of heroin. Hillel was fucking gizacked. They told me that the first fifteen hundred dollars' worth of drugs had already been consumed; so I started scooping and grabbing and snatching and saturating and got so loaded I was in no shape to be part of a creative process.

Poor Cliff was off in the corner of the studio, tinkering with what was then a

brand-new device, a drum machine. You would hit the pads to create a prepro-
grammed drum sound, and you could record your own sounds so you could play
the drums with whatever sound you wanted. Cliff's favorite was a baby crying. It
was a low-tech device, but Cliff was fiddling with it as obsessively as we were with
the drugs, laughing in a strange, nervous fashion. He looked at me and said, "I
could play with this thing for ten years. This is like a whole band within itself." I
remember thinking, "That's what he wants to do. He's sick of this circus, and he's
looking at this machine and seeing his future."

It was obvious that Cliff's heart was no longer in the band. He didn't quit, but
we sensed that he didn't want to continue, so Flea visited him and gave him the
bad news. He took it pretty hard and had bitter feelings for a couple of years. But
then Jack Irons, our original drummer, decided to come back to the band, which
was as much of a shocker to me as when Hillel came back. Something must have
happened with What Is This to shake Jack's loyalty, because he was not the kind
of person to leave something for a better career opportunity. Whatever, he missed
us and he loved us and he wanted to play music with us. So he came back and we
began to write music again as the original foursome.

Then someone else came back into my life. About a month had gone by since
I split with Jennifer. I was still shooting a lot of heroin and cocaine, not learning
anything. I wasn't growing as a person. I wasn't setting goals or working on my
character defects. I was just a fucked-up drug addict.

One night about three in the morning, there was a knock at my door on Carmen Street. It was Jennifer. She was working as a go-go dancer at a club, and it
was obvious that she bad come right from work, because she was dressed up in a
thousand different colors, with feathers and boots and chains and crazy makeup
that must have taken her a few hours to apply.

"Please just let me in. I miss you. I miss you," she begged. "No chance," I
said. "Just go. Don't get me in trouble, don't start yelling. I don't need cops at
my house."

I closed the door and went back to sleep. When I woke up, I saw Jennifer curled
up on the welcome mat outside my door, sound asleep. This went on for the next
few weeks: Every night she'd come up and either knock or curl up and go to sleep
on my doorstep. I even started going out my kitchen window and climbing down
a huge lemon tree that was right outside (and which came in handy when I scored
some Persian heroin, which was oil-based and had to be cooked up in lemon juice).

One night I succumbed. I can't remember if I gave in to her love or if I was so bad off that I needed twenty bucks or if she came offering drugs or whatever sad, sick, and bizarre circumstance it was, but I let her in and we picked up where we left off. High as kites together, back into the mix of a totally dysfunctional but passionate relationship. So passionate that it would be documented on a video that became a cult classic in the underground dub scene of L.A.

It happened one night at the Roxy. Some people had organized a benefit for Sea Shepherd, a hard-core version of Greenpeace, and the Chili Peppers were asked to play. The theme of the night was that every band and would cover a Jimi Hendrix song. There was a great bill that included Mike Watt, our friend Tree, and Fishbone, so we were psyched to play.

When I showed up at the gig, Fishbone was about to go on. Earlier there had been some discussion of Jennifer singing backup with Fishbone, but I kiboshed it. "You are not going to go onstage with *that* guy." Fishbone took the stage, and I made my way to the balcony. When I looked down, there was Jennifer onstage. That was not good. Now I had to make her pay for disrespecting me like that in front of my friends. At the same time, I kept my focus, because what really mattered to me was that I sing "Foxy Lady" well. Right before we were scheduled to go onstage, this young hippie girl walked backstage. She had brown hair, was really pretty, and had these huge tits poking through her tank top that couldn't help but be in everybody's face.

A lightbulb went off in my head. I went over and whispered in her ear: "We're going to do 'Foxy Lady,' and when we get to the end of the song, when we're freaking out onstage, I want you to come out and dance with me naked." Two can play the same game. The hippie goddess agreed. We went out and killed "Foxy Lady." It was like our band could have levitated. The drums were happening. Flea was digging in. Hillel was orbiting. I was giving it everything I had.

I almost forgot there was supposed to be a surprise guest. We came to the end of the song, and this slinky young hippie walked onstage. She hadn't gotten completely naked, but she was topless, and her big tits were just *to*-ing and *fro*-ing across the stage. She came up to me and started to do her hippie shimmy next to me. Norwood, the bass player from Fishbone, came out to join us, and we sandwiched this semi-naked girl.

Suddenly, a figure flew onstage as if shot out of a cannon. It was Jennifer. She grabbed Norwood, who's a big man, and tossed him aside like a rag doll. Then she grabbed the girl and literally threw her off the stage. Meanwhile, the band kept going. I realized that I was about to become the recipient of some serious pain. By then I had wound up on the floor on my back, singing the outro. And there was Jennifer, coming at me with fists and feet, punching and connecting and going for my crotch with her boots. I was trying to block the punches, all the while not missing a note. She kicked my ass till I finished the song and somehow escaped and ran off into the night.

Between my dysfunctional girlfriend and my dysfunctional platonic friend and my dysfunctional self, my life continued on a downward spiral. We had settled on a producer for our third album, Michael Beinhom. He was a very intelligent fellow from New York who was into all of the same music that we were and had produced a hit by Herbie Hancock called "Rockit." But I was stuck in my Groundhog year, waking up every morning to the same gray reality of copping to feel right. I went on another horrible heroin run with Kim and stopped being productive. I was withering away, mentally, spiritually, physically, creatively— everything was fading out. Sometimes doing heroin was nice and dreamy and eu- phoric and carefree, almost romantic-feeling. In reality, I was dying and couldn't quite see that from being so deep in my own forest.

The few times I showed up at rehearsal, I wasn't bringing anything to the ta- ble. I didn't have the same drive or desire to come up with ideas and lyrics. They were still in me, but the process was thwarted, numbed out. We'd written some music for the third album, maybe four or five songs, but we needed a lot more. The whole band was suffering from Hillel and me being on drugs, but I was the much more obvious candidate to put the onus on, because I was literally asleep at rehearsal.

One day I showed up at rehearsal, and Jack and Hillel and Flea, who probably loved me more than any three guys on earth, said, "Anthony, we're kicking you out of the band. We want to play music and you obviously don't, so you have to go. We're going to get a different singer and go on, so you're out of here."

I had a brief moment of clarity when I saw that they had every right in the world to fire me. It was an obvious move, like cutting off your damn foot because it was gangrened, so the rest of your body wouldn't die. I just wanted to be re- membered and acknowledged for those two or three years that I had been in the Red Hot Chili Peppers as a founding member, a guy who started something, a guy who made two records; whatever else came after that was theirs. Part of me was genuine in letting go of the band. But what made it so easy for me to accept was that now I knew I had zero responsibilities, and I could go off with Kim and get loaded.

Much to their amazement, I shrugged and said, "You guys are right. I apologize for not contributing what I should have been contributing this whole time. It's a crying shame, but I understand completely, and I wish you guys the best of luck."

And I left.

Once I didn't have anywhere to report to, it went from worse to worse than worse. Kim and I went for it. We were getting more desperate, and we owed too much money to the drug dealers around Hollywood, so we started walking from her home, which was not far from downtown Los Angeles, to known drug neighborhoods, mainly Sixth and Union. We went down and started introducing ourselves to these different street characters. I met a pretty talented hustler right off the bat. He was this scurvy street urchin, an out-of-control white-trash drug addict who was moving deftly in the downtown Latino drug world. He became our liaison to all the other connections. He still lived with his parents in this little wooden house. The kid was covered with track marks and abscesses and disease from head to toe, but he was a master of the downtown corners. Kim and I were always such petty punkass low-budget buyers that he would always do us right. We trusted this guy. We'd buy bindles of cocaine and bindles of heroin and walk a couple of blocks into these residential neighborhoods and shoot up right there on the street. We still had an air of invincibility and invisibility, so we thought we couldn't be touched.

About a week after I was terminated from the band, I had a defining moment of sadness. I was talking to Bob Forest, and he told me that my ex-band had been nominated for L.A. band of the year at the first annual *L.A. Weekly* Music Awards. For our circle, that was similar to getting nominated for an Oscar, so it was pretty exciting. Bob asked me if I was going to go to the ceremony. I told him I wasn't talking to the guys, so I couldn't imagine showing up.

But the awards show happened to be at the Variety Arts Theatre, a classic, old venue right smack downtown. Coincidentally, I was in the same neighborhood that night, trying to hustle more drugs for my money than anyone wanted to give me. I was down to my last ten dollars, which is not a good feeling, because on a night like that, you want to be inebriated, and instead I was barely high. I remember doing a speedball with some gang dealer guys when I realized the *L.A. Weekly* event was going on.

I stumbled into the lobby of the theater in a bit of a haze. It seemed unusually dark inside, and there was hardly anyone there, because the show was in progress. The doors that led down the aisles of the theater were open, so I leaned up against one of those doors and started scanning the audience for my old bandmates. Sure enough, they were in the front. I hadn't been there for more than a minute when I ran into someone I knew who said, "Man, you shouldn't be here. This is going to be really sad for you."

Just then they announced the winner of L.A. band of the year: "The Red Hot Chili Peppers." "We won! We won the damn award!" I cheered to myself. I looked over at the guys, and they all had big grins and a pep in their step as they marched up onstage in their fancy suits and hats. Each guy got his award and made a little speech like "Thank you, *L.A. Weekly*. Thank you, L.A. We rock. We'll see you next year." Not one of them mentioned our brother Anthony who did this with us and who deserved a part of this award. It was like I had never been there those last three years. Not a fucking peep about the guy they had kicked out two weeks before. No "Rest in peace," no "May God save his soul," no nothing.

It was a poetically tragic, bizarre, and surreal moment for me. I understood getting kicked out; but I could not understand why on earth they didn't have the heart to give me a shout from the podium. I was too numb to feel sorry for myself. I was just trying desperately not to think about how bad I had fucked up and trying to escape any responsibility or reckoning. So I just said, "Ah, fuck them," to myself and tried to borrow five dollars from someone in the lobby so I could go out and continue to get high.

Money for drugs was a real issue for us, but one day Kim got a big check, and we went out and got a ton of smack and went back to her place to do it. I got so high and felt so good that I said to Kim, "I got to get off this stuff." Sometimes when you get that high, you think you're going to feel that good for the rest of your life, and you actually believe you can get off dope; you can't imagine that euphoria ever going away.

I'm going to call my mom, go back to Michigan, and get on methadone," I told Kim. As far as I knew, that was the cure for addiction.

We were drooling and way too high for anyone's good, but Kim thought it was a great idea, so I picked up the phone and dialed my mom. "You're not going to believe this, but I have a pretty bad heroin problem here, and I'd like to come back to Michigan and get on methadone, but I don't have a penny to my name," I said.

I'm sure my mom was in shock, but she immediately tried to act together and rational. She must have sensed that my life was on the line and that if she flipped out and got judgmental, I would never come home. Of course, if she could have seen the way we were living, she would have had to be committed to a mental asylum.

She made the arrangements, and the next day the ticket arrived, but we couldn't stop getting high. The day of the flight came, but we had been getting high all night and when it was time to go to the airport, we were incapable of getting it together. I called up my mom and made up some stupid lie about why I couldn't leave that day, but I'd change the ticket to the next day. That went on and on, and each time it was "I'm coming tomorrow, I'm coming tomorrow," while Kim and I were up in her house getting plastered.

Finally, I made up my mind to leave, but I had to do one last run and get really good and loaded right before the flight so I could be high the whole way home. The morning of the latest flight came around, and we went downtown to buy a bunch of balloons of dope and some coke.

Kim was driving an old Falcon that she had borrowed, and I kept jumping in and out of the car, looking for good deals on the street, filling the pockets of my trench coat with heroin, cocaine, spoons, cotton, syringes, you name it. I was out on one of the downtown streets when I saw someone that could be useful to me on the other side of the street. I crossed in the middle of the block, and before I knew it, a cop barked out, "Hey, buddy, you in the trench coat. Why don't you come over here?"

Out of the corner of my eye, I saw Kim parked behind the wheel of the Falcon. She slumped down and started moaning.

I weighed 120 pounds if I was lucky, and my hair was one big helmet of matted hair, like an elephant ear. I was wearing this trench coat that was hanging off my body, and my skin was a strange shade of yellow and green. I also had on canvas high-top sneakers, which were black and red and filled with marker drawings that I'd done. On the top of one of the shoes, I had drawn a pretty nice Star of David about the size of a silver dollar. Oh, and I had dark glasses on.

I was so busted.

By now the cop had backup.

"We saw you jaywalking back there, and you look a little suspicious," the first cop said. "Why don't you go ahead and show us your ID?"

"Uh, I don't have an ID, but my name is Anthony Kiedis, and I'm actually late getting to the airport to get on a plane and go to see my mom . . ." I stammered.

While this interrogation was going on, the other cop was systematically searching me inch by inch, starting with my sneakers and socks.

I was telling the first cop my date of birth and place of birth and address, and he was writing it all down, keeping me distracted while his partner searched me. The partner was up to my pants, going through the pockets, pulling out whatever scraps of paper and junk I had with me. He even went into the mini pocket, and I was getting more and more nervous because he was getting closer to my side pocket, which was packed with bad news.

"Does this jacket have an inside pocket?" the second cop asked. I started stalling and showed them my plane ticket and whatever else I had in the inside pockets.

Just as he had exhausted all the other pockets and was about to start in on the ones that were loaded, his partner looked down at my sneakers and said, "Are you Jewish? Why do you have the Star of David on your sneaker?"

I looked up and saw his name tag. It read COHEN.

"No, but my best friend in the world is Jewish, and we both have a thing for the Star of David," I said.

Cohen looked at his partner, who was about to find my stash, and said, "Kowalski, let him go."

"What?" Kowalski said.

"Let me talk to him for a second," Cohen said, and pulled me aside. "Look, you shouldn't be down here," he whispered to me. "Whatever you're up to, it's not working for you, so why don't you go get on that plane and get out of here. I don't ever want see you down here again."

I nodded and, as soon as the light changed, ran across the street, and that was the morning I made it to the airport.

By the rime the flight arrived in Michigan I was still loaded on the drugs. I saw my mother in the waiting area and walked up to her, but she looked right past me because I looked like I had stepped out of a grave.

"Hi, Mom," I said meekly. The look of shock and horror and fear and sadness and disbelief on her face was unbearable. "Let's go straight to the clinic," I said.

We drove to the building and asked a worker where the methadone clinic was. They told us that the state of Michigan had discontinued the use of methadone six months prior to my arrival. That was really, really bad news for me, because normally, I would go hustle something somewhere. But I had no game left. I didn't have a penny in my pocket, and I could barely walk.

The counselor offered to admit me to a long-term treatment center, but that was a year's commitment. I would have rather gone out on the curb and died than check in for a year.

"The only other alternative is the Salvation Army," the guy said, "but there's no detox there."

We drove to a seedy part of Grand Rapids, and I checked in to the Salvation Army. "Thank you, we'll have your son back to you in twenty days," they said, and my mom left. I was at a loss. They took me to a big room and gave me a cot. I looked around and saw white kids, black kids, Hispanic kids, alcoholic kids, dope-fiend kids, crack kids, and a smattering of older guys. I fit right in.

I was facing cold turkey. I knew what to expect, because I'd been through it already. I knew I was going to be sick to my stomach, that every single bone in my body was going to hurt. When you're kicking, your eyelashes hurt, your eyebrows hurt, your elbows hurt, your knees hurt, your ankles hurt, your neck hurts, your head hurts, your back hurts, it all hurts. Parts of your body you didn't know could experience pain, experience it. There's a bad taste in your mouth. For a week your nose is running uncontrollably. I didn't throw up that much, but the worst agony was not being able to sleep. I couldn't get a wink the whole twenty days. I'd stay up all night and wander the hallways and go sit in the lounge and watch late-night TV. For the first few days I couldn't eat, but I got my appetite back and started to put some meat on my bones.

After a few days, a staff member came up to me and said, "You have to go to a meeting every day you're here." It was cold and snowing outside, and I was feeling pretty miserable, so I accepted my fate and marched along with all the other kids into this little room. I was not in a great state of comprehension, because I was in physical pain and emotionally agonized, but I sat down in the meeting and saw the twelve steps up on the wall. I was trying to read them, but I couldn't focus my eyes. I was trying to listen to these people, but I couldn't focus my ears.

I had mocked anything that had to do with sobriety or recovery for my whole life. I'd see stickers that said ONE DAY AT A TIME and I'd be like "Fuck that." I was a hustler, and a con artist, and a scammer, and a fiend, and a liar, and a cheat, and a thief, all these things, so naturally, I started looking for the scam. Was it a money thing? A God thing? A religion thing? What the fuck was going on here?

But as I sat in that meeting, I felt something in the room that made sense to me. It was nothing but a bunch of guys like me, helping one another get off drugs and find a new way of life. I was keen on discovering the loophole, but there wasn't one. I thought, "Oh my God, these people are coming from the same place as me, but they don't get high anymore, and they don't look desperate, and they're joking about shit that most people would send you to jail for talking about." One girl got up and started talking about not being able to stop smoking crack even though she had a kid. She'd had to give her kid to her mother. I was thinking, "Yeah, I'd do the same. I'd be leaving the kid with the mom and disappearing. I did the same thing with my band."

This was not a cult, not a scam, not a fad, not a trick, not an out-to-get-your-buck type of thing; this was just dope fiends helping dope fiends. Some of them were clean and some of them were getting clean because they were talking to the ones who got clean, and they were being honest about it and unafraid to say how fucked up they were. It flashed on me that if I did this, I could be clean.

I stayed there for the twenty days, not sleeping but going to meetings every day and listening and reading the books and gleaning a few of the basic principles.

After twenty days, I went back to my mom's house in Lowell, feeling a hell of a lot different than when I came. At age twenty-four, I was totally clean for the first time since I was eleven years old. I was able to sleep through the night, and my mom and I celebrated the next day. My stepdad, Steve, was real supportive, and so were my sisters. I was feeling pretty good, oddly in acceptance of the damage that I had created. There's a whole lot of optimism in those meetings, with people being freed from self-imposed prisons, so everything seemed fresh and new.

Steve had some old weights lying around the house, and I rebuilt them and did some weight lifting. I took long walks and played with the dog. It had been so long since I'd felt normal, and wasn't chasing something or calling someone or meeting someone in the middle of the night to talk him out of a bag of something. Amazingly, none of that was on my mind at all.

During my stay at the Salvation Army, I realized that if I didn't want to keep doing what I had been doing that I'd have to let go of Jennifer. I really wanted to stay sober, and I wasn't blaming her for my problem, but I knew that if I was with her, my odds of staying dean would be diminished.

I kept going to meetings while I was at my mom's house, and I learned that alcoholism/drug addiction is a bona fide illness. When you recognize that there's a name and a description for this condition that you thought was insanity, you've identified the problem, and now you can do something about it.

There's a real psychological relief that comes from discovering what's wrong with you and why you've been trying to medicate the hell out of yourself since you were old enough to find medicine. I wasn't too dear on the concepts in the beginning, and I still wanted to cut corners and do things my way and take some short cuts and not do all of the work that was asked of me, but I did like the feeling and I did identify hugely. I also felt waves of compassion for all of these other poor motherfuckers who were destroying their lives. I looked at the people in the meetings and saw beautiful young women who had become skeletons because they couldn't stop using. I saw other people who loved their families but couldn't stop. That was what attracted me. I decided that I wanted to be part of something where these people had a chance of getting well, of getting their lives back.

After being in Michigan a month, I decided to give Flea a call to check in. We exchanged greetings, and then I told him about the cold turkey and the meetings and the fact that I didn't get high anymore.

"What do you mean, you don't get high?" Flea said. "You're not doing anything? Not even pot?"

"Nope. I don't even want to. It's called sobriety, and I'm loving it," I said.

"That's insane. I'm so happy for you," he said.

I asked him how it was going with the band, and he told me that they'd hired a new singer who had a bunch of tattoos, but I could tell in his voice that they weren't happy with him. I didn't really care. In no way or shape or form was I trying to get back in the band.

Flea must have heard something in my voice that first call, something that he hadn't heard since we were in high school. It's amazing to me, because it wasn't like me not to be angling my way back into the band as soon as I felt good. But I honestly didn't care then if I went back to the band or not. It was a real take-it-or-leave-it feeling, which is really not me, because I'm a control freak, and I want what I want and I want it immediately. However, at that moment I was relieved of all of the self-obsessed, driven behavior.

A few days later, Flea called me. "Do you think you'd want to come back here and maybe play a couple of songs and see how it feels to be back in the band?" he asked.

That was the first time I had even considered that as a possibility. I blurted out, "Wow, hmmm. Yeah, I would. There's really nothing else that I'd want to do."

"Okay, come back, and let's get to work," Flea said.

I got on the plane to go home, riding a whole new wave of enthusiasm for my new life. I decided to write a song about my month-long experience of going to meetings, getting clean, and winning this battle of addiction. I look back on it, and it seems naive, but it's exactly where I was at that point of my life. I took out a pad of paper, looked out the window at the clouds, and started channeling this river of wordology that was cascading toward me. [Lyrics that would become the song "Fight Like a Brave."]

When I got back to L.A., within two months I was shooting heroin and cocaine again. My sobriety hadn't stuck for a long time, but now I knew there was a way out of the madness if I wanted it and if I was willing to do the work to get it. I had been given the tools; I just didn't want to use them yet.

X X X X

EPILOGUE / MIKE DOUGHTY
SCARY FAKE JOY

EXCERPT FROM
The Book Of Drugs: A Memoir

AUTHOR
Mike Doughty

Mike Doughty, the former leader of Soul Coughing, is a songwriter, blogger and poet.

✕ ✕ ✕ ✕

*"I went back to the kitchen, got the Pringles,
came back, handed the canister to the girl, sat down,
then decided I wanted to smoke, lit a cigarette, and,
upon ashing, discovered the first of the four cigarettes
I'd lit in the past three and a half minutes still
burning in the ashtray on the end table."*

THE SAMPLER PLAYER drove the van sometimes. He'd get particularly stoned for this. Nobody paid any thought to it, because we all assumed that you drove better high. People still believe this. I have friends in their late thirties who believe, genuinely, that weed makes you more perceptive at the wheel. I read about some study on some blog the other day presenting data that, at the very least, it was just as safe as driving not-stoned.

OK. So. I remember this one time doing bong hits with a girl. It was during the first Gulf War. The media were jazzed about there being a war—first real one in twenty years, right?—so they had canceled all the shows and had three anchors talking about the same unchanging information, sans commercials, until two in the morning. Eventually we tired of it; we turned the sound off and listened to CDs, loving the moments when the lips of the anchor synched, almost-kind-of, to the music.

I lit a cigarette. (I smoked three packs a day. A morning pack, an evening pack, and then another pack rationed through the intervening hours; I had ashtrays placed at five-foot intervals in my house.) I put it in the ashtray, then got down on the floor to pick out a CD. Flipping through the rack, I decided I wanted to smoke. I lit a cigarette; put it in an ashtray on a speaker as I got out my copy of *Sign 'O' the Times*. The girl I was getting high with asked if I still had those Pringles from before. Sure, I said. I walked to the kitchen, lighting a cigarette on the way. When I got to the kitchen, I put the cigarette in an ashtray by the sink and opened the fridge. Blinked at the fridge's innards for a second. I got out a grape soda and walked back towards the couch.

Want some grape soda? I asked the girl.

"The Pringles?" she asked.

Oh, right, right. I went back to the kitchen, got the Pringles, came back, handed the canister to the girl, sat down, then decided I wanted to smoke, lit a cigarette, and, upon ashing, discovered the first of the four cigarettes I'd lit in the past three and a half minutes still burning in the ashtray on the end table.

There are a number of people in the world who believe that in this state I could *drive better.*

Weed was sustenance. We were never without it. Really and truly *never.* My bandmates were high constantly, and I resented the hell out of them for it, because weed fucked up my singing, thus limiting my intake. We had terrible days when all we had was shitty weed, shwag weed. Dark agitation would come over us; the other three would actually fight among *themselves.*

Purportedly, weed isn't what people call *physically* addictive—the expression implies bodily withdrawal when you stop using—but to me, the distinction is more or less superfluous. To me, addiction is mostly a state of being inherent in the addict that can translate to choices that stimulate the brain's pleasure centers which most people can pick up and put down at will, like sex, sugar, gambling. I have no expertise in the biology of weed withdrawal. I do know that just having *bad* weed discombobulated us in the extreme.

Weed addicts are alone among drug users in that they think their shit is cute. I heard an anecdote once about a guy working in a studio, and there was somebody sleeping under a blanket on a couch; the guy whips off the blanket and gets up, and it's a legendary outlaw country music star. The storyteller goes on, like, "He fired up a joint and whoohoo! Wake-and-bake! Whoohoo awesome!" I don't think that story would go, "The first thing he did when he was awake was chop out a line of blow!" Or, "He downed a shot of tequila when he woke up, 'cause he had the shakes!"

I did a vocal on a song by a techno band from Manchester (do you call it a band when all the music making is done in the studio, and live, it's three guys standing behind machines, watching data turn into music, like Laverne and Shirley watching the bottles on the quality control line?). They flew me to Britain to shoot a video.

The set was an abandoned airstrip. The German lady directing the video made me chase a truck, until I was wheezing, lip-synch in front of flame jets, and lie on the cold, wet asphalt. All the band had to do was stand in a triangular formation in their mod jogging suits, looking past the camera, regally.

They had a potbellied guy named Rufus with them, who didn't dress groovily and had an unfashionable mustache. "Do you want some pyooaah?" Huh? "Some pyooaah, mate." Oh, *pure.* Pure what?

"Whizz, mate, pure whizz." Rufus held up a bag of white powder. I didn't know what "whizz" was, but I sniffed some anyway. It was something other than cocaine—probably speed? My displeasure at lying on an airstrip in the drizzle dispelled.

There was a girl cast as the girl in the video. I wasn't that attracted to her. She was, in fact, the German lady's pinch-hitter for the girl role—the model who was originally cast dropped out, and this woman was somebody who worked in a production company the German director was affiliated with. She was a half-Chinese girl with an extremely snooty-sounding English accent, incongruously named Françoise. Her friends called her by the last syllable of that name: Swaz.

How do you say that name when making love to her? Well, it's sexier than the phlegmy charms of Breggggggkkkkkggggggggya.

We were taken to a trailer, where a gay guy with an Afro and circular glasses wielding blush and eye shadow had transformed Swaz into a glamor icon. Her sudden transformation into a beauty was disquieting.

In the makeup chair, I said, "They want me made up to look like a dead man."

"Really?!"

No, I said, not really.

He got sullen.

We were seated in the cab of the truck I had chased, for shots in which I lip-synched while Swaz pretended to drive. They shot one angle, then another from the side, then one from the front, then a close-up. Then the German lady said, "And now it is time you and Swaz vill have a snog."

We were startled. Did they tell us beforehand that the job description included making out with a stranger? Cameras rolled.

I leaned in and gave her a real kiss. My lips brushed hers, and I budged in closer. Her mouth yielded. A long, soulful, all enveloping kiss.

In the car back to London we talked about poetry, and then we met the next day; she came over to my hotel room and took a shower with the bathroom door open. I watched her soap herself up, scrub herself off.

At some point in the six hours we hung out, it was decided that I was going to abandon New York and come live with her in London.

I went back to Brooklyn. She called me, blind drunk, when I was throwing my stuff into boxes, and slurred over and over, "Are you going to save me? Are you going to save me?" Unnerving. I told her to stop, she kept repeating it, I pleaded with her, Stop, please stop, but she kept saying, "Are you going to save me? Are you going to save me?"

I boxed up my life and went anyway.

Swaz and I would get high and say words back and forth to each other.
Swear, I said.
"Swah," she responded.
There, I said.
"Thah," she responded.

We went to see a refurbished version of *Star Wars*. I learned that the English put sugar on their popcorn, and they ran a parade of arty commercials before the previews.

The movie started. "Is Han Solo Luke's brother?" Swaz asked. "Or was it—Obi Wan Kenobi is Luke's uncle? . . ."

No, I said. Darth Vader is Luke's father.

"DARTH VADER IS LUKE'S FATHER?!" cried Swaz in the middle of the theater.

I was a terrible boyfriend. I'd get home from tour and not want to do anything but lie on the couch—of which Swaz had two, called the Major Couch and the Minor Couch. I sat on the Major Couch, smoked weed, and ate the Cumberland bangers that Swaz cooked for me.

Swaz was a terrible performance poet. There's a certain kind of would-be artist who chooses poetry because of its materials: to make a film, you need a bunch of people, a camera, lights, a script; to write a song, you need a guitar or a piano, and you need to learn how to play; to write a poem, you need a piece of paper and half an hour. Swaz's performance involved undulating while she intoned in a ridiculous sexy-fairy voice. In poetry, she found a way to vend her sexiness.

She performed around London, sometimes just a few blocks from our place. I could've gone and been good and clapped and kissed her. But I never went. Lousy, lousy boyfriend.

Since then, she's become a kind of quasi-academic. She gives performance poetry workshops all over Britain, and the world: Bogota, Sarajevo, Dublin. Vending your sexiness works in any medium.

At that time in Britain, it had become near impossible to find good drugs, unless it was cocaine. Swaz had the country's last decent Ecstasy connection, a bug-eyed, chubby guy named Alfonso who seemed totally hapless and sometimes wore a bolo tie over a Hawaiian shirt.

I was in a club, sitting on the floor, rolling my jaw around and obsessively feeling my skull. A guy came up, shouting over the music.

"Whadeegetyapah," he said.

Ha ha, what? Ha ha.

"Where did you "get your pill," he repeated.

Alfonso!

"What? Who?"

This guy named Alfonso. Ha ha ha.

"Where is he?"

He's, ummm, I don't know, he lives . . .

"Did you get it here?"

No, no, we called him. My eyes crossed and uncrossed.

"You don't give a fuck, do you, you daft cunt?"

Ha ha ha.

"You fucking twat, you don"t even know where the fuck you are, do you?"

Ha ha ha. Eyes rolling and rolling.

(I don't do E anymore. I'll hang out with you when you're on E. But if you start rubbing your face and telling me how amazing your face feels, I *will* make fun of you.)

Alfonso called, sounding coked up and disturbed. He said he wanted to be an artist, he wanted to design CD covers; you make CDs, can I design your CD cover?

Um, Alfonso, why don't you bring some art over next time?

"Can I come over right now?"

Ah, no, right now we're . . . um, we're . . .

"I want to make a positive change in my life," Alfonso said. You could hear his heart pounding in his throat.

Swaz told me that she heard voices. She had sudden, bug-eyed outbursts: she'd burst into tears and shriek at me. She had an evil streak. She'd say something innocuous that would devastate, and she pretended she wasn't trying to hurt me.

I'd go back to North America to play shows, mostly in brown, cold cities on flat terrain; at the end I'd fly from Columbus or Cedar Rapids back to London. I would be exhausted by the weeks on the road with the band that hated me. I smoked lots of weed and barely wanted to move off the Major Couch. Swaz mocked me cruelly for being crippled. She was a versatile mocker.

We went out to clubs, taking Alfonso's pills. We heard all the great Jungle DJs of London, a scene in full flower. We dropped the pills, the high came up, and I desperately tried to get away from Swaz. I was frightened when my druggy eyes looked into hers. She reached out and pulled me to her face. She kissed me. She'd been dutifully swigging water, as a cautious E-taker is supposed to: the inside of her mouth was cold.

I fled, and went around asking for sips of peoples' drinks, greeting everybody with ostentatious fake love, being the most annoying person on Ecstasy you could imagine. Particularly considering how unapologetically E'd-up I was, when everybody else in the place was probably on adulterated cocaine.

When I got back to Swaz's, and the high was coming off, I hated myself for the idiotic, chemical affection.

She poured me a glass of Scotch to ease the internal clatter. I refused, but she was persistent. I drank.

It tasted like adulthood. *This is really nice*, I thought. The jitters smoothed.

I thought: *As coffee is a vehicle to help me transport from the sleeping state to the waking state, maybe alcohol is something to carry me from waking back to sleep again.*

I flew to East Lansing for two weeks opening shows for Dave Matthews.

I put one of Alfonso's pills on my amp during sound check at the Boston Garden. Halfway through the set, between songs, I stepped back to the amp and gulped. I wanted to be coming up as soon as the show was over.

We played to a crowd that had mostly not shown up yet. There were pockets of people in the chairs on the arena's floor—people who paid big bucks for the good seats—who mostly drank their beer, looking bored. The people in the cheap sections were more likely to show up for the opening act: after the tunes, we'd hear a muted roar from the back of the hall.

I began to feel the glow. We clambered down the stairs and into the strange middle ground behind the stage, with big road cases gathered together like cattle, cables running from the stage to generators somewhere, Dave Matthews's techs in states of distraction. By the monitors there was a tiny TV screen hooked up to a camera, currently showing an empty drummer's stool. The Guy's kit was so huge, jungled with cymbals, chimes, tom-toms, that they needed the TV screen to communicate.

There was one lonely guy sitting at a computer. His job was to feed lyrics into the teleprompter. I thought: *Who does this guy drink with when he gets on the tour bus at night?*

Our dressing room was a visiting-team locker room. There were empty massage tables and stationary bikes; the lockers had been covered with white sheets. A guy from Warner Bros. Stood by the sandwich platter. He had horn-rimmed glasses and an aw-shucks, kid from the cul-de-sac, Encyclopedia Brown demeanor. The high ratcheted up and I started to think he realized I was oozing into another state of being. He seemed weirdly menacing. He engaged me in some good-show-excited-for-New-York-tomorrow? chat; my eyes must've been ping-pong balls.

I got more googly-eyed as he chatted; I hopped up on one of the stationary bikes and started pedaling. Idly, then furiously. I stopped pedaling, and the force of the exertion shot an intense blast of drugs—when you're on E, and you move intensely, then stop, you feel like you've ignited. This is why E goes so perfectly with dancing. My body shook in pleasure and disorientation. Encyclopedia Brown was still talking. I dismounted and walked off midsentence.

Dave Matthews took the stage to grand hurrahs. I walked out of the barricades and into the crowd, looked up at the people in the stands, the spotlights tracing over them. The whole place seemed to be breathing in unison.

I was grabbed by a girl in a hippie dress and pulled into the seats. "Dance with us!"
Are you on E? I asked idiotically.

"No! We're drunk!" she said. My bones were noodles.

I felt like a vice-presidential candidate. I walked the rings of the stadium, slapping hands with fans here or there who recognized me. I was by myself, on drugs, grinningly holding up the all-access pass on a lanyard around my neck to security as they stepped up to block my way. They parted resentfully. This is what I wanted to do with my life. Be outrageously high, be absolutely alone except for the random high fives and yelped *You're awesome*'s.

Our bus was parked with a dozen other buses in a concrete chamber beneath the stadium. One weirdness of an arena tour is that you go to sleep on the bus at night as it heads to the next show, and then wake up inside a hockey stadium, in a giant grey room—some of them big as a double football field—lit with yellow fluorescence, neither in daytime nor night, in the loud thrumming of all the buses' generators. Once you had your coffee in you, you had to clamber all over the arena searching for an exit to see what kind of day it was.

Our bus was rented from a company that painted the same murals on all their buses—a beach scene, in a purple sunset, with gentle waves, driftwood, and a beached rowboat—with subtle variations of the elements in the picture, like a puzzle in *Highlights* magazine. There were several buses from the company on this tour. After one night, early on, when I looked in panic from bus to muraled bus, not knowing which one was mine, I memorized an aggregation of seagulls to know which one to get into.

As the bus pulled out of the arena that night, I was in the back lounge of the bus. The E began to wear off, and in grief I gulped another. I came up as the sun came up. Not knowing what else to do, I took off all my clothes. I lay on the banquette, savoring the ever-diminishing buzz. Each time I felt it subside a level, I would get up and manically improvise weird calisthenics, causing a rush. Each rush less satisfying than the one before it.

In New York, we played Madison Square Garden. I had one E left. Dave brought me onstage to do something with the band—I improvised an onomatopoetic melody: frighteningly manic, scary fake joy. I danced circles around Dave—literally. I'm guessing now that every member of the band was staring at me with bayonets in their eyes, this freak who had seized their stage. I was oblivious. I introduced each of them in detail—though I couldn't remember some of their last names—by their star sign and their affinity for hiking or swimming. The audience—fucking sold-out Madison Square Garden—looked like a sea of love lapping at the stage.

The second night I smoked weed: the jam was more contemplative. I scorned myself for wasting that one E on the drive out of Boston. Luke had come to the show, and I took him on my customary perambulation. We stopped on one of the upper levels to watch the music a little. There was a fifteen-year-old hippie girl dancing. She turned around and saw me. Her eyes lit up. I realized that I was wearing the same clothes I had worn onstage with Dave, and having essentially been in the Dave Matthews Band, I was a celebrity. I playfully shushed her: don't reveal my secret identity. She screamed. In seconds I was dogpiled by fifteen-year-old girls. Like a Monkee. Luke yanked me to safety.

✕

The buses traveled as a caravan. One night, at 3AM, all the buses stopped for an hour. We found out that the concourse bus had seen a car flip over, rumbling into a ditch. One of the concourse kids was trained as an EMT, and he ran out onto the median and held the head of the driver up, keeping his broken neck aligned.

Apparently he cracked corny jokes for twenty minutes until the ambulance arrived, to keep the guy from going into shock. "He'll probably never walk again," said the kid, "but it was a good night."

I was supereffusive with the EMT kid, called him a superhero. The next night, and every night for the remainder of the tour, he would come into our dressing room—uninvited—drink our beer, grin cheesy grins, and make schmoozy, repetitive small talk about the night he saved a life.

We played New York on the tour's last night. I met a cute blonde girl from the hedge-fund belt of Connecticut and brought her back to my apartment. I crushed Ecstasy pills, cut the powder into lines, and we sniffed them up.

I put Marvin Gaye on. "Why are we listening to this *old* music," the girl said. "Do you have any Sublime?"

I kept sniffing the lines, and she, nervously, kept sniffing them alongside me, trying to keep up. As we were fucking, I noticed she was frowning. I came, and she ran to the bathroom, where she lay on the cool floor moaning.

What do I do if the girl dies? I thought.

No compassion.

"I'll be OK," she kept saying. I went up on my roof, naked, freaked out on the E, feeling radiant under the New York sky, which had been turned green by the city's ambient light.

Stanley Ray and I went to a comedy show at Largo, on Fairfax, every Monday night when we were in Los Angeles making the record. Patton Oswalt, David Cross, Paul F. Tompkins, Sarah Silverman, Todd Barry, all these amazing comedians playing this small room. The then-unknown Jack Black's Tenacious D would debut at that show, alas, the week after I left California.

Stanley Ray and I got stoned before the show in the car. We were both at the point where getting high barely got us high: we just got paranoid and groggy. "Why do we do this?" said Stanley Ray. "It doesn't make anything better. Isn't that what addiction is, when you keep getting high, but it doesn't do anything, and you don't want to, but can't stop?"

What? I said. That's ludicrous.

✕ ✕ ✕ ✕

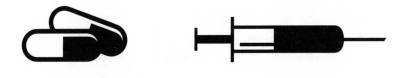

ACKNOWLEDGEMENTS

Many thanks to the following people who were instrumental during the conception and construction of this book:

Howie Abrams, Sarah Birdsey, Alexander Bordelon, John Blake,
Frederick T. Courtright, Michael Croland, Michael Croy, Alicia Dercole,
Walter Einenkel, Jade Hoye, Lucas Hoye, Richard Hoye, Wenonah Hoye,
Elizabeth Ishii, Ken Ishii, Rei Ishii, Alex Kazemi, Gabriel Kuo, Jodi Lahaye,
Noah Levenson, Beth Metrick, Pauline Neuwirth, Laura Piasio,
The Permissions Department at HarperCollins, Jeroen Puyk,
Jamie Roberts, Ellyn Solis, Marcus Turner, Rosie Virgo, Erwin Walbeek,
Cees Wessels, Eric Wybenga, and Patricia Zline.

✕ ✕ ✕ ✕